MONTMORENCY'S
❊ REVENGE ❊

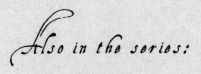

MONTMORENCY'S REVENGE

ELEANOR UPDALE

SCHOLASTIC INC.

New York Toronto London Auckland Sydney
Mexico City New Delhi Hong Kong Buenos Aires

This book was originally published in Great Britain in
2006 by Scholastic Ltd., and in the United States by
Orchard Books in 2007.

ISBN-13: 978-0-439-81374-7
ISBN-10: 0-439-81374-3

12 11 10 9 8 7 6 5 4 3 2 1   8 9 10 11 12 13/0

Printed in the U.S.A.   40

First Scholastic paperback printing, March 2008

The display type was set in Aqualine.
The text type was set in 12.5-point Venetian301 BT.
Illustrations © 2006 by Nick Hardcastle
Book design by Tim Hall

Like all the Montmorency stories, this one mixes real and fictional characters and events. And once again it is dedicated, with my love, to Jim, Andrew, Catherine, and Flora.

Contents

CHAPTER I

≫

GLENDARVIE CASTLE, SCOTLAND
JANUARY 1901

Lord Francis Fox-Selwyn felt the pressure of the blade against his head. He closed his eyes and grasped the arms of his chair.

"Go on. Just do it," he said, trying to sound brave. There was a pause, then a stinging sensation, and he knew he was bleeding.

"You stupid fool!"

"It's not my fault," said Tom, flinging the razor into a pot of soapy water. "I've never done this before. Do it yourself!"

"Do I look as if I've got eyes in the back of my head?"

Tom laughed. "I don't know yet. Your hair's in the way."

"Well, have another go," said Frank, calming down. "But be careful. That hurt."

Tom tried again, more gently this time, wiping the razor on his leather apron and scraping away every tuft from Frank's scalp. The newly exposed skin was a pale, sickly shade of gray. Frank held up the hand mirror.

"See? I told you. I'm unrecognizable. I could go anywhere like this, and no one would know that it's me."

In the reflection, Frank could see the door opening and Montmorency's face dropping from a smile into horror as he saw the bald head and then the clumps of ginger curls scattered about the floor.

"What on earth is going on? Frank! What have you done to yourself?"

"It's a disguise. Everyone thinks I've got to stay hidden. But see, I could help you find Uncle George's killers. I'm completely transformed."

Montmorency was firm. "No, Frank. You're not. You look a bit strange, it's true. But you'll never be able to disguise yourself completely. Nature's seen to that. Your red hair is always going to show through." He stood behind Frank and guided his hand so that they could both see in the mirror. "Look at your eyebrows. Your pale lashes."

"I can dye them. One of the maids has some stuff. You can tell her hair isn't really black. Only yesterday, when she bent to clean out the grate, I could see a lighter color at the roots."

"Exactly," said Montmorency. "And the same would be true for you. Except it's worse than that. Your pale skin and your freckles would give you away at once."

"I could use makeup, or scarves, or something," said Frank as his father, Gus, Duke of Monaburn, came in. Gus was even more shocked than Montmorency. He was angry.

"Frank! You idiot! What sort of game is this?"

"It's not a game, Father. It's serious. I'm changing myself so I can do something about Uncle George."

"Don't be ridiculous. You of all people have to keep out of sight." The duke looked at Tom, who was still holding the razor. "Did you do this? Did you mutilate him?"

Frank dived to Tom's defense. "I told him to."

"And Tom can't think for himself, I suppose?"

"Of course I can," said Tom. "And I thought it was a good idea."

"Stupid boy! Do you want to put him in danger again?"

Frank grabbed the razor. "It has nothing to do with Tom. It's my decision, and I've got to do something or I'll go mad." He dipped the razor into the water and started scraping away at his eyebrows.

"Stop it!" cried the duke. He turned to Tom, still shouting. "You thought it was a good idea? Well, see what you've done. Look at him now!"

"Stop picking on Tom," said Frank. "Stop blaming him for everything, Dad. You're always criticizing Tom."

With no eyebrows, Frank seemed crazed and wild, his face round and puffy, coloring up with rage. Tom pushed his way out of the room.

"I was only trying to help," he said, slamming the door as he stomped off into the backyard, where embarrassed servants could hear the raised voices of the other three men even though the windows were closed tight against the winter cold. Tom ran to the stables. Most of the horses were gone. The rest of the family were out for a ride. But they had left his favorite, a young gray, and he jumped onto its back, not bothering with a saddle or bridle. He rode fast to the edge of the estate, half thinking of escaping forever: of finding some way of returning to the simplicity of Tarimond, his island home. But he urged the beast to a stop as they reached the boundary with the road. Over the top of the hedge, he caught sight of a dark figure wrapped in a heavy cloak, limping along towards the castle gates. The man shouted up to Tom, his breath freezing into white vapor in the cold air: "Is this Glendarvie Castle?"

"Yes," said Tom.

"And the people here? Fox-Selwyn?"

"That's the family name," said Tom, still bitter after the quarrel. "But that's not enough for them. Rightly speaking, you should say 'His Grace the Duke of Monaburn,' 'the Marquess of Rosseley,' 'Lord this and the Honorable that.'"

"You work here?" asked the stranger.

Tom realized that in his disheveled state, with his sleeves rolled up and his apron flapping, he looked more like a disgruntled stable boy than the heir to a fortune. The truth was that he was virtually one of the family — he'd inherited a huge legacy from Frank's uncle, Lord George Fox-Selwyn, who had been brutally murdered not six months before.

The man spoke again before Tom could reply. "And Lord Francis Fox-Selwyn. What does he look like? About your age, I think?"

"No. Older," said Tom. He was still too angry to think properly, to realize that he had no reason to engage in conversation with a passing traveler. "He's older. And right now he looks mad. Crazy." Tom stopped himself, suddenly alive to the danger he and his friends might be in. *Who was this man?* What was Tom doing answering his impertinent questions?

They both looked up sharply as a dog started barking. A second later they could hear wheels and hooves, and a carriage pulled around a bend in the road and through the gates to make its way towards the castle.

"That's odd," said Tom. "No one's expected." He turned back. The inquisitive stranger was gone.

CHAPTER 2

≫

THE INSPECTOR

*T*om galloped across the fields, knowing he could make it back to the castle before the carriage arrived. The stable yard was full of activity. Harvey, the chief family servant, had seen the carriage meandering along the drive and was organizing a reception for the unexpected guest. Tom tried to tell him about the limping man.

"I haven't got time for that just now, sir. There's somebody coming."

"But he was asking questions. I think we ought to find out who he is."

"I'll get someone to go down to the village and see if he's been spotted there," said Harvey. "And I'll make sure everyone keeps an eye out for intruders. Now you go upstairs and get yourself cleaned up. Lunch is almost ready, and it looks as if you've got company. The duke won't like it if you go in looking like that."

"The duke doesn't like me, whatever I look like," said Tom.

Harvey knew his place and said nothing, but his kind smile showed that he understood. Tom went upstairs to his room as the mystery coach and horses were led into the yard behind him.

He washed and put on more presentable clothes. His mother was still in control of the money he had inherited and would be for another seven years, until he was twenty-one, but she had used some of it to buy him the sort of outfits the Fox-Selwyns had worn in their youth. Tom was getting used to starched collars and shiny shoes after a lifetime of rough work clothes at home on the remote island of Tarimond.

He could hear voices from the library downstairs. The anger of a few minutes before had turned to a more polite but serious tone. From his window, he could see the stable lads tending to the horses that had brought the unexpected visitor to Glendarvie. He didn't recognize the coach. It wasn't a neighbor who had disturbed the family argument.

Tom went downstairs and hovered outside the door of the library. He could hear Montmorency, the duke, and another man with an English accent. A maid entered with a tray of tea, and the duke caught sight of Tom through the open door. He looked guiltily at the boy and beckoned him to join them.

"Tom," he said in a much calmer voice than before. "This is Inspector Howard from Scotland Yard. Inspector Howard, Tom Evans."

Tom shook hands with the policeman, who looked familiar.

He addressed the boy with all the respect due to his apparent class and none of the contempt usually given to people his age. "We have met before, sir. Last summer. In London. After that unfortunate business."

"Oh yes," said Tom. "You came to ask Frank questions." He remembered how the police had spent days drawing information from Frank after the shootout at the Hippodrome theater, which had led to the smashing of an anarchist plot.

"Indeed. Lord Francis Fox-Selwyn was most helpful then," said Inspector Howard. "And I am hoping that he can help us again now."

"I'm sure he'll be only too pleased," said Tom. But the duke interrupted him.

"Inspector, you must realize that my son has undergone a terrible ordeal. We have taken great trouble to keep him out of the public eye and to make him safe from anyone who might wish him ill. After my brother's death, we are all, to some extent, liable to be in danger. Our only prudent course of action is to live quietly and out of the way."

"I understand," said Howard. "But I fear that your son may be indispensable to our efforts." The inspector stopped. He could not disguise his alarm as Frank came in, smartly dressed now but still looking bizarre after his radical shave. "My Lord," said Howard awkwardly. "A pleasure to see you again, I'm sure."

In his surprise at seeing the policeman, Frank had quite forgotten about his bald head and missing eyebrows. His mind was back on the horrors of the previous summer, when he had nearly lost his life.

"How do you do, Inspector? What brings you here? I over-heard you saying that I could help you."

"I have been explaining to His Grace and Mr. Montmorency."

The duke interrupted again. "And if you don't want to repeat yourself several times over, I suggest you save the full story until the family sits down for lunch. We are all involved in this, and I don't want secrets kept from anyone. Even young Tom here."

Montmorency saw how pleased Tom was by the duke's implied acknowledgment of his place among the Fox-Selwyns. It was clear they assumed Tom was George's child. Montmorency had still not admitted that Tom was his son, and, as ever, the time did not seem right. Particularly as Tom had news for them all.

"I saw a strange man on the edge of the estate." He told them the story of his encounter.

"This is worrying," said the inspector. "We are going to have to be even more careful than I thought."

"We should search the grounds," said the duke. "Really, Tom, you should have told us sooner."

"Go easy on the boy, Gus," said Montmorency. "We haven't given him a chance to say anything till now."

"And Harvey and his men are looking already," said Tom. "I told him straight away."

As he spoke, a drop of water fell from the ceiling onto Frank's bald head. The drip became a stream, and everyone started rushing around, looking for something to catch the flood. Montmorency emptied the coal scuttle into the hearth and dragged it across, sending Tom to the kitchen to find someone with a bucket and mop. Then he dashed upstairs.

"It's Robert," he cried as he left the room. "He's left the taps running again."

CHAPTER 3

≫

THE SHOWER

*M*ontmorency flung open the door of Doctor Robert Farcett's room. At least it wasn't locked. The catch had been broken a week before when Montmorency had forced it in similar circumstances. Once again, the chilly bedchamber was full of steam from the adjacent bathroom. Through the mist, Montmorency could see the grand tub. Over the top, a brass showerhead the size of a dinner plate sent down a powerful torrent. As Montmorency expected, his old friend was standing with water beating hard against his body. He must have been there for ages. The bath was full and overflowing onto the floor. Montmorency grabbed a towel and approached.

"Robert. Robert. It's me. Turn off the taps, Robert, and come out."

Doctor Farcett didn't move. His thin voice barely penetrated the roar of the water.

"I've dropped the soap. I can't get clean. I've dropped the soap."

Montmorency took off his jacket and rolled up his right sleeve. He reached through the spray to turn off the taps and pulled out the plug.

"It's all right, Robert," he said, holding out the towel. "Step out now, and we'll get you dry." He helped his friend lift his feet onto the sopping bathmat and tied the towel around his middle. "There you are now; all is well. We'll just get this mopped up, shall we?" and he pulled the bedspread onto the floor to soak up some of the water.

Farcett spoke again, very quietly. "But I'm not clean, Montmorency. I'm not clean."

"Yes you are, Robert. You're cleaner than anyone else in the house. Now let's get some clothes on you. It's nearly time for lunch."

Farcett did as he was told, meticulously dressing in his smart city clothes. Montmorency watched the pathetic figure before him. Robert hadn't been himself since the news of Maggie Goudie's death.

Maggie had been the nurse at the infirmary on the island of Tarimond, far away to the west of Scotland. Farcett had loved her but never took the chance to tell her before she was killed by the X-rays he had been researching in the hope of professional glory. Farcett had taken her death badly and resolved to withdraw to Tarimond, hoping to make amends by devoting himself to a life of humble day-to-day medicine. But Maggie's tragedy had been followed by another. Lord George Fox-Selwyn, the duke's twin brother and beloved friend of both Montmorency and Farcett, had been grotesquely murdered. Montmorency and the Fox-Selwyns had been devastated by that loss, and they had all traveled to Tarimond in the faint hope of finding some shelter from their horror.

In their grief, they hadn't noticed the effect that the events were having on the doctor. He had always been obsessed with hygiene. Ever since they first met him, they had laughed about how he was forever washing his hands. But just before Christmas, it became clear to everyone that his obsession was out of control. He would wash and dry himself and then start over again, repeating and repeating his ablutions, however cold the water and however clean his skin. Washing was taking over his life completely. Washing and tidying. He spent hours rearranging the equipment in Tarimond's little infirmary: rolling and unrolling bandages, then boiling them to kill the germs he thought he'd passed on from his hands. The bottles in the medicine cabinet shone with polishing. But he hadn't seen a patient in months. Even his body had changed. Usually athletic and forceful, he now seemed smaller, younger, more vulnerable.

It was partly for Robert's sake that they had all moved from Tarimond to Glendarvie, the Fox-Selwyn family home in the lush heart of Banffshire. Without really lying, they had told Farcett they wanted a change of scene for Christmas, and he had agreed to come with them. But in truth, Montmorency and the duke had hoped that the move to the mainland would restore Robert to full sanity. There were times when he seemed almost normal, capable of urbane conversation and able to observe all the conventions of polite society. But sitting on the bed, with water drenching the floorboards and dripping through the ceiling of the room below, Montmorency knew the plan hadn't worked and that with this second flood at Glendarvie, the time had come to get Robert a specialist's care. As the doctor fiddled with his fingernails, trying to

dislodge some nonexistent dirt, Montmorency found the courage to speak.

"Robert, you can't go on like this. You need help."

"No, it's all right. I can clean it up myself."

"I don't mean the water, Robert. And you know I don't."
Doctor Farcett stared ahead, unresponsive. Montmorency
continued. "Robert, I've got to be honest with you. Here
in this very house you helped me when I was at my worst.
You've seen me in the grip of drugs and despair, and you
forced me to change. Now it's my turn to help you. You
must see a doctor."

"But I *am* a doctor, Montmorency. I can't admit that I'm
ill. At least not in this way. I know what's happening to me. I've
had patients who have lost their minds. I envy them. They
didn't understand the process; some of them were completely
isolated from their real selves, quite unaware that anything
was wrong. But I have these moments — days even — of
lucidity. I'm cursed with being able to observe myself. And yet
I can't control what I do. I know I need to see a specialist, but I
also know what that will involve. Believe me, Montmorency,
the treatment and the stigma that goes with it can be worse
than the disease."

"But you must have seen people get better. You can get
better, too."

"Why? Why should I want to?"

"So that you can be my friend. So that you can help me
avenge George's death."

"And Maggie's death? Isn't this illness her revenge on me?"

"Don't be stupid. Maggie would want you to be happy. And to continue with your work."

"But if I admit that I'm mentally sick, no one will accept me as a doctor. I need to go away to a proper hospital, Montmorency. But if I do that, word will get out, and I will never be able to return to my old world. I'm stuck with this affliction. And it's no more than I deserve."

"Then we'll get a doctor to come to you. Do you know of anyone? There must be somebody not too far from here?"

Doctor Farcett sighed and reluctantly came up with a name. "I've read of a Professor Frost. He's director of that new mental hospital at Strathgillon. But I don't know him. Just that he's supposed to be very good."

There was a surge of noise from downstairs, with doors banging and the occasional burst of female chatter. The rest of the family was back from riding. The gong sounded. It was time to go downstairs for lunch.

Doctor Farcett walked over to the basin and started washing and rewashing his hands.

CHAPTER 4

≫

LUNCH

*I*nspector Howard joined the family for lunch. He sat between the duke, who presided at the head of the table, and the new Marchioness of Rosseley: Angelina (the Italian wife of Frank's brother, Alexander). Montmorency was on her left, next to Tom, who took the last place on that side. The duchess (Gus's new wife, Beatrice) sat at the foot of the table, opposite her husband. Next to her came Alexander, then Tom's mother, Vi, Doctor Farcett, and finally Frank, allowed to sit higher up than usual, next to the duke, so that he could face the inspector and take a full part in what promised to be a very serious conversation. The family confined themselves to light pleasantries while the first course was being served. Then, when all the waiters had left the room, the duke turned to the policeman, speaking in a voice loud enough to cut through everyone else's chatter.

"So, Inspector. Perhaps we should go back to the beginning. Please tell us exactly why you have come."

The inspector put down his soupspoon. "First, I must apologize for not giving you any warning of my visit. I did contemplate calling you on the telephone or sending a telegram, but I could not take the risk of being overheard by the operator or betrayed by a delivery boy. It is important that no one knows why I have come or that I have asked your family to help me."

The duchess forgave any social faux pas. "We quite understand, Inspector. Are you implying that our safety is at risk?"

"Not directly, no, ma'am. But there is a threat to the safety of others, and I have to admit that if you help me with my task of saving them, you may find yourselves in some peril."

Alexander joined in. "Our family has been through a great deal, Inspector. My uncle died trying to save others. Are you sure we are the only people who can help?"

"I'm afraid so," said the inspector, looking around to make sure that the servants were all out of the room. "And I need the help of Lord Francis Fox-Selwyn in particular."

"Good," said Frank. "Does it mean I'll have to come to London? Perhaps from there I could track down the people who killed Uncle George. Have you made any progress on that, Inspector Howard?"

"No, sir. I'm afraid it's not a matter for Scotland Yard. Your uncle was murdered in Italy, and the investigation is in the hands of the Italians and our ambassador there."

"But Inspector, the Italians haven't gotten anywhere trying to catch Moretti. He disappeared on the day he sent Uncle George's body back from Florence. We're sure he pulled the trigger, but they just let him slip away, even though he must have been trying to protect the assassin who killed their king."

"Well, sir, I can see that is a great concern to you, but it's not something over which I have any control."

"And there's more," said Frank. "Moretti can't have been acting alone. Like all the rest of those anarchists, he was under the spell of Malpensa. There's no doubt about it. Malpensa was the one who stirred them all up, even if he never had the courage to do his own dirty work. It stands to reason that they've both found their way out of Italy. I know Malpensa had contacts in London. I want to go there and see if I can find out where he is now."

The duke interrupted. "No, Frank. We've taken a big enough step letting you come here. We can't risk you being recognized. Perhaps Alexander could help instead. He's going to London anyway. Inspector, Alexander is taking up a post at the Foreign Office in the spring. Is that soon enough for you?"

"I'm afraid it might not be, Your Grace. It is Lord Francis Fox-Selwyn who can be of most assistance to us, and we need him now. In a way, he just told you why. Let me explain." He lowered his voice. "Her Majesty is very ill."

"Well, I don't see how we can help with that," said the duke. "I'm sure she has the best of physicians."

"I fear that no doctor can help her for long. It may seem callous, but we have to think ahead. Arrangements are being made for her funeral."

Frank realized where the inspector was leading. "And you remembered what I said, didn't you, about the anarchists planning an attack on the mourners?"

"What's that?" asked the duke.

Inspector Howard answered. "When I was questioning your son after the events at the Hippodrome, he told me what he had heard when he was with the anarchists in America. There was a specific threat from Malpensa to target our royal family when they gathered for Queen Victoria's funeral ceremony."

"So, Frank has already helped you," said the duke. "You know who to look out for. Surely you have plenty of people who can do the job?"

"I'm afraid we do not. To be honest, our sources of intelligence are poor. We have no hard evidence of a plot, but that may say more about us than about our opponents. Something might be going on of which we are completely unaware. As you know, our international resources have been greatly burdened by the South African war. And I'm sorry to have to remind you, but the one person who knew most about these anarchists, who had trailed them across Europe . . ."

"Was Uncle George," said Frank. "And he is dead."

"Indeed so," said the inspector. "We have descriptions of the man Malpensa, of course, and even a photograph of Moretti, taken when he was curator of La Specola museum in Florence . . ."

"Damn him!" The duke cursed at the mention of his brother's murderer.

The inspector continued. "But it seems to us that the person who knows Malpensa best, and who might recognize any sympathizers in London, is Lord Francis Fox-Selwyn."

"Please call me Frank. And you're right. I've seen Malpensa face to face. And I worked in the ice-cream factory among the Italians in London. I know how Malpensa's supporters in this country think and behave. I have to go to look for them."

Tom's mother, Vi, spoke up. "I saw Malpensa, too, remember. On Christmas Day last year, in Paterson, New Jersey. I'd recognize him again. I can help."

"And Inspector," said Angelina, "I don't know if you are aware, but my father, Mario Baldo, is the police chief in Florence. I could talk to him on your behalf."

"Thank you, madam. As I said, the government is already in contact with the Italian authorities through the usual channels, but who knows, that may be useful. Yet, if I may be so bold, madam, may I urge caution should you be writing home. I am sure your father is of the utmost dependability, but letters might be intercepted. I can't overemphasize the need for absolute discretion."

Montmorency agreed. "Of course, Inspector. We all understand. And I'm sure we'll all do whatever we can. I may not have seen Malpensa, but I saw Moretti countless times. We all did, in Florence. And I worked with Frank in the ice-cream factory in London. I could pick out troublemakers. I could come."

The duke was growing angrier as everyone continued to defy him. "And they could just as easily pick you out, Montmorency! Moretti could recognize you if you dressed as a gentleman, and the factory workers would know you in rough clothes."

"But they think *I'm* dead," said Frank. "The anarchists knew me only as the man who died in the gunfight outside the Hippodrome. They don't know he — I — was also Lord Francis Fox-Selwyn."

"But they know that Lord Francis Fox-Selwyn exists," said

the duke. "They know that they killed his uncle. They must be wondering when any or all of us will come after them. Who knows? They may even be watching us now. They might have people keeping track of where we are and what we do."

Tom tried to speak, but the duke cut him off and continued.

"That's just something we have to live with. I can't pretend to be someone else. Everybody knows who I am, who Beatrice is, who Alex is, and Moretti can even tell the other anarchists about Montmorency. But we can protect Frank. Even if they find his name in a reference book, they don't know where he is. They don't know he was the young man who accompanied Montmorency and George in Florence, and they don't know that he double-crossed them and foiled their plot to blow up the Hippodrome."

"Which is why I can help, Dad," Frank insisted. "It's why I must go to London!"

Tom tried to intervene again. The duke snapped back. "Will you shut up, Tom! This is family business."

"I'm sorry," said Tom, "but I really have to speak. That man I told you about . . ."

"Yes," said the inspector. "I'd like to hear a bit more about him. What did he look like?"

"It's hard to say. He was all wrapped up in a cloak. He had a limp."

"What!" gasped Frank. "Why didn't you say so? Don't you realize? It's Malpensa! He had a bad leg. Did he sound Italian?"

"I don't know," said Tom. "He didn't say much. He was asking about the family. And he asked me about you, Frank. Asked what you were like."

"And you told him, I suppose," said the duke bitterly.

"Well no. I mean, I did say something, but I don't think I gave anything away."

"What *did* you say?" asked Montmorency. "Think hard, Tom. Tell us exactly."

Tom blushed. "I said he was older than me . . . and a bit mad."

"Oh for goodness' sake!" said the duke. "Stupid boy!"

The remains of the soup were going cold. The duchess rang the bell, and everyone sat in silence as the plates were cleared. The duke was breathing heavily, his rage building as he tried to look calm.

When the door was shut and the servants were gone, Montmorency made sure he was the first to talk. "Well done, Tom," he said. "I think you may have made it possible for Frank to help the inspector. Forgive me. I'm thinking as I speak, but it seems to me, Tom, that you have given us the basis of a plan that will work."

CHAPTER 5

≫

MONTMORENCY'S PLAN

*B*eatrice tried to keep the conversation going as the servants circulated with plates of beef and dishes of vegetables. She ostentatiously changed the subject and avoided calling the inspector by his official title in front of the servants.

"Was the road icy on your way here, Mr. Howard?" she asked.

"Only in patches. My driver said we were very lucky. He could sense snow in the air."

"We thought so, too, out with the horses, didn't we, Angelina?"

"Alex said so," said Angelina. "But I've spent all my life in Italy. This is my first winter here. I don't know your Scottish seasons yet."

"What do you think, Robert?" said the duchess. She was aware that the doctor had said nothing since they had sat down and was anxious to distract him from what he was doing: rubbing his cutlery on his napkin, even though it was perfectly clean.

"Me?" said Doctor Farcett without looking up. "How should I know? It seems a little warmer today. I think it's been too cold for snow this last week."

The last of the gravy was being served, and Harvey was touring the table, filling up water and wine glasses. Beatrice thanked him and motioned for the servants to go. "Please. Just leave the dishes on the sideboard. We can help ourselves if we want any more. I will ring when we are ready for dessert."

"Very good, ma'am," said Harvey, ushering the maids out of the door and closing it firmly behind him. He could see that serious matters would be under discussion once the servants were out of the way.

"So, Montmorency," said the duke, "what's this plan of yours? It had better be a good one."

"Well, as I said, we'll have to work out the details, but my instinct tells me it will work." Montmorency looked across to Doctor Farcett, who was slicing up the potatoes on his plate into perfectly formed tiny dice. "Robert, my plan involves you. It touches on what we were talking about upstairs. Do you mind if I talk about this here, in front of everybody?"

"Not a bit," said Doctor Farcett, still concentrating on his plate. "Though it's hard to see how I can help anyone." He looked up at last and stared at the inspector. "I'm sure you'll have noticed a change in me since we first met, Inspector?"

Inspector Howard politely tried to deny it, but Farcett cut him off, unblinking and with a false smile that disturbed everyone around the table. "I know I'm ill," he said. "Talk about me all you like."

Montmorency carried on. "Thank you, Robert. That's very good of you." He turned to Inspector Howard. "Inspector,

Doctor Farcett has suffered a tremendous upset to his nerves. He is in need of care — care I fear we cannot provide, even here at Glendarvie. I have spoken to him about it, and he knows it is time for him to go to a special hospital."

The duke cut in, appalled at the idea of an acquaintance entering a mental institution. "But he can't! He'd never get any patients again. What's the point of him getting better only to become an outcast?"

"Gus!" cried the duchess, angry at his honesty.

Montmorency interrupted. "I'm coming to that. But Gus, not all asylums are terrible places. George and I hid in one in Austria once, when some bandits were on our trail. It was a kindly, peaceful place."

"I'm not going to Austria," said Robert, dipping his napkin into his water glass to clean an imperceptible speck of gravy from his shirt.

"I'm not suggesting that you should," said Montmorency. "I think you should go somewhere very near here. Robert, you yourself have mentioned a place called Strathgillon."

"I've heard of it," said the duke. "I gave some money when they were building it, I think. One of the doctors wrote boasting about it and asking for donations. It's got farms and workshops and things — to give the lunatics something to do."

"Gus!" said the duchess. "Robert isn't a lunatic!"

The doctor stared ahead, frightening everyone at the table but saying nothing. The duke raised his eyebrows, indicating that he thought his point was proved.

"Anyway," he said, "what's all this got to do with helping the inspector and letting Frank go to London?"

Montmorency took a sip of wine and began to explain. "My idea is that Robert will go to Strathgillon, but under a false name. Everyone there will think he is Lord Francis Fox-Selwyn."

"What!" said Gus. "My son in an asylum? Have you gone mad?"

Frank couldn't help laughing at the duke's unfortunate choice of words. "Dad, I think I can see where this is leading. It sounds pretty sane to me."

Montmorency continued. "So Robert would go to Strathgillon. There he could get treatment and be restored to us as the wonderful man we all know him to be when he is well. No one need ever know that he has been there. Meanwhile, if we put it out that Frank is the patient, anyone looking for him will think he is safely under lock and key and unable to pursue George's killers. The real Frank can come to London with me and help the inspector. Everyone else in the family can go about their normal business. We have no reason to suspect that the anarchists actually plan to attack any of us. My guess is that they are more scared of us than we are of them. The anarchists probably want to make sure that we are not on their trail. If they think Frank is locked up in an asylum, they'll stop worrying about him."

"But Robert is more than twice Frank's age," said the duke,

still resisting the logic of the plan. "I know he looks young —
but not *that* young."

"That's where Tom has done us all a favor," said Montmorency.
"Remember what he said to the stranger this morning? That
Frank was older — and crazy? If that man was Malpensa,
he'll believe it when he hears that Lord Francis Fox-Selwyn
has been taken to Strathgillon, and if he goes there to check,
Robert will fit the description."

"So you're proposing that we get a whole hospital of
people to conspire in this deception?" said the duke, still
unconvinced.

"No. There need be no conspiracy. The staff at the hospital will keep the secret best if they believe it to be the truth.
I suggest that tomorrow, Robert should enter the hospital
under Frank's name. And that we do nothing to limit the
gossip that will follow his admission."

"And have you no thought for our family name?" said Gus.
"After all we have been through, do we want people thinking
we've got a nutcase among us?"

Alexander intervened, calmly, surprising everyone with his
words. "Father, everyone who bears the family name is here.
Let each of us say what we think of this plan. You all know
how much I dislike disorder and dishonor." He looked at
Frank and across to Tom. "I know that some of you laugh
about me. You think that I'm stodgy and staid — too concerned with propriety and form. I will be head of this family
one day. I think my view should count for quite a lot. And I

say that we should do it. Is our family's reputation more important than the safety of royalty? Don't forget that Inspector Howard is asking us to help protect them — not to indulge our own quest for revenge! And if the price of saving the Prince of Wales and his relations is a public perception that Frank is mad, then I think it is a price we should pay."

"And you, Frank?" said Montmorency. "It's your identity we're playing with here. What do you think?"

"I have no difficulty in making a decision. I have a choice between my name being locked in an institution and my body being free or my whole self being confined here or on Tarimond forever. I want to help — I want to help the queen's family and the nation. But I can't pretend that I don't also want to get out there to avenge Uncle George. And I don't care if people think I'm barmy. If I can't join in, I really will go mad!"

The duke turned to the ladies. "Angelina?"

"I agree with my husband. And if the madness is not a problem for my brother-in-law, I don't see why it should be for me."

"Beatrice?"

The duchess responded with gentleness. "Gus, I know why this is breaking your heart. You are right to care about the family name, and you are realistic in thinking that people will regard even a hint of insanity as a mark against us. But Gus, do we really care about those people? Do we really value our reputation above the safety of the realm? Of course not. And my darling, I know that the asylum is not the real reason you are so angry and opposed to this plan." She shifted her gaze to Frank, sitting alongside Gus. "Frank. Believe me. Your father is concerned for you. We nearly lost you, Frank, just a few months ago. He cannot bear the thought that you might be in danger again. I agree with him. But I know your stubbornness is every bit as strong as his, and if you want to go, I don't think we should stand in your way."

"So that's the last word then?" said the duke testily. "I see I am outnumbered. Proceed with your plan, Montmorency."

The duchess interrupted. "But there is someone else we should ask, surely? Robert, are you prepared to go into the hospital? Are you content to do this for Frank?"

"I'm grateful to you all for making it so easy for me," said the doctor.

"And will you be able to keep up the pretense? Will you remember always to be Lord Francis Fox-Selwyn and not Doctor Robert Farcett?"

"Doctor Robert Farcett is no more," he replied. "I am Lord Francis Fox-Selwyn."

Inspector Howard cleared his throat. "Well, ladies and gentlemen," he said, "I cannot tell you how grateful I am for your cooperation. I would like to get things moving as soon as possible. Perhaps we could make detailed plans before the day is out?"

"I will make a telephone call to Strathgillon after lunch,"

said the duke. "Presumably, in this case, we hope that the operator will be listening in?"

"Indeed, Your Grace," said the inspector. "But after that, I think you should all keep your use of the telephone to a minimum."

The duchess rang the bell for dessert.

CHAPTER 6

≫

KITCHEN TALK

Down in the kitchen, Cook was alarmed. "They've hardly touched their food," she said. "It was a beautiful joint. What a waste!" She dipped her finger in the gravy to check the flavor. "I wonder what was wrong with it."

"Nothing wrong with the food, if you ask me," said Harvey. "It's that visitor. He's brought bad news, I'll be bound."

"Who is he? Turning up out of the blue like that in the middle of winter?"

"I don't know. English. Looks a professional sort of chap. Didn't introduce himself to me when he arrived, just gave me a sealed envelope to hand to the duke."

"But they seemed to know him, didn't they?" said one of the maids.

"I heard the duchess call him Mr. Howard," said another.

"What do you think he is? A lawyer? A doctor?"

"Did you ask the coachman?"

"Didn't say a word. Very stiff and formal. Maybe we'll get something out of him when he comes in from the stables for his lunch. If you ask me, they're here about something pretty private."

"They might be something to do with the government," said Cook. "Master Alex is going to work for them in London, after all."

"You shouldn't call him 'Master Alex,' Cook," said Harvey. "He's the Marquess of Rosseley now. He's over twenty-one and married, for goodness' sake."

"Seems like only yesterday that he and young Francis would pop in here to steal sugar lumps," she replied. "Happy days. Before their mama died. Before they lost their uncle George."

The maids were still speculating about the visitor.

"Maybe that man's come about something to do with old George."

"Or about poor Doctor Farcett. They must all have noticed. He's gone mad with grief."

"Oh, they'll have noticed all right," said Cook. "They just try to look normal when we're around. I think he's the reason they came back from Tarimond so sudden."

Harvey stayed quiet while Cook and the maids played with ideas.

"But he's a doctor. He must be used to people dying. And anyway, he wasn't nearly as friendly with George as Mr. Montmorency was."

"No, but it wasn't just George, see. That young Tom told me. The doctor had a lady friend on Tarimond. A woman called Maggie. Died while they were all away last year. He blames himself for it. Can't see why."

"Poor man. No wonder he's gone halfway 'round the bend."

"That's enough now!" said Harvey brusquely, putting an end to their chatter. He didn't want to think about Maggie's death. He'd heard all about it in letters from his family on

Tarimond. But he had lost Maggie years before, when she had turned down his offer of marriage and refused to follow him from Tarimond to Glendarvie. He was glad now that hard work had deprived him of the luxury of losing his own mind.

He scraped the doctor's neat little squares of potato into the trash. What a morning! A family argument, a flood, and an unexpected guest. He had completely forgotten about the stranger Tom had seen on the road outside the gates.

CHAPTER 7

≫

THE TELEPHONE CALL

*G*us, Montmorency, Frank, and Inspector Howard were in the library. Gus went over to the wall by the window and lifted a heavy cloth off the telephone. It was a wooden box with a mouthpiece in the middle, a separate earpiece balanced on a hook to one side, and a little black handle on the other.

"The housekeeper insists on keeping it covered up," said Gus. "She says it just collects dust otherwise. All these little nooks and crannies. And the maids don't like having to clean it. I see their point. I'm not sure I like having all this electricity around."

"It's quite safe," said Montmorency. "George had it specially made by one of the top men. It was the latest model then. There's one just like it in the house in London, and that hasn't done anyone any harm."

"Well, I never wanted it," said Gus, fiddling with the earpiece. "We have to have that ugly wire running across the grounds for a start. George thought it would be a good way of keeping in touch, but he was never at the other end if I called, and there's hardly anyone up here to call. I'm not sure I can remember how to do it." He leaned towards the mouthpiece. "Hello! Hello?"

"You have to turn the handle to get the power going," said Montmorency. "Then they should answer at the exchange."

"Exchange!" said Frank. "It's Mrs. McDuff at the post office. Let's hope she's listening for a call."

"I remember now," said Gus. "You need about three hands." He moved the earpiece to his left ear, turned the handle, and waited. Nothing happened. He tried again a few times. "Confounded thing!" he said. "Never works. Where is the wretched woman?" His voice suddenly changed to a tone Montmorency had never heard him use before. It was grand, and yet ingratiating at the same time, and rather slow, with every consonant clipped as if he were making a public announcement. He addressed Mrs. McDuff by her official title. "Operator? Ah, operator. This is the Duke of Monaburn speaking. I wish to make a telephone call. Kindly connect me to the director of the Strathgillon Mental Asylum."

There was a pause. Montmorency and the others could hear the faint sound of a woman's voice from the earpiece, which Gus held a few inches from his head. Then the duke spoke in that unusual voice once more.

"No, I do not have the number."

Another pause. Then Gus continued. "Very well. I will wait."

He let go of the earpiece and turned to the others. "She is going to make the connection and call me back. Then we should be able to talk to the doctor."

The squeaky voice was still coming out of the earpiece dangling down the wall. "Dad," said Frank. "I think the operator wants to speak to you again."

The duke raised the earpiece to his mouth. "Hello?" he shouted into it. "Hello!"

"Dad, she's not in that part. You have to speak into the box."

The duke covered up his embarrassment by shouting back at Frank just as he turned to face the mouthpiece. "Shut up, you fool," he yelled into the machine. "I know what I'm doing!"

The woman's voice grew louder. Even Montmorency, a few feet away, could tell that her formal cry of "Hello caller, hello caller!" was mixed with shock and surprise. He calmly guided Gus's hand so that the receiver was against his ear.

The duke could hear the woman again and put his "telephone voice" back on. "Yes. This is the Duke of Monaburn speaking."

The other voice was muffled as Gus listened to the reply. Then he carefully replaced the earpiece on its hook. "Goodbye," he said. "Good-bye."

"Dad, you're supposed to say good-bye *before* you end the call."

"But she told me to hang up. I had to replace the receiver so she can call me back."

"Never mind," said Montmorency. "At least you've set things in motion. Now all we have to do is wait for the hospital to come on the line."

"And that's when I ruin your reputation, Frank," said Gus. "Are you sure about this?"

"Certain, Dad. I want you to do it. For Uncle George and for Doctor Farcett."

They all jumped as the bell on the wall rang loudly. Gus got flustered, trying to wind the handle again. Frank stopped him just in time.

"No, Dad. Don't touch that this time. Just say hello."

"Hello," said the duke. "This is the Duke of Monaburn speaking."

They could hear the distant female voice again.

"Yes, please," said the duke. "Put him on."

Now the voice at the other end was deeper, obviously male. The duke spoke again, very loudly.

"This is the Duke of Monaburn speaking. Good afternoon, Professor Frost. I have a matter of the utmost delicacy, and of some urgency, to discuss with you."

Huddling by her telephone equipment at the post office, Mrs. McDuff knew she should not listen in. But somehow she couldn't stop herself. After all, she needed to make sure that the connection didn't break down. At the end of the call, she realized that she could never tell anyone what she had heard. That evening she moved on to her other job, at the bar of the local hotel. Trade was slow. There was only the quiet, dark stranger in the corner and her old friend Betty Cameron, who'd dropped in to discuss the flower committee for the church. Mrs. McDuff found herself passing on the duke's news, in strictest confidence of course. By the end of the day, everyone on the flower committee knew about it. And the lone guest was up in his room, scouring his map to find Strathgillon.

CHAPTER 8

≫

SNOW

*E*veryone at the castle went to bed ready for the next day. Doctor Farcett's bags were packed, and Inspector Howard's driver had been briefed on the best route to Strathgillon. Cook had prepared a little hamper for the journey, and Montmorency and Frank were ready to leave for London with the inspector as soon as his carriage returned. But next morning all their plans had to change. Just after six, the telephone bell rang, its unfamiliar noise terrifying the maid who was laying a fire in the library grate. Frank ran downstairs in his pajamas to answer the call. It was the first test of Montmorency's strategy. Frank could not admit who he really was.

"Hello," said the voice at the other end of the phone. "This is Professor Frost at Strathgillon. To whom am I speaking, please?"

Frank thought fast and gave his brother's name. "This is the Marquess of Rosseley, Doctor. How may I help you? Are you calling about my brother?"

"Indeed yes, sir. I am sorry to disturb you so early, but I hope he has not already left. We have had a severe snowstorm here. All the roads are blocked."

Frank wiped away some of the condensation on the window with his sleeve. It was still dark, but he could see that it must have been snowing all night. The driveway had disappeared, and fat snowflakes were still falling, diagonally, driven by a sharp north wind. "Same here, too," he said. "It looks as if we won't be making the journey today. Shall we call again when there's a thaw at this end?"

"Yes, and I will keep in touch from here. Do you need any help with the patient?"

"I believe we can cope, if it's not for too long," said Frank. As he spoke, he heard the thump and bang of hot water making its way through air-locked pipes to the upstairs bathroom. Doctor Farcett was having his first wash of the day.

One by one the family woke, saw the snow, and realized the inevitable delay to their plans. They were cross at first, but the extra time made it possible for them to discuss in more detail exactly what they were all going to do. Overnight, Montmorency, Frank, and Inspector Howard had all been brooding on Tom's encounter with the stranger, and when Harvey came into the breakfast room with extra fuel for the fire, Montmorency asked him if his search had turned up anything.

Harvey was embarrassed. There hadn't been a search. But fortunately, Nancy, one of the maids, had gone down to the village the night before, and Harvey had overheard her talking in the kitchen about the dark man who had been settling his bill at the hotel when she arrived. The duke sent for the girl, and she nervously answered questions from the inspector as the family ate their porridge, toast, and sausages.

Inspector Howard asked for a description.

"He was foreign, I think," she said. "At least not from around here. I couldn't make out exactly what he was saying."

"Was he tall, short, dark . . . ?"

"The hood of his cape was up, but I could see he had black hair and a bit of a beard. And he was tall but kind of bent over. He had a stick."

"That's him," said Tom. "That's the man I saw."

"And he was leaving?" said Howard briskly, silencing Tom and hoping he would take the hint not to speak in front of a servant. "Did you hear where he was going and how?"

"He wanted a ride way up past Elgin," said Nancy. "It must have been important for him to go right away. He had plenty of money. That's why the carrier agreed to take him at night. It's good he got away when he did, really. Otherwise he'd have been caught in this snow. Perhaps he could tell it was coming."

"And did you hear a name? Did anyone at the hotel say who he was?"

"No. They were talking about him after he left. He'd only been there a day and never gave any details. Never even slept in the bed. But he paid for the night even so."

"Thank you, Nancy," said the duke. "You may go."

As soon as the door was closed, he turned to Tom. "So you think that's the man you saw yesterday?"

"Yes. That's him."

"It's Malpensa," said Frank. "I'm sure of it. And it sounds as if he's making for Strathgillon."

"We were right. He wants to check up on you, Frank," said

39

Montmorency. "He's making sure you're no threat to him or his organization. Maybe I should go to Strathgillon, too. I want to get my hands on him."

"No," said Inspector Howard, more curtly than he had dared speak before. "I know you hold him partly responsible for Lord George Fox-Selwyn's death, and I can understand that you want to do something about that. But this is England . . ."

"Scotland, actually," the duke interrupted, annoyed as usual at the way English people forgot about the border.

"Forgive me, Your Grace." The inspector cleared his throat. "Here in Britain we do things properly. We have the rule of law. I can't be party to a private vendetta, and in any case I need this Malpensa — if that's who he is — alive. I need to see where he goes, what he does, who he mixes with, how he gets messages to and fro."

"So are you going to go to Strathgillon, then?"

"Yes, I think I will. If I travel with the patient, I may be taken for a doctor. But I can't stay. I have to go back to London in case there are any developments involving Her Majesty. I will need to leave someone behind and to set up a means of communicating with them." He turned to Vi, Tom's mother, who had been sitting quietly, taking everything in. "Madam. It occurs to me that your son might be the person to take on this task. He knows what this stranger looks like, and he has already told us that he believes the man mistook him for a servant. I wonder if Tom might enter the hospital posing as some sort of assistant to Doctor Farcett."

Now the doctor interrupted. "You mean Lord Francis Fox-Selwyn."

"Thank you for the correction, Doctor. You are right. We must all refer to you by that name now." He returned to his main point. "As I was saying, Tom here could fit in and let us know of developments at Strathgillon."

Gus looked at Tom and his mother. "What do you say, Vi? Will you let him do it?"

"Yes, if I can go too," she said. "I don't want to leave him on his own. He's only fourteen, after all. And you know, I would be able to tell if that man really is Malpensa. I'm the only one apart from Frank who's seen his face."

"Maybe Vi could pose as a nurse," Montmorency suggested. "She's worked in the infirmary on Tarimond. And we've seen before what a good actress she is."

The duke liked the idea. "I could write a letter saying that I insist on 'my son' having familiar people around him. What do you think, Inspector? Will they swallow that?"

"I'm sure any request from you will be treated with the utmost respect, Your Grace," said Inspector Howard. "In view of your rank — and of course you will be paying the bill."

There was an embarrassed silence. No one had given the matter of money a moment's thought up to that point. Doctor Farcett began rocking backward and forward in his chair.

"I must pay. I must pay," he chanted. "I am not fit to take your money."

Gus was calm but firm in his reply. "Don't be ridiculous, Robert. Inspector Howard is right. The accounts must come to me, or the whole stratagem will fail. You just concentrate on getting better. When you are well, we can discuss the matter again, but for now, this is my contribution to the enterprise. I know I was against all this at first, but I want you all to understand that if it's going ahead, you can count on me. I'm beginning to see why George found this sort of thing so exciting. I just wish we could get moving." He walked over to the fireplace and threw an extra log on the blaze. "Let's hope a thaw sets in soon."

CHAPTER 9

≫

AGOSTINO GRASSO

*F*ar away, across the Atlantic, a much smaller fire was burning in a tiny, dirty grate. "Agostino Grasso" was feeling the cold. He had never been a rich man, but just six months before, as Antonio Moretti, curator of La Specola museum in Florence, he had wanted for nothing, and both his home and his workplace had been comfortable and warm. Now here he was, in Paterson, New Jersey, with a new name and no job. He had never expected to end up like this. His old self, Antonio Moretti, had always been one row back from the front line of the anarchists' struggle. He had helped them, shielded them from the authorities, given them a base in his museum; but he had never intended to hurt anyone directly. Not until those Englishmen — Montmorency and Fox-Selwyn — had accidentally stumbled into his world.

Then he had been trapped. He had known that the really clever one — Lord George Fox-Selwyn, who took such care to appear as a bumbling fool — would eventually work out what was going on and that George would be ruthless when he discovered a plan to kill the Italian king. It could only be a matter of time before George worked out that Moretti was involved.

Moretti had waited as long as he could, while George, still believing Moretti to be his friend, unwittingly gave a running commentary on the progress of his investigations. But inevitably, the point came when Moretti had decided to be ruthless himself. He had stopped Lord George Fox-Selwyn from foiling the plot against the king, stopped him with hot bullets straight into his back. And then a kind of madness had set in. He had crated up the corpse and sent it, pickled in preserving fluid, to London. He knew as he sealed the tank, as he calmly arranged the documents for shipping, as he supervised the transport of the cargo to the docks, that he was saying goodbye to his old life. Montmorency would realize who had done the deed, and Montmorency would be after him. In the aftermath of the king's assassination, Moretti could not risk contacting Malpensa or any other anarchists in his homeland for help. So he had changed his name to Agostino Grasso and joined the flood of Italians making for the New World. Surely Montmorency would never find him there.

Moretti couldn't have known that his hiding place was the one part of America that Montmorency knew well. To his dying moment, George, who so successfully portrayed himself as a gifted amateur, had behaved with consummate professionalism. He had never betrayed the whereabouts of Montmorency and Frank, even to Moretti, whom he mistakenly thought of as a charming companion. And he had not once let slip that Frank, the disheveled young man who had accompanied him and Montmorency on their trip to Florence, was in fact his nephew, Lord Francis Fox-Selwyn. Moretti, like all the other anarchists, thought Frank had died heroically, in a failed terrorist attack in London. Moretti, too, had stayed quiet about the lad — thinking he was keeping Fox-Selwyn off the scent. And so Moretti had never made the link between Frank and Francis. That was why he could relax in Paterson. Why on earth would the family of a dead English aristocrat, murdered in Italy, think of looking for his murderer in the United States?

He could relax, but he was cold. He really must get a job. His landlord had found him one when he first arrived: toiling in the silk works down by the rushing water of the Passaic River. But Moretti, or rather "Agostino Grasso," wasn't built for that kind of thing. Short, round, and unable to function without his powerful glasses, he had been a disaster in the workshop. He was too slow and weak, had dropped heavy bales of material, and made elementary mistakes from exhaustion at the end of each shift. He had tried hard, and the workforce of Italian immigrants had enjoyed his company and his tales from home. But it had been no surprise when the foreman had sacked him just before Christmas, when his chubby hands had failed to keep pace with a rattling machine and he had lost the company hundreds of dollars worth of production.

Moretti's skills were academic. He knew he could never display his extensive knowledge of natural history — that would be too much of a giveaway — but he was orderly, methodical, neat, and good at languages. He wanted to find work in a bank, a school, a college, or a library. He sat down with some notepaper he had brought from Italy and drafted a recommendation for himself. He used a false address, shifting his old hometown from Florence to Rome. Ditching his own tiny handwriting for a bold, flowing script, he wrote of "Agostino Grasso's" diligence, patience, and reliability. He endorsed Grasso's enterprise in setting off for the new world after the "tragedy" of losing his (nonexistent) wife. And he signed the letter with the fictitious name of the director of an invented institution, thoughtfully adding a translation of the original Italian underneath.

After that, he needed to make himself look better. The months in the factory had worn his clothes almost to tatters. And he knew where he might find something smarter. In a house along the road lived a woman whose husband was locked up far away in an Italian prison. Gaetano Bresci, who had traveled to Italy to kill King Umberto in July, had left behind a wife and child in America. Moretti would introduce himself to Bresci's wife and ask whether "Agostino Grasso" could have the use of his clothes. She was bound to understand, especially when he explained that he had personally intercepted and disposed of an Englishman on her husband's tail. She might even turn out to be a good cook. He was hungry and could do with a decent meal.

CHAPTER 10

≫

CODE MAKING

*I*n the library at Glendarvie, Tom's mother, Vi, wanted to know what was expected of her. "So when we're there, at the hospital," she asked, "what exactly are we looking for?"

Montmorency replied, "Well, you're looking for changes in Robert, of course . . ."

"Lord Francis Fox-Selwyn," said Robert, always anxious to assume his new identity.

Montmorency continued. "Looking for changes in the patient. After all, we'll want to hear all his news if we can't visit him. But you must watch to see if anyone is trying to make contact — trying to track down the real Frank. We hope that stranger outside was just inquisitive — seeking to put a face to a name in a reference book — but we have to be ready. If the anarchists ever found out that our Lord Francis and their Frank are one and the same, Frank would be in danger, and so too would Robert, for as long as he bears the name of Fox-Selwyn. You would have to raise the alarm if anything happened at Strathgillon."

"How? How would I do that? The inspector has already told us not to write letters or use the telephone or telegraph."

Inspector Howard was thoughtful. "I think you could send a few messages, but you'd have to put it all into some sort of code."

Tom interrupted him. "I know one already. You give every letter of the alphabet a number, and then you write lists of numbers instead of words. It takes ages, though."

"Yes," said the inspector. "And it's not very secure. It's obvious that you're trying to hide something and that particular cipher is very easily cracked. It's much better to secrete the real message in a communication that looks perfectly normal."

The duke spoke. "Well, if Frank really were in the hospital I should certainly expect regular bulletins on his progress. Perhaps Vi could write to me, or even telephone, and hide important information among all the medical detail."

"That's probably the best way," said Inspector Howard. "But it's likely to be harder than you think. It's got to be obvious enough for His Grace to pick up on the message, but sufficiently unclear for a spy to miss it."

"Maybe we should have a trial run," said Vi, and she and the duke spent a jolly half hour exchanging bogus notes.

Vi started. "Little to report. Some improvement in spirits following unexpected visit from doctor in black cloak."

Frank was unimpressed. "Too obvious, Vi. If Malpensa got ahold of that one, he'd recognize himself straight away!"

"It needs to be a real code," said Alexander. "I can see what you're doing, disguising Malpensa as a doctor, but try something else. 'Visitor,' perhaps."

"That's just as bad, surely," said Gus. "How about 'friend'?"

"Or don't say it's a person at all," said Montmorency. "What about 'infection'?"

"I like that," said Frank. "Then if Malpensa hangs around

you could say 'infection persists.' Or, if he goes, 'infection cleared up.'"

"I see," said the duke. "But there's just one thing."

"What's that?" asked Frank.

"What is Vi supposed to write when she really does mean that Robert has an infection or is getting better?"

They all laughed and played around with codes for a good while before Montmorency came up with an idea. When Vi really meant what she said, she would sign the letters "V. Evans." When the message was in code, it would be "Evans" alone. Messages back would say "Monaburn" when encrypted, and a simple, aristocratic "M" when not.

"That's clear then," said the duke with weary relief. "So long as we both get it the right way around."

Frank had his head in his hands. "Oh, Dad. Let's just hope there isn't much of significance to report. I don't think you are a natural spy."

"You're right," said the duke. "George had all the talent in that department, I'm afraid."

The gong sounded for lunch, and they started moving towards the dining room. Montmorency took Frank to one side. "That was fun," he said, "but it's made me realize that we are going to need codes of our own."

"You mean when we're tracking the people who killed Uncle George?"

"Think about it during the meal, and we'll have a chat this afternoon."

By teatime, Montmorency and Frank were ready to reveal

their scheme to the others. Everyone sat around the fire in the library, trying to keep warm as Montmorency laid out the details.

"Before I start, let me say that this code is only to be used when absolutely necessary. If our targets see it too often, they will be able to work out who is who, and the code will be useless. Forgive us, Inspector, I know you want us to concentrate primarily on the threat to the Crown, but you will understand if we prepare ourselves in case we come across our own, private, enemies. The chances are that the two are the same, anyway. So here is our list: And to make it easier to remember, we've constructed a mnemonic."

"A what?" squealed Vi.

"Something to make it easier to remember," said Frank.

"You know," said Alex, "like 'Every Good Boy Does Fine' to remind you of EGBDF on the musical scale."

"Exactly," said Montmorency. "And with our system all you need to think of to get started is one word: REVENGE. We've drawn up a chart to make it easier for you to learn."

Frank held up a large piece of paper, with words arranged on a grid.

R	REX	CROWN	REGINALD
E	EVIL	ANARCHISTS	EVELYN
V	VICTIM	FRANK	VICTOR
E	ENGINE	MALPENSA	ENID
N	NATURALIST	MORETTI	NATHANIEL
G	GRIEVING	MONTMORENCY	GRISELDA
E	EMPIRE	HOWARD	EMILY

Gus let out a loud sigh. "What on earth does all that mean?" he asked. "I can tell already that it's going to be too much for me."

"A little tricky, perhaps," said Montmorency. "But too much for our opponents, we hope. I'll take you through it in stages. Look at just the first two columns for now." He pointed at the chart with a silver spoon. "Here's the mnemonic. Now repeat this after me:

REX will be saved from the
EVIL force and the
VICTIM will be avenged when the
ENGINE and the
NATURALIST are caught by the
GRIEVING on behalf of the
EMPIRE."

The duke sighed again. Montmorency tried to get him into the spirit of the enterprise. "Come on, Gus. Give it a go. You can see it all written here. Just repeat it a few times to get it into your head."

They all chanted out the strange sentence like children in a classroom.

"Thank you," said Montmorency when he felt they had memorized it. "Now, here's what it all means. We've given code names to the most important people we might want to talk about. We've decided that those names should be as unlike their real names as possible, but you'll be able to remember them because they all start with the same letters as their description in the mnemonic." He moved his spoon along to the last two columns of his chart.

Frank took over the explanation. "The first one is very easy. Rex obviously means 'king' or possibly the queen while she is still alive."

"Oh Lord!" said Gus in a stage whisper.

"Concentrate, Dad. It really is simpler than it looks. Now. When referring to the monarch we shall always call her, or him, REGINALD."

Montmorency took over. "So, let's go back to the mnemonic. REX will be saved from the EVIL force." He pointed to the chart again. "You see? The evil force is the anarchist movement. In our code, they are Evelyn."

Frank took the next part. "REX will be saved from the EVIL force and the VICTIM will be avenged. Now, I know we are all victims of what happened to Uncle George, and that he was the biggest victim of all, but for our purposes in London, that word VICTIM refers to me, and my code name will be VICTOR."

"I can see how it works," said the duchess. "But what's all this coming up about an engine?"

"Ah," said Montmorency. "Whom do you think we have in mind when we talk about the 'engine' of the evil force — the motivator of the anarchists?"

"Malpensa?" said Vi.

"Precisely. The ENGINE is Malpensa. So his code name must begin with En."

"Enid!" said Alexander, looking at the chart.

"You got there before me, Alex," said Montmorency. "We thought it a suitably demeaning name for him. It should help to make us all a little less impressed by him, don't you think?"

Tom had got the idea and was moving on. "The ENGINE and the NATURALIST. Well, the naturalist must be Moretti. He worked in a museum of natural history."

Angelina interrupted. "And the 'Na' in naturalist gives us NATHANIEL."

"But the ENGINE and the NATURALIST are caught by the GRIEVING. Who is that?"

"That's me," said Montmorency. "So I'm . . ."

"GRISELDA!" Vi laughed.

"I'm glad you think that's an unexpected name for me," said Montmorency. "Just one more to go. The last 'E' of Revenge. Who can still remember how it goes?"

This time Gus took a turn. "REX will be saved from the EVIL force and the VICTIM will be avenged when the ENGINE and the NATURALIST are caught by the GRIEVING on behalf of the EMPIRE."

Everybody clapped.

"So, EMPIRE is the word," said Frank. "And, Inspector Howard, we hope you don't mind if, to mark your role as the upholder of the empire, we give you the code name of EMILY."

The policeman blushed. "No, no. I can see what you are trying to achieve. Emily will do nicely, thank you. I had a great-aunt Emily, and I was very fond of her."

"That's settled, then," said Montmorency. "Have another

look at the chart, everyone, and run through the mnemonic in your minds. Then we will put it to the test."

They passed around the chart.

"So how might a message read?" asked the duke.

"Try it, Gus," Montmorency replied. "Try saying, 'The anarchists are planning to disrupt the coronation, and I believe Moretti is involved, under Malpensa's direction.'"

Gus took his time and then came out with: "Evelyn is planning to disrupt the coronation, and I believe Nathaniel is involved, under Enid's direction."

"Well, you've got it right, Dad," said Frank. "But you could make it more secretive. You don't have to be so literal. I think we'd all know what you meant if you said, '*It seems Evelyn is determined to ensure that Nathaniel spoils the party, and I shouldn't be surprised if Enid is egging him on.*'"

"Which is the sort of gossip one hears all the time!" said the duchess. "In fact, if we were going to pass on that kind of message, it would probably sound best coming from me."

"I can see you've all got the idea," said Montmorency. "Let's test one another from time to time. All those E's are a pest, but I liked the idea of basing it all on the word 'revenge.' In spite of your reservations, Inspector, it does remind the rest of us of what this is all about."

"I'll turn a blind eye, sir," said Inspector Howard. "But don't expect any of my men to help you out in a family feud. And I can't offer any protection if you break the English law."

"Well, the chances are that we'll be able to deal with these men abroad anyway. And if we do find them at home, I promise we will be discreet."

"I'm afraid I can't hear you, sir," said the inspector diplomatically. "I seem to have gone a little deaf. I can only thank you for your assistance in helping us counter the enemies of the queen and the empire."

"And the sooner this snow melts, the sooner we can start," said Montmorency, tearing up the chart and throwing the pieces onto the fire. "Now, Tom, tell me the new name for Moretti."

"Moretti. He's the naturalist, isn't he? So he's Nathaniel."

"Well done, Tom. And the inspector?"

"He's the empire. So he's Emily."

"And Enid, Gus?"

"Well, it comes from evil, doesn't it?" The duke corrected himself quickly: "No, not evil, that's the anarchists. They're Evelyn, aren't they? Enid must be engine. Engine. The man behind it all. Malpensa. He's Enid, I think."

"Yes, Gus, you got there in the end. Now, practice, everyone, practice. We can't afford to get this wrong. And don't forget, the man we now call Enid may be closer than we think. We'll be depending on you, Vi and Tom, to tell us if he turns up at Strathgillon. If only this snow would go away."

Stranded at an inn on the way to Strathgillon, the quiet stranger was thinking the same thought.

CHAPTER II

≫

STRATHGILLON HOSPITAL

Two days later, Montmorency was awakened by a noise on the roof, as if someone was walking across the tiles in heavy boots. But who would do such a thing? Had Malpensa returned to seek out Frank? Down below, Gus's elderly dog, Tess, started barking in a sweet attempt to protect the household. Montmorency went to the window. He could see nothing in the early-morning darkness, but then the noise came again, and something gray and heavy scraped across the glass a few inches from his face. It was frightening, but after a second of horror he realized it was good. A thick sheet of snow had detached itself from the roof and fallen to the ground. The thaw had begun, and Robert would be able to make the journey to Strathgillon soon.

By midmorning, Harvey and his men had cleared a path to the gate, and a phone call to the hospital had established that the roads were open there, too. Doctor Farcett had a last long bath before climbing into the coach with Inspector Howard, Vi, and Tom.

"Good-bye, Robert," said Montmorency. There was no reply. "Robert, good-bye," he repeated, but still the doctor did not look up. Montmorency realized with some anxiety that Farcett had already adopted his new identity, perhaps a little more convincingly than was strictly necessary at this stage. Was this charade perhaps too much for his fragile mind? Was he losing track of who he really was? Montmorency tried again. "Lord Francis Fox-Selwyn?" he said, and Robert's head rose at last. "Have a good trip, my lord!" said Montmorency, humoring him, and Robert nodded calmly as the horses began to move.

Inspector Howard shouted a last farewell. "We'll leave for London as soon as I get back," he said.

Strathgillon Hospital looked magical at the foot of a wooded hillside still touched by snow. Built in the same baronial style as Glendarvie Castle, its high round towers and sweeping arches made it look like the home of an aristocrat. Only the high wall along the road and the bars across the windows gave away its true purpose. The driveway snaked through farmland, where patients could be seen clearing away snow and scattering turnips for the sheep, which could find no sustenance in the frozen ground. Huge barns indicated that other livestock was probably kept here, too, closed away now for protection from the weather. The driver pulled up outside the tall double doors at the front of the hospital, and Inspector Howard left the others in the carriage as he went to ring the bell. Someone must have seen them coming. The door opened as he reached out for the bell pull, and a middle-aged man in a white coat emerged to greet him.

"Good afternoon!" he said, shaking Inspector Howard's hand. "I presume you have brought Lord Francis Fox-Selwyn? Doctor . . . ?"

"Howard," said the inspector, happy to go along with the assumption that he was a medical man and glad not to have to initiate the lie himself. "He is in the carriage. I suggest we move him inside right away."

"Of course," said the doctor. "I'm Peter Frost, by the way. Director of Strathgillon. Should I send a porter to help restrain him?"

"No. He's perfectly docile. I think you will find him a cooperative patient," said Inspector Howard, "though he is uncomfortable in the company of strangers. That is why His Grace has sent two of his personal servants to ease his transition into hospital life. Mrs. Vi Evans has some nursing experience, and her son, Tom, can attend to his lordship's personal needs. It is the duke's wish that they should lodge with him. He will pay for their board, of course."

"That is somewhat irregular, but we are happy to abide by His Grace's wishes." Professor Frost could hardly say no. His institution was still young, and he could not pass up the chance to gain acceptance, and even publicity, among moneyed patients by accommodating such an illustrious client.

Vi and Tom helped bring Doctor Farcett and his luggage into the building, settling him down in an armchair near the fire. Professor Frost talked to him kindly but a little louder and more slowly than he would have done had he realized that his patient was in fact a fellow medical man. He gave a short resume of his methods at Strathgillon. "We don't believe in locking people in cells here, nor in tying their hands or bullying them. We will work hard together, but we will take good care of you. You must be tired after your journey. I have already ordered some tea." Still taking Inspector Howard for a doctor, Frost urged him to one side. "His Grace the Duke of Monaburn has acquainted me with the particulars of His Lordship's case. But perhaps you would care to give me your own opinion."

"I am no expert in your field," said Inspector Howard (truthfully). "But the basic facts are these. His lordship has become increasingly preoccupied with washing. His obsession is preventing him from leading a normal life. He blames himself for many things that are not his fault. His father, the duke, is concerned that he may become a danger to himself, but we are in agreement that he is probably no danger to others. He has been through several demanding experiences of late. You may have heard that his uncle, Lord George Fox-Selwyn, of whom he was extremely fond, died suddenly last summer. He has been profoundly changed by grief."

"I can see that," said Frost, "even without having known him before. He has the careworn look of someone older than his true years. It's hard to believe that he is indeed the duke's younger son."

"That is one reason for the duke's concern," said Inspector Howard, trying to deflect any suspicion. "He is quite unrecognizable as the old Francis. The duke wants his son back again. And he does not want him to suffer extra indignities in addition to those brought about by his condition."

"I understand. And you have come to the right place. We do not believe in punishing the mentally sick, nor in treating them as if they were subhuman. Lord Francis Fox-Selwyn will be comfortable with us, I can assure you. But we do have two rules. He will have to confront his fears, and he will have to work. I am a great believer in the curative power of open air and exertion. It seems to me that the best way to challenge his fear of dirt will be to assign him to the piggery. When he sees that he can muck out the sties without falling sick, he should be able to return to normal habits."

"So you think you may cure him quite quickly?" asked the inspector, secretly disappointed, as he hoped the real Lord Francis Fox-Selwyn would be officially out of circulation for some time.

"Well, I wouldn't necessarily use the word 'quick,' but I'm sure we will get there in the end, especially if we get to the bottom of what has really caused the problem. Now where's that tea I promised you?"

He rang the bell, and a tall swarthy woman entered with a tray of cups.

"Forgive the delay, Professor. The water took a while to boil, it being so cold."

"That's quite all right, Belinda," said the professor kindly. "Just put down the tray, and you can get back to your duties."

The woman left the room, and Frost turned back to the inspector. "That lady is another of our patients. When she came here, she was afraid to talk to anyone. She would not even set foot outside her bedroom from sheer fear. Even I had to speak to her through a grille in the door. You saw for yourself how relaxed she was encountering four strangers. I think that's an indication that my methods work."

Professor Frost could see that his new patient was listening in, and he walked towards his chair. "My Lord, may I call you Francis? You may have noticed that I addressed Belinda by her Christian name. We find here that it helps to break down barriers between ourselves and the patients and between the patients themselves. Of course, if you prefer to be known by your full title . . ."

"Not at all," said Robert, with the first words he had uttered since leaving Glendarvie. "Do call me Francis. Indeed, you must call me Francis. I am Lord Francis Fox-Selwyn. Francis is my name. Francis. Yes. Francis."

"Agreed," said Professor Frost, intrigued by his new patient's manner. He turned quietly to Inspector Howard. "This repetition of his name. Very interesting, isn't it? It's almost as if he needs to reassure himself of his identity." Then he smiled at Farcett. "Now, Francis, if you and your assistants will follow me, I will show you to your room."

Vi and Tom collected the luggage. Inspector Howard wanted to get away before Professor Frost realized he was not a doctor. "I'm afraid I must go at once," he said. "I have important business in London, already delayed by the bad weather." And, taking his leave of the others, he returned to the carriage and started back down the driveway. At the first village, he noticed an inn, saw that it might be his last chance for some hours to get something to eat, and asked the driver to stop, promising that it would be only a short interruption to their journey.

He was welcomed by a kindly woman who offered him a seat by the fire. Another guest was already there, with a plate of steak pie and vegetables balanced on a rickety table in front of him. He didn't look local. In fact, he didn't look British at all. Several days' growth of beard obscured most of his face. His clothes were dark, worn, and spattered by travel. And behind him on a hook hung a long black cloak and a powerful pair of binoculars. Inspector Howard could hardly believe his luck. He was face to face with Malpensa.

CHAPTER 12

≫

THE SEEDS OF DECEIT

*I*nspector Howard struggled to look calm as he worked out a strategy for dealing with the man before him. He must do nothing to reveal that he was a policeman, and he must give away as little as possible while obtaining the maximum information. He toyed for a moment with the idea of taking Malpensa into custody, but he knew he could not. This was Scotland, where his English powers had no effect. And anyway, on what grounds could he arrest the man? He had nothing but suspicions: a vague idea that Malpensa might be planning an attack on the royal family. But there was no evidence.

Evidence was what he needed, and he was more likely to get that if Malpensa were watched and reported on. Maybe later Howard would approach the local authorities and take them into his confidence, asking them to put a tail on him. But would there be time? They were miles from the nearest town and still farther from any sophisticated police force. No, Inspector Howard must find out what he could now and leave the rest to Vi and Tom. At least the real Frank was safe at Glendarvie, and his decoy, Robert Farcett, securely locked away at Strathgillon. He reassured himself that it was unlikely Malpensa would do any physical harm here. He was probably just trying to pin down exactly where all George Fox-Selwyn's family were so that he and his allies could dodge any attempt at retribution for George's death.

Inspector Howard was still trying to think of an opening question when Malpensa spoke first. His accent was odd, unplaceable, but definitely not British. "I saw your carriage pass up to the hospital and back. Are you a doctor?"

It was a more direct question than Inspector Howard was prepared for. He decided to pretend to be a doctor and perhaps reinforce the story Malpensa had already heard at Glendarvie. "Yes, I was accompanying a patient. He has just been admitted."

"The patient was a man?"

"Indeed, but you will appreciate that I cannot talk about him. These matters are extremely delicate, as I'm sure you know."

"I understand. It must be a great shame for the family to have one of their number so stricken."

"A tragedy. But I really cannot say any more. What brings you here?"

He was surprised by the reply. "I am a birdwatcher. There are species in these parts that are seen nowhere else in Europe."

"And you have traveled here in such bad weather just to see them?"

"Yes. Although the weather was better when I set off. But the snow can be a help, in fact. The birds stand out so well against the whiteness. It is easier for me to pick them out with my binoculars."

Aha! thought Howard. *He's a canny one. He's got an explanation for owning binoculars. Obviously up to no good. He's spent some time working out his story all right.* Howard tried to sound charming, casually interested in the stranger's hobby. "Oh, binoculars! Do you know I've never actually used a pair. Could I possibly have a look?"

The other man calmly rose and took down the binoculars from the peg. Howard made a great play of not understanding how the focus worked — though he had used many a pair in his time — and took the opportunity to examine them as closely as possible. They were an unfamiliar brand.

"Edgecomb Mystic. Is that the best manufacturer? Not a company I've heard of."

"American," said the stranger. "I brought them over with me when I came."

"So you are an American!" said Howard. "I couldn't place the accent."

"I've been living in America for some time," said the man. "I'm from Hungary, originally."

Howard took the opportunity to find out more, though he didn't believe for one minute that the man really was from Hungary or America. He reached out his hand to make a formal introduction. "Charles Aston," he said, plucking as an alias the name of the first man he'd arrested.

"Max Bartok," said his companion, shaking hands confidently. Howard noted that the stranger was a professional. He had worked out every detail of his false identity.

The woman arrived with a plate of food for the inspector. He ate it quickly, interspersing mouthfuls with answers to questions from "Bartok." *He's clever, this Malpensa,* thought Howard. *He makes it all seem so natural and urbane. Just two affable people meeting by chance and discussing the affairs of the day. He makes it sound normal to be interested in the health of the queen and the prospect of a new king.* But Howard was circumspect in his replies, all the time memorizing Malpensa's facial features, ready to do a sketch as soon as he was alone.

The stranger was showing a close interest in the queen's funeral. "I expect that crowned heads from all over Europe will be in attendance," he said.

"No doubt, and representatives from across the empire, too."

"Apparently, if she dies at Osborne House on the Isle of Wight, her body will be taken by boat to the mainland, by train to London, and then on to Windsor for burial. It could take several days."

Howard was alarmed that Malpensa was so well informed. The details of the queen's condition had been kept from the newspapers, and the funeral arrangements would not be made public until after her death. Malpensa must have contacts at the highest level. But Howard was determined not to give away his suspicions or inadvertently to confirm what Malpensa said. "It might well take a long time. But it will be a great and solemn occasion in the life of our nation," said Howard. "I have no knowledge of what the plans are. And it doesn't really feel seemly to discuss them while Her Majesty is still alive."

"I'm sorry," said Malpensa. "Forgive the insensitivity of a foreigner."

Moments later, Howard's driver entered the room, a stain on his chin revealing that the barmaid had given him some pie as well. "Excuse me for interrupting, sir, but I'm worried about the weather, and we really must get back on the road if we are to reach Glendarvie tonight."

Howard noticed a flicker of relief in Malpensa's face. No doubt he was glad of the confirmation that Howard had come from Glendarvie and that his "patient" must indeed have been Lord Francis Fox-Selwyn.

Howard rose reluctantly. He would have liked to find out more about Malpensa and his plans, but he knew his driver was right, and now more than ever he felt he must get back to London to make sure the funeral procession would be safe. "Yes, I'm afraid I must be getting along," he said. He couldn't bring himself to shake hands with Malpensa again, but forced himself to say, "Very nice to have met you, Mr. Bartok." And he added one more question. "Are you staying in the area long?"

"Well, that's really up to the birds, not me. I'll stay until I spot the species I've come to see. But I must admit, if the queen dies, I'd like to go to London to see the funeral."

I'm sure you would, thought Howard. *But I'll make sure you stay here, well out of the way.*

Back in the carriage, he wrote a note to Vi.

Very important to guard against infection. Signs of disease in locality. Enid may visit soon.

He sealed it, put on a stamp, and asked the driver to stop at the next mailbox so he could drop it in. She should get it in the morning. He hoped she would remember what it really meant.

CHAPTER 13

≫

MOTHER AND SON

At Strathgillon, Vi and Tom were allocated a room next door to Robert Farcett. They were also given a key. It unlocked the bathroom opposite, and they had strict instructions to use it only to let themselves in. Robert himself — or Francis, as everyone in the hospital called him — was not allowed anywhere near running water. He had a chamber pot in his room, which Vi was in charge of emptying and cleaning, but not even a jug and basin for his own use. Once a day, he was allowed, accompanied, to take a shower for a set number of minutes timed on a special clock. He was not permitted to shave and soon had a bristly beard, which hid his true identity perfectly. For the first few days, he stayed in his room, occasionally visited by Professor Frost, who withstood all his pleadings for soap and shampoo. Farcett cried openly and rubbed his body with anything he could find: the sheets, the curtains, even his own rather grubby clothes. Vi thought it was cruel not to allow him at least to clean his teeth and make his mouth feel fresh, but Professor Frost explained to her that his method depended on depriving the obsessive of his passion, and that this early stage of the treatment had to be endured, no matter how horrible it was for all concerned.

The patient said very little during that time, and by the end of the first week, even his moaning had stopped. He became easier to manage and was gradually allowed to join the rest of the patients for meals. It was hard for Vi to see this as an improvement. The dull, shuffling figure she escorted to the vast dining room bore no relation to the lively man she had known for fifteen years or even to the troubled figure who had spent Christmas at Glendarvie. Every now and then she would take Inspector Howard's note from her apron pocket. She remembered the code and knew it must mean that Malpensa was nearby, but she worried in case the words about infection were true. What if there were a risk? Shouldn't she be keeping her patient clean?

While she was confined indoors with Robert, she had sent Tom outside, with instructions to look out for Malpensa but to take extreme care. He had walked all around the grounds with an eye out for intruders. He'd gotten to know a number of the patients. Some of them talked pure nonsense to him. Others said nothing but rocked or jiggled with nervous tics. Some seemed to him the sanest people he had ever met. But there was no sign of Malpensa. Once or twice he had a strong feeling that he was being watched, but whether by an outsider or one of the patients he could not tell.

At night, he and his mother talked. They discussed the hospital, the patients, their own home on the island of Tarimond, and their friends in London and Glendarvie. Eventually the long-evaded topic came up. In the security of the darkened room, Vi found a way of telling Tom exactly who his father was. They had been laughing about Alexander and his punctilious correctness, and then moved on to the duke.

Memories of his attempts to use the telephone made them chuckle, but then Tom grew more serious, complaining about how Gus was always finding fault with him, even though, after George's death, he had insisted on taking Tom into the bosom of the family.

"He's angry, Mam, isn't he? He's disappointed in me."

"Why should he be disappointed, Tom?"

"Because I'm not good enough. Not enough like George."

"But why should you be like George?" asked Vi, well aware of what Tom's answer would be.

"Because George was my father, wasn't he, Mam? Don't worry. I've worked it out. Otherwise, why would he have left me all his money?"

Vi knew she couldn't lie to Tom. She stared up into the darkness and found the courage to speak. "No. George may have thought of you like a son, Tom, but he wasn't your father. I know I should have talked to you about this before, but it's been so hard. The moment has never seemed right, and I didn't want to do it on my own."

"You mean you wanted my real father to be there? Who is he? Do I know him? Do you know where he is?"

"Yes, Tom, we both know him very well. Tom darling, I know he won't mind me telling you now. Your father is Montmorency."

Tom was silent. Then he was angry. "And he knows this? And he's never said anything? All this time I've been hoping it was him, and he's never even hinted . . ."

"Tom, he's only been sure himself for about a year. I never

told him, and when I did, it was just when you were most angry with him — when you were cross because he was in love with that girl, Mary, in America."

"But you still should have said something."

"I know. It's easy to say that now, but the time was never right. And then George died, and then Robert got ill. . . ."

"What does he matter? What concern is it of his?"

Vi was silent for a moment. "It's just that he's very fond of you, too, you know. I thought it might upset him to see you belonging entirely to someone else. Before, it was as if they all shared you. They all gave you presents and things, all spent time with you when you were growing up on Tarimond. I thought three adoptive fathers were better than just one."

"No! You fool!" shouted Tom. "Don't you know I've been worrying about this for years?"

"I didn't know you were worrying. . . ."

"Because I didn't tell you. Because I didn't want to upset you!"

"Please don't be angry, Tom. Can't you see this is what I feared?"

Now Tom was quiet. When he finally spoke, the question took Vi by surprise. "I'll have to give the money back, won't I?"

"No, Tom, you won't. George never said he was your father, even in his will. And anyway, who would you give the money to? All his family have more than they know what to do with anyway."

"But we must tell Gus. We must tell him I am not one of his family. Maybe then he might even like me more."

Vi reached out to stroke Tom's hair. "The duke loves you, Tom. We all get exasperated by people we love. But you are right. He should know the truth. I'll write to Montmorency to tell him that you know everything and ask him to break the news to Gus."

"Montmorency's probably in London by now," said Tom. "In George's old house."

"Yes, he probably is. That's how generous George was, Tom. He left his home to Montmorency, who was certainly no relative at all."

"And his property on Tarimond went to you, Mam."

"Yes, to me. And I was never more than a very good friend."

"So I can keep the money?"

"Yes. Keep it. But serve George's memory with pride. You know that Montmorency and Frank are going to try to track down the men who killed George. You may be young, but you must do everything possible to help them. Keep on watching for Malpensa, and see if you can find out anything about where he intends to go next."

"Of course I will," said Tom. "I will help my father in any way I can."

"Good boy. Now get some sleep. If you hear me rustling around, I'll be writing that letter to Montmorency."

"So next time I see him, I can call him 'Father'?" asked Tom.

"Yes, and I'm sure he will be delighted to call you 'son.'"

They both tried, unsuccessfully, to sleep.

"Mam?"

"Yes."

"Montmorency was a bad man once. A liar and a thief. He told me."

"I know. I knew him when he was poor."

"Does that mean I'll be bad one day?"

"Not necessarily, Tom. You have a choice. I've changed myself, and Montmorency has changed, too. You can decide to be good. And with your advantages in life, it would be a disgrace to be anything else."

"I promise to be good, Mam."

"I'm pleased. Why not start now by going to sleep."

"Good night, Mam."

"Good night."

"Thank you for telling me."

CHAPTER 14

≫

LONDON LIVES

Down in London, Montmorency and Frank were settling into the house they both knew so well. It was Lord George Fox-Selwyn's old home, now Montmorency's London base. Chivers, the butler, and Cook, who had been with the family many years, were both glad to greet them, hoping that the household might develop a peaceful routine after the horrors of the previous summer. But Montmorency knew that, like George before him, he had to take the two trusted servants partly into his confidence, and his first announcement told them that life was not going to be quiet: Lord Francis Fox-Selwyn was never to be addressed by his real name.

Frank had arrived looking quite different from usual, wearing worn-out clothes, with a hat pulled down to cover his eyes. When the cab stopped, he had jumped down to help unload the baggage, as if he were a servant. Montmorency soon explained to Cook and Chivers that for the foreseeable future that was exactly what Frank would be.

They had made a plan in their last few days at Glendarvie and refined it on the journey south with Inspector Howard. Frank needed a disguise, and Montmorency had fallen back on his own past to determine what it should be. Years before, Montmorency had lived at the grand Marimion Hotel with a bogus manservant, Scarper, played by himself. Now he would have another Scarper in his life. Frank insisted on keeping the name. This time, Montmorency would be spared the nerve-wracking exhaustion of switching between the two roles. Frank would become Scarper, completely disguised physically, so that no one recognized him as his former self.

They foresaw problems, of course. Frank's red hair was, as Montmorency had predicted, the main one. At Glendarvie, just a couple of days after the big shave, it was growing out unmistakably ginger. Even his pale eyebrows were starting to reappear. They had to resort to dye. Montmorency had offered to flirt with one of the parlor girls to get some, but in the end, the duchess had sent her own maid to buy large quantities, pretending that she wanted to look more like Angelina, Alex's dark Italian wife. After one attempt, the duke flamboyantly refused to let her color her hair again, and Frank inherited the mixture, as planned. At first, he'd intended to let his hair grow, but he realized that the palaver involved in dying long hair would be too much for him, so he decided he would shave his head once a week and just rub in a little color every morning.

He had, however, resolved to grow a short beard. Dyed black, it changed the balance of his face radically, covering most of his freckles, and it made him look older, too. Luckily, not much hair grew on his body, but where it did, he had to dye that as well — just in case he was captured, said Montmorency. You never knew what depths of degradation the enemy might inflict on you. Soon, Frank found his new morning routine of razors, brushes, and swabs quite familiar, and he borrowed a hip flask from Montmorency to keep in a trouser pocket wherever he went, filled with dye just in case he should ever be caught far from home.

Frank had made another decision, and it pleased him, at least in the short term. He would get fat. It might take a while, but he would eat all the food he could, to fool anyone who might remember the lanky teenager he had been when last in London. He told Cook about his plan as soon as he arrived there, and she had a roly-poly pudding steaming on the stove in no time. It was all good fun. But Frank knew that the serious side of things had to begin, and, lying awake in the servants' quarters on his first night back in the capital, he remembered the raw fear he had felt when in danger before. After all his bravado, he was scared — the next day, he would be on his own.

He and Montmorency had agreed with Inspector Howard that they would split up to do some elementary groundwork and meet to discuss their findings the following morning. Montmorency went to his club, Bargles, to see how far the secret preparations for the queen's funeral had permeated London gossip. He was appalled. Within the comfortable, slightly battered sanctuary of the dining rooms and bars, people who expected to have duties at the event swapped information openly. News of the queen's condition had been kept out of the papers, but a senior editor happily passed it on to his illustrious companions over a brandy after lunch. His information was corroborated by a Member of Parliament whose butler had a friend in the queen's household, who wrote regularly from the Isle of Wight. A recently retired general joked about an official letter he had received, asking him to stand by to return, in full uniform, to help command the troops who would line the processional route. And one of the richest men in England, owner of cloth mills in the north, boasted that his company would be providing tents for visiting soldiers who would be sleeping in London's parks.

Standing back from it all and listening, Montmorency realized how each of these minor transgressions of propriety, made in a spirit of conviviality and meant only to reassure each hearer of his own trustworthiness, added together to become useful information for an enemy. He could see how a loose word here or there might touch the ear of a servant at Bargles and find its way out into the places where opponents of the Crown ate and drank. There need be no malice on the part of the gossipers anywhere along the line. It was that final listener, huddled in a murky pub, that they would have to worry about. Montmorency was glad he had not invited Inspector Howard to join him at Bargles to discuss their own plans in private.

While Montmorency was at his club, Frank walked the East London streets, revisiting his old haunts in Clerkenwell and wandering among the Italian immigrants who settled around Snow Hill. The derelict site of the ice-cream factory where he'd worked was still there. It had closed after the strike he and Montmorency had started to get themselves out of trouble nearly two years before. Now its windows were smashed, and there were holes in the roof where tiles had been stolen. He walked into the old kitchen, scene of hard work and humiliation for him when he was little more than a boy. Weeds were growing through the flagstones on the floor, bravely defying the icy air.

But it was people he was looking for, and there was nobody there. The houses were derelict. The workers had lost them when their jobs had gone. So he made for a street market and visited pubs and pie shops, but he saw no one he recognized. He had imagined himself coming face to face with someone he'd known in his time posing as a political firebrand in the factory. He had worried that they might see through his disguise. But in the end, it wasn't tested. The only human contact he had that day was the odd accidental nudge from people who wanted him to get out of the way. He seemed invisible, and in a way, it was a relief. But as he wandered, he realized how unprepared he was. What would he have said about himself if anyone had started up a conversation? Without the cover of a job, how could he blend in and listen to people without them wondering why he was there?

At the end of the long and fruitless day, Montmorency invited him up from the servants' quarters for a glass of port in the drawing room.

"So. How is my old friend Scarper?" said Montmorency playfully.

"What's his first name?" asked Frank. "Don't tell me that he didn't have one, like you."

Montmorency was evasive. "Well he didn't, actually," he

said. "Though Vi came up with Bert once, in an emergency. I used it again in the ice-cream factory, remember? I never liked that name, though. Made me sound a bit stupid. I think you should choose something for yourself."

"I've always hated being called Francis. Too effeminate, I think, and hopeless with Fox-Selwyn to follow. It's like some sort of elocution exercise. You should try saying it when you're drunk."

"I hope you've never had to, Frank."

"Well, perhaps once or twice . . . but I've always fancied something stronger, like Oscar, or Edward, or Jack."

"I like Jack. Oscar's too flowery for the kind of man you're pretending to be. Jack's good. Jack. Short for John. You could say it was your mother's pet name for you when you were a kiddie. It always does to build yourself a bit of a life history. I found that out the hard way. Didn't work enough on mine either as Scarper or as Montmorency. I had to do too much bluffing, especially in the early years. Even now, there are huge chunks I haven't really worked out."

"Like what?"

"You know. Where I went to school, where my family got its money, that sort of thing."

"And your first name of course. Montmorency's Christian name, I mean. Surely you've had plenty of time to think that one up."

"Oh yes, I did that. But I made a bit of a mistake."

"What do you mean? You had every name in the world to choose from."

"I know, but I couldn't settle on one, and when George first took me to Bargles, the word somehow got around that I was called Xavier. Nothing to do with me. It's just that George kept introducing me as his 'savior' after I'd helped him out, and some of the people there got the wrong end of the stick.

"Then when I needed a passport all of a sudden, someone at the club said he'd fix it for me, and Xavier was the name that went down. I was stuck with it. But I hate it, and I've never used it since. All the people I'm really close to have just got used to calling me Montmorency. It's become a sort of nickname on its own."

"Xavier!" said Frank. "Very exotic! I'm surprised you don't use it. It would be a great hit with the ladies, I'm sure. Haven't you ever told anyone? Not even that girl in America? Mary? You must have told her?"

Montmorency looked embarrassed. "Yes. I told Mary. It didn't seem right not to. I wanted to marry her. But I didn't tell her much else. I didn't tell her about the thieving, about living in the sewers, about how my whole existence is based on lies." He paused, looking away from Frank and into the fireplace. "I wonder what she's doing now."

"Why don't you write and ask?"

"Honestly, Frank! You've heard how we parted. Vi must have told you about the fight up at the Bayfield house in Paterson. How Cissie drove a wedge between us."

"Not really. She wouldn't go into detail. Neither would Tom. They just seemed relieved that you weren't going to stay in America. But what have you got to lose now? If she still doesn't want to know you, she won't reply. But if she does, she'll write. And anyway, she might be useful to us. Remember where she lives — Paterson, New Jersey — the epicenter of anarchist activity in America. Suppose Moretti has gone there? She could help us find him."

"I won't have her mixed up in dangerous things like that!"

"I'm not saying that she should creep around listening at doors with a gun in her hand. But if he's there, she might have seen him or heard about him. There's no one else in Paterson we could ask. You could draw a picture of Moretti and send it to Mary. It's worth a try. I doubt if he's using his real name. Like you and me, he'll have changed that."

"I know," said Montmorency. "I had thought of looking for Moretti in Paterson, but my pride wouldn't let me go back. And it's a long shot anyway. He may still be in Italy, or he could be anywhere in the world. Always assuming that he's still alive. Sending George's body back in that tank was the act of a madman. Maybe he's taken his own life. But perhaps I will write. Give me some time to think about it."

"And while you're waiting," said Frank, trying to change the mood, "let's do some work on our personal histories. It seems to me that it doesn't have to be as difficult as you've been suggesting."

"Why not?"

"Because all we have to do is swap. You can have my family background, and I can have yours. We'll change the names, of course — say that your relations are dead, your school closed down, and so on — but the meat of it all is there. It shouldn't be hard for you. You've been fabricating bits and pieces for years, and you've seen exactly how my family lives. But I need to know more about you. You've already told me about life in that orphanage — the Foundling Hospital. But what happened next? Where were you after you left and before you invented Montmorency? How long was that gap?"

"Years. Quite a few years. For some of them, I was in prison. I wouldn't put that into your story of yourself."

"But before prison?"

"I started off in service — most Foundling Hospital children did. I was a bootboy in a house in Spitalfields. If I'd known how I'd end up, I would have taken more interest in what was going on upstairs, but I just got on with things: polishing, mending, running errands. I was the lowest of the low. I suppose I might have worked my way up if I'd stayed, but I got the sack."

"Why?"

"They said I was a thief. Some silver was missing." His voice suddenly turned more youthful, as if he were traveling back to his past. "It wasn't me, though, I swear."

"So they sacked you."

"Yes, and then I really did start thieving. I had to, to stay alive."

"And where did you live?"

"Here and there. People would take me in. Other thieves,

older people who wanted someone else to do the dangerous work. I was good. I was quick. Until I got unlucky. I was living with a man called Baines when I was caught."

"And did you have friends? Did you have girls? Did you have children?"

Montmorency laughed. "The first two, but no children!" His voice dropped. "At least, not then."

Frank sensed embarrassment in the air and didn't push the point. He could hear himself sounding a little too cheery as he returned to the subject of his new identity. "Well, you've certainly given me some material to work with there! If I add your experiences to mine in the factories in London and Paterson, I should be able to paint a pretty convincing picture."

"But of course, don't say you were in the ice-cream factory or in the silk works. You mustn't be too precise, just in case someone links you with the old Frank."

"Of course I won't."

"And if you do find the need to talk about yourself, keep it simple. Don't give any more information than is necessary to avoid the impression that you're being evasive. Listen to the way people talk. Very few give their whole life history — and those who do are usually crushing bores. People just deal in brushstrokes. You won't often find yourself having to give a full account of your background. Unless you fall into the hands of the police, of course."

"And we're working with them this time!" said Frank.

"Yes, and we've got that meeting with Inspector Howard

tomorrow. He must be up to his eyes in it now that the kaiser has decided to make a last visit to the queen, but he said he'd meet us at noon, and we'd better be there."

"I still think it's a strange place for a rendezvous," said Frank.

"Not at all," said Montmorency. "It's rather a clever idea of Howard's. Somewhere private, but where people come and go all day long. And anyway, I'm looking forward to seeing what it looks like inside."

"Well, I'm off to bed," said Frank. "I'll get myself to sleep thinking out the story of my life."

"Good night then . . . Jack Scarper," said Montmorency.

"Do you know?" said Frank. "If this disguise is going to work, you'd better call me that all the time. Even here, when we're on our own, and when you're talking about me to other people, like Inspector Howard. Otherwise, there will come a moment when you say the wrong thing and my real name comes out."

"You want me to call you Jack?"

"Yes. Always. Jack Scarper or Jack for short. Remember, Frank is supposed to be at Strathgillon."

"All right, Jack. I'll try. Now you get some sleep. And don't forget to do your eyebrows in the morning. I'll just stay up a little longer."

He took some paper from the writing desk and started composing a letter to Mary Gibson, in Paterson, New Jersey.

CHAPTER 15

≫

WESTMINSTER SCHOOL

*M*ontmorency and Jack Scarper arrived early, Jack walking a little behind his master, carrying a pile of books. Big Ben chimed a quarter to twelve as they passed beside the ancient, soot-stained majesty of Westminster Abbey and through the archway of a new building into Dean's Yard. Montmorency remembered the directions Inspector Howard had given him and followed the pathway around to the left until another, smaller arch brought them to the ramshackle collection of buildings that made up Westminster School. Boys and masters were passing to and fro, but no one paid the strangers any attention until a tall, thin man in a tattered black gown approached and said quietly, "Mr. Montmorency, I presume. Do come this way." He took Montmorency and Jack up some stone steps and through a warren of corridors to a small room. "Welcome to Westminster," he said when the door was closed. "I am Matthew Joskyns, head of Classics and volunteer librarian. I'm sure Inspector Howard will be here in a minute."

There was a knock on the door.

"Is that you, Howard?"

A high-pitched voice answered. "No, sir."

"Who is it then?"

"Milsom, sir."

"Go away, Milsom."

"But you told me to show you my homework, sir."

"Not now, Milsom. Go away, and count yourself lucky that you have until two o'clock to improve it."

"Yes, sir. Thank you, sir."

"That will do, Milsom. No need for gratitude. I will show no mercy at two."

Mr. Joskyns had his back to Jack and Montmorency, but years of experience as a schoolteacher had trained him to sense suppressed giggling.

"You find this little scene amusing, gentlemen? Perhaps you are reminded of your own schooldays. One has to be a trifle harsh sometimes. Nothing else gets results. I fear only extreme violence will improve young Milsom's Greek."

There was another tap on the door.

"Go away, Milsom. I said two o'clock."

The handle turned slowly, and Inspector Howard put his head around the door.

"I hardly dare come in!" he joked. "I feel as if I should bend over and prepare for a whacking!"

"Sorry, Howard, old boy," said Joskyns. "I thought you were one of the scum. Close the door. I assure you we shall not be interrupted again."

"I see you have met my associates," said Inspector Howard. "Thank you so much for letting us use you as cover."

"That's quite all right. I have told the staff and the porter that you will be visiting me to help catalog the library. But you need not worry. No one will take the slightest notice of you. Nobody ever acknowledges visitors here. It can be a bit of a problem when it's someone important, but I'm sure you'll be glad to be ignored. Now you don't need me listening in to what you have to say. I'm off to watch the monsters eating. I will make certain you are undisturbed."

"Good man, Joskyns," said Howard, when the schoolmaster had gone. "Don't be put off by his manner. He does quite a lot of work for us. Informally of course. He says we can use this room whenever we like."

"Did you go to school here?" asked Montmorency.

"Oh no," said Howard. "My education was rather more humble, and this place doesn't turn out many policemen. But it has produced some very effective government agents. I met Joskyns through Westminster Abbey. I worship there — it's very handy for Scotland Yard. The dean introduced us a few years back. This school started off as part of the Abbey, you know. But enough of all that. How are you getting on with your investigations? My lord?"

"Please don't call me that. I'm Jack now. Jack Scarper. I can't keep switching between one name and the other."

"I'm sorry, Jack," said Inspector Howard. "Forgive me. Of course, it is best if we all behave as if the real Lord Francis Fox-Selwyn is in the hospital in Scotland."

"And to be honest," said Jack, "I'm beginning to wonder if *I* wouldn't be more use at Strathgillon. At least we know that's where Malpensa is. We've made a huge mistake, you know. I could have dealt with him there. We'd have gotten our revenge, and you wouldn't have to worry about him plotting an atrocity at the funeral."

"Now calm down, Jack," said Inspector Howard. "I take it that you didn't find anything of importance yesterday?"

"Nothing. And that's my point. What exactly are we looking for here? I was just drifting around, waiting for something or somebody to come to my attention. It's hopeless. A complete waste of time."

"I'm afraid that's what police work is sometimes like, Fr — I mean Jack," said Howard. "There's a lot of slog involved. All over London I've got people doing exactly what you are complaining about."

"Then why do you need me?"

"I've told you before. Because you know names. You can recognize people. We have to do everything in our power to intercept anyone who might make trouble at the queen's funeral. And frankly — if you don't mind me using that word — I think I may have a duty to keep you here. I can't let you go to Scotland if I think you might commit a crime. Particularly if that crime might be murder."

Jack sighed angrily, and Montmorency interrupted. "I quite understand, Howard. But how are you getting on with Malpensa? Are you sure he hasn't left Strathgillon?"

"Oh yes, he's still in Scotland. I decided to bend the rules and send up one of my own men to trail him, to stop him getting to Doctor Farcett, and to keep him away from London. Our man's a real birdwatcher in his spare time, so he's gone to the same hotel with his own binoculars. We have to be very careful about communications, of course, but when last we heard, Malpensa was still there, watching the hospital grounds."

"So we're just letting him go about as normal?" said Jack. "As if we don't know who he is?"

"Believe me, it's for the best," said Howard. "At least until he shows any sign of leaving Strathgillon."

"Which he's bound to do, isn't he?" said Jack. "We don't know why he's putting so much effort into finding me in Scotland, but surely it can't be as important as whatever he has planned for the funeral. He's certain to leave Strathgillon eventually."

"And if that happens, my man will swoop down and bring in the local force if necessary. We will intercept trains if we have to. But in the meantime, Malpensa must be left thinking he's free. That way, if he tries to communicate with anyone in London, we'll hear about it, and we can follow the message to its destination. That's where you'll come in, Jack. You may find yourself on the trail of a real killer. Believe me, Malpensa is where we need him, and we need him alive."

"And what's the latest news about the queen?" Montmorency asked.

"She's sinking, and the kaiser is definitely going to try to visit before she dies."

"Why is he so interested in her?" asked Jack.

"He is her oldest grandchild, of course," said Howard.

"And he'll want to show the Prince of Wales just how

important he is," added Montmorency. "He may be sorry that his grandmother's dying, but there's international power at play here, too."

"The problem for us," said Howard, "is that he's likely to bring a whole load of German secret service men with him."

"That's understandable, I suppose," said Montmorency. "After all, the anarchists killed the king of Italy and Empress Elizabeth. They must realize how much danger the kaiser could be in here."

"Of course," said the inspector. "But if we're not careful, we might all end up chasing each other's tails."

"Well, at least we know where Malpensa is," said Montmorency.

"Yes, that's a comfort," said Howard. "But we still have to keep our eyes open for troublemakers in London. And, you know, there's more than one way of doing that, Jack." The inspector lifted a pile of ledgers onto the table. "You were complaining earlier that pounding the streets was getting you nowhere. Well, now you're going to find out about another side of police work." He opened the first book. Each page was ruled into columns filled in with dense rows of tiny handwriting.

"What's that?" Montmorency asked.

"It's the parish register for the Italian church in Clerkenwell. We'll have to go through it quickly because they don't know we've got it, if you get my meaning."

"You've stolen it?" said Jack.

"I don't like to use that word, Jack. But borrowed it, yes."

"And we are going to look through it for names?"

"You are, Jack. You're the one who knows who these people are. I want names and addresses of people my men can trail."

"But it will take forever," said Jack, flicking through the pages.

"I hope not. I've got the electoral roll here as well, and if I can persuade the authorities, we should have the register of births, marriages, and deaths by the end of the week. When you've been through all those, we'll move on to property records, court reports, and the membership logs of sports clubs and so on. Then, if we've got time, we'll work our way through the adjacent districts and outward across the city."

Jack slumped in his chair. This wasn't the life of spying and danger he had envisioned when he'd begged to be allowed to go to London.

"I'll help," said Montmorency. "I'm sure I would recognize a few names from the factory."

"No doubt Jack will welcome some company from time to time," said Howard. "But Montmorency, I want you to continue keeping an ear to the ground elsewhere. Stay in circulation. Let me know what they're saying at that club of yours. I want to hear what information is making the rounds, and I want to know if anyone has seen or heard anything unusual. Lead as normal a life as you can. Don't do anything to arouse suspicion. No one must know you are working for me. And remember, if you must contact anyone else, stick to your codes and keep messages to a minimum."

Jack could not disguise his jealousy of Montmorency and his disappointment at landing such a dreary job.

"This really is a vital task, Jack," said the inspector, stroking the leather binding of one of the ledgers. "I wouldn't ask you to do it otherwise."

"But if I find a lead," said Jack, "someone else will follow it up?"

"Probably. But I'll try to make sure you are involved as much as possible. And of course what you do in your spare time is your own affair."

"It doesn't look as if I'll have much of that," moaned Jack.

As Big Ben chimed a quarter to two, they rose to leave Mr. Joskyns's room. Walking along the corridor, they met Joskyns himself, his black robe now bearing the marks of lunch. He carried a thin cane under his arm.

"Ah, gentlemen!" he said. "And how is the catalog today?"

"It seems there may be even more work to do than we thought," said Inspector Howard. "Young Jack Scarper here will come every day until the task is complete, and if you don't mind, the three of us would like to meet here in the evenings to compare notes."

"Capital!" said Joskyns. "I'm sure your efforts will prove most worthwhile. Now, I will bid you good day. I have work of my own to do." He flexed the cane mischievously and bared his teeth. "Milsom will be here in a minute."

The visitors continued on their way. They stood aside to let the nervous, inky schoolboy pass as he hurried to arrive at Joskyns's study on the first stroke of two.

CHAPTER 16

≫

THE PIGS

Farcett could smell the piggery long before he got there. Professor Frost and Tom were accompanying him on his first session at his new job. Frost had explained that eventually he would find it perfectly possible to muck out all the filth from the enclosure, but for now, all he had to do was go in, place the swill in the feeding trough, and return to the hospital dining room without washing. Tramping across the field in borrowed boots, Farcett could think of only that last instruction. No washing. The dirt. The germs. He was more frightened of them than of the muddy beasts who faced him as he looked over the low brick wall of the sty.

Tom was carrying a bucket of scraps from the kitchen. That was repulsive enough, but now the sight of the filthy animals wallowing in their own mess made Farcett recoil. He turned away, ready to go back to his room in the hospital.

Professor Frost took the bucket from Tom and stood across Farcett's path. "Here you are, Francis. Just go in and tip the food into the trough."

Farcett stood still, beginning to shake. He said nothing.

"Take it, Francis. Then we can all go back for tea."

"Tea?" said Farcett. "How can we eat when we've been here?"

"People have been doing it for centuries, Francis," said the professor, forcing the bucket into Farcett's hand. "Come on, we need to keep these pigs alive, you know. They're very important to the hospital. They get rid of our waste, they give us fertilizer for the farm, and, in the end, we turn them into food. The least we can do is to give them some nourishment in return."

Farcett faced the sty again. Tom positioned himself, ready to open the gate. Farcett moved forward, gingerly, his hand shaking so fiercely that cabbage leaves and old potatoes started tumbling from the top of the bucket. He felt a shove in the small of his back as Frost urged him through into the stinking enclosure. The pigs darted forward, snuffling and honking around him, jostling one another to get at the food. He bent to pour the leftovers into the trough. Something skittered against his leg. He tried to steady himself just as another pig — a big, pink female — approached from the opposite side. His feet slid away from beneath him, and he landed on his back in the slurry, covered with the contents of the swill bin. The animals snuffled up to him, greedily picking off the tidbits from his clothes.

In no time all, the food was gone, and Farcett tried to lift himself out of the sludge, but his feet couldn't get a grip on the slithery ground. With every kick, his clothes were ground deeper into the mess. In the end, Tom came to his rescue, gripping the wall with one hand and reaching out the other to pull Farcett up.

Farcett wiped his hands against the wall, trying to rub the slurry away. "I can't believe that any animal wants to live like this," he said. "Someone should give this place a good clean out." As he said it, he caught the eye of the big pink beast. For a second, he thought he detected a look of agreement on her chubby face.

"Well, Francis," said the professor, "if you don't like their conditions, you can do something about it. Cleaning them out is your job now. I wasn't expecting you to get quite so involved so quickly." He looked at Farcett's stinking clothes. "Perhaps on this occasion, I can permit you to have a proper wash. Just a quick one, though. Tom, you take the bucket back to the kitchen and then go and ask your mother to start running a bath."

Farcett secured the gate to keep the pigs in their smelly home. He smiled back at the friendly pig. Thanks to her it looked as if he would be clean again. He promised himself that he would come back the next day to return the favor.

"Well done, Francis," said the professor as they set off across the farm to the main hospital building.

Ahead of them, Tom turned the corner from the piggery and walked quickly up the path, swinging the empty swill bucket. He saw a movement in the bushes, went closer, and recognized the stranger from Glendarvie. He was wearing the same grubby cape. This time he had binoculars around his neck.

"Remember me?" he whispered to Tom. "Can you talk?"

Tom didn't know what to say. It was clear the man had taken him for a servant once again. And in truth, Tom did have jobs to do. He had to get back to the hospital. But he couldn't pass up the chance to talk to Malpensa, to see what he wanted. "I'm in a hurry," he said. "I have to get to the kitchen. What are you doing here? What do you want?"

Malpensa pointed at the two distant figures making their way up the hill towards them. He handed Tom the binoculars. "Look through here," he said. "You see those two men?"

At first all Tom could see was leaves and sky, but eventually he focused on the professor and Robert Farcett. Then he quickly scanned the land around them. You couldn't see the piggery from there. The bend in the path was too sharp. Malpensa could know nothing of what had just happened.

Malpensa spoke again. "The one on the right. He is Lord Francis Fox-Selwyn, is he not?"

Tom homed in on the men again. Farcett looked odd alongside the neat cleanliness of the white-coated professor. His hair and beard were matted with mud, and his arms were jerking wildly as he struggled to sweep the dirt off his clothes. "Yes," said Tom. "That is Lord Francis Fox-Selwyn."

Malpensa took back the glasses and looked himself. "Mad?" he asked.

"Oh yes," said Tom, "quite, quite mad. Lives in a world of his own. No use to anyone now." He could sense Malpensa's disappointment. He was glad he had had a chance to reinforce the deception they were playing on him, but knew he must avoid allowing Malpensa to make contact, just in case Farcett let them all down and gave away the truth. He gently pushed Malpensa back towards the hedge. "That's the professor with him," he said. "The top man here. I'll be in trouble if he sees me talking to you."

"That's all right, I'll go," said Malpensa. "Like you say, Lord Francis Fox-Selwyn is no use to anyone now."

"And won't be for a very long time," said Tom. "If ever." As he spoke, he wondered if it sounded too obvious that he was lying. He tried to cover up his mistake. "Will I see you again?" he asked.

"Oh yes, I'll be back," said Malpensa. "I need to speak to his lordship when he is well enough."

"Why do you want to see him?" asked Tom.

Malpensa took no notice of the question. He pulled a wallet from his pocket and handed Tom a ten-shilling note. "For your trouble," he said. "I am staying at the inn in the village. Bring me word of any improvement. Bartok is my name." He looked down the path and saw the two men getting nearer. "Now, get along to the kitchen before they see us. And don't say a word."

The last instruction was given with a threatening grimace that Tom would not forget. Malpensa turned and vanished into the undergrowth, and Tom ran on to the hospital, just as he had been told. When he got there, he told Vi all about Malpensa, the pigs, and Doctor Farcett's bath. As she went about the business of sorting out the soap and towels, she started composing in her head a coded message to the duke. She couldn't decide whether it was good or bad news. Malpensa had revealed himself. She and Tom could keep an eye on him now. He seemed to accept that Robert Farcett was Lord

Francis Fox-Selwyn and that Francis was a useless prisoner at Strathgillon. It appeared that he wanted information from Francis, rather than to hurt him. But Malpensa had given Tom ten shillings — a fortune for a servant boy in rural Scotland. That information must be important to Malpensa, which meant that something serious was being planned. She couldn't work out how it all fit together, but her note to Gus would end with the suggestion that "Emily" (Inspector Howard, in London) should be made aware of "the onset of infection" as soon as possible.

CHAPTER 17

≫

DUCHESS DETECTIVE

At Glendarvie, Gus, the Duke of Monaburn, was deciphering coded messages from London and Strathgillon. "It's no good," he said to Beatrice, who was checking to see that he'd got it right. "They're all working very hard and keeping their eyes open, but in the end, what have they achieved? Montmorency and Frank haven't come across a single anarchist, and even though Tom has seen Malpensa, we haven't really got any useful information from him."

"All the same," said Beatrice, "you'd better do as Vi says and let Inspector Howard know. If you write to Montmorency, he will pass on the news."

Gus dipped his pen into the inkwell and started drafting the message. "Oh, how I hate this code!" he said. "I get my Emilys muddled up with my Evelyns, and Victor the Victim confused with Grieving Griselda. Once you add in all this 'infection' stuff from Vi, it's hard to make any sense at all."

"Let me do it," said Beatrice, taking the pen. And she dashed off a couple of pages of gossipy notes that managed to hide the crucial details among what read like family chat.

"You're really good at this," said the duke. "Maybe you should be out there looking for those killers!"

Beatrice knew he didn't really mean it, but his joking aside gave her the chance to make a suggestion that had been brewing in her mind for a while. "Perhaps that wouldn't be a bad idea," she said. "You're right; the others haven't made much progress in Britain. I've been wondering whether Angelina and I should go to Italy. After all, we know that's where a lot of these anarchists come from. I'd like to check on the house in Florence, and I'm sure Angelina would enjoy a visit to her family. And while we are there, we can keep a lookout for trouble — perhaps even find out where Moretti has gone."

"Have you gone raving mad?" asked Gus angrily. "Do you think for one minute that I would let you expose yourselves to such danger? I couldn't possibly allow you to go there alone."

"But we needn't be alone. Angelina's father is a policeman, after all. He could make sure we were safe. And I've got plenty of friends there. In fact, I was thinking of visiting the Vanninis. You remember? The people whose son's a painter? I want to see what his work is like. Perhaps we could put a little business his way. It looks as if you're going to have to have your portrait done soon."

"Don't remind me," said Gus, looking around at the pictures of his forebears that lined the walls. "I've got no choice, I suppose. Every Duke of Monaburn has commissioned a portrait to mark a coronation."

"I think it's a lovely tradition," said Beatrice. "And I want this one to be a work of real quality, Gus. Not just a daub by some local boy. Let me go and see the Vannini's studio."

"I'm still not sure. I shouldn't let you travel when there might be madmen on the loose."

"Then come with us, Gus, and see if you can find any leads to George's killers."

"I've told you before. I'm no good at all that cloak and dagger stuff. I'm sorry. It's absolutely out of the question. And in any case, if the queen dies, I'll be stuck in England. I'll have to go down south for the funeral, and then there'll be a coronation at some stage after that. Special meetings of the House of Lords, and so on. I couldn't possibly go to Italy now."

"I could," said a voice from the doorway. It was Gus's son, Alexander.

"Alex, you startled me," said the duchess. "How long have you been standing there?"

"Just a couple of minutes. But long enough to get the drift of what you've been saying. You really shouldn't have left the door open, you know. We have to be careful." He closed the door behind him and walked to the table, picking up the coded notes. It took him no time at all to work out what they really meant. "I think Beatrice is right, Dad," he said. "There's nothing to be lost by our going to Florence. I know Angelina would like to go back, and I could do a little digging around while we're there."

"But you might not be safe," said Gus. "We know Malpensa has been looking for Frank. How do we know the anarchists aren't after you, too? You are just as much George's nephew as he is."

"We've been through all this before, Dad. If those people want to get any of us, they can do it here as easily as anywhere else. I think Montmorency was right, back at the beginning of all this, when he guessed that Malpensa just wanted to find out where Frank was. He and his men may be keeping an eye on us all, but I don't think they'll hurt me. And what could be more natural than for me to visit the home of my wife and my stepmother? I promise not to draw attention to myself. You know me, Dad. I'm not like Frank or George. There won't be any fireworks."

The duke pondered for a minute, then reluctantly gave his assent. "All right, you can go. But Alexander, I'm counting on you to keep everybody safe. Look, if the queen doesn't recover, I'll have to go down to London anyway. Why don't we all get ready now and set off together as soon as we can? I'll see you off to the continent and then stay at Montmorency's until the funeral is over."

Beatrice went to tell Harvey and the housekeeper to make all the necessary arrangements, while Alexander added a postscript to her coded message to Montmorency. He folded and sealed it and rang for a servant to saddle him a horse. He was determined to play a bigger part in the quest for revenge, and he would start by mailing the letter himself.

CHAPTER 18

≫

LOYALTY

The royal family had managed to keep the true gravity of the queen's illness out of the papers, but the public had started to read the signs. Victoria's relatives were gathering at Osborne House, her residence on the Isle of Wight, and when her grandson, the German kaiser, hurried there to join them, the queen's doctors knew that their bulletins had to start reflecting her true condition. Victoria was intermittently unaware of her surroundings. She was having difficulty swallowing and sometimes needed oxygen to help her breathe. In short, she was dying of old age. The doctors' announcements did not rule out all hope, but everyone knew the end was near. Shops began discreetly to take orders for mourning clothes. Society women prepared wardrobes in which everything, right down to their underclothes, would be black. At Glendarvie, that meant no change. The Fox-Selwyn family accepted that their private grief for George would slip seamlessly into public mourning for the queen. At least it made packing easy for the trip to Italy. Even Angelina, born Italian but now British by marriage to Alexander, felt she should go home in the new black uniform of her adopted country.

In London, Inspector Howard was at the heart of consultations about the funeral. Queen Victoria had made her wishes clear. She wanted the ceremony in St. George's Chapel, at Windsor Castle, and then to be buried at the nearby Frogmore mausoleum, built for the body of her beloved husband, Albert, forty years before. Officially, no precise arrangements would be announced until the queen was dead, but everyone knew that plans had to be prepared and precautions taken to protect illustrious mourners from all over the world. Victoria had been on the throne for so long — more than sixty years — that no one in authority had any direct experience of such an event. Squabbles were breaking out between courtiers in the households of the dying queen and the Prince of Wales, who would soon be king.

Inspector Howard was told to pay special attention to policing the crowds without preventing the people from observing the spectacle and paying their respects. But he was worried. At the inn near Strathgillon, Malpensa had shown a frightening degree of knowledge of what would happen. He knew things that had only been shared with top officials and representatives of foreign governments who would need to get their leaders swiftly across the globe to Britain when the queen died. Malpensa had been right: The queen's coffin would be taken by ship from the Isle of Wight to Portsmouth. From there it would go by train to Victoria Station, cross London in a solemn procession to Paddington, and then travel by rail again to Windsor for the full funeral service and burial. The whole thing would take four days. Four days of ceremony and danger that would stretch the police and surveillance services to the limit. Montmorency and Jack Scarper would be part of the team: watching, waiting, and, if necessary, pouncing on anyone who might be a threat to royal or public safety.

For Jack, that meant leafing through lists and painstakingly checking the details on thousands of filing cards. Occasionally, he came across a familiar name, and he passed on the details to Inspector Howard. At last, he was even allowed to go out with the team who went to check on a suspect: Luigi Benedetti, an old friend from the ice-cream factory.

Jack and the two Scotland Yard men crept along in the dark near Farringdon Street station, down a back alley to the railroad track. It was exhilarating for Jack to feel his heart pumping with excitement and fear after days of sitting in the stuffy room at Westminster. He didn't mind the cold drizzle or the chill wind. Silently, they climbed over garden walls, until they reached the back door of Luigi's house. It gave way easily to the pressure from a policeman's shoulder. The frame was rotten, and the hinges dropped away with a crash.

All three men flattened themselves against the wall, expecting Benedetti to emerge, perhaps armed, to see who was breaking in. But no one came. Jack slid along the wall to the gaping doorway and looked inside. The house was empty. There was no furniture, only a few piles of rubbish and some dead birds. They tried to get out by the front door. It had been boarded over from the outside and wouldn't budge. Jack was furious. The card index was long out of date. If Luigi had ever lived in the house, he certainly didn't now. Another wasted day. More hopes dashed.

To make things worse, Beatrice's coded letter was waiting at Montmorency's house when he got back. Montmorency was preoccupied with the news of the duchess's trip to Italy and Gus's impending arrival in London, but Jack focused on the message from Vi. "It's crazy!" he said. "We're messing around here in London, and Malpensa has gotten right into the grounds at Strathgillon."

Montmorency tried to calm him down. "Don't worry about it. You heard what Inspector Howard said. He has Malpensa under control."

"Well, I'm fed up with playing by Howard's rules. I've just been wasting my time here, chasing people who've long since moved away. I've done my bit for the government. I'm going up to Scotland, and I'm going to deal with Malpensa myself."

"Don't be stupid. You can't leave London now. The queen may die at any time."

"What do I care about that? George is dead already, and we've done nothing about it. Malpensa nearly caused my death outside the Hippodrome, and I've just slunk away into the shadows. I'm ashamed. I've been a coward. A useless clerk doing a pointless job the police can't be bothered to do themselves. And as for you, you've just been swanning around London — your old indulgent self!"

"That's enough!" shouted Montmorency, as Jack kicked over the side table, knocking a decanter of whisky onto the floor. "It's not my fault we haven't had any luck. We have to help Inspector Howard. We must try. We would never forgive ourselves if anything happened to the royal family."

"Well, I would!" shouted Jack. "And I'll tell you something else. I'd never forgive myself if nothing happened to Malpensa. I'm going up to Scotland, and I'm leaving now!"

Jack dashed through the front hall, picking up Montmorency's wallet as he passed, and slammed the front door behind him. Montmorency, penniless, got into the street in time to see him turning the corner in a cab. Montmorency had no hope of reaching King's Cross Station before the sleeper train was due to leave for Scotland. He went back into the house and telephoned Westminster School.

Jack had boarded the train and was settling into his sleeping compartment when the door opened. He was about to get his ticket out when he realized that it wasn't the attendant, but Matthew Joskyns, the schoolmaster, who was coming towards him. Confused, he opened his mouth to speak, but before he could utter a sound, his breath was stopped by a large soft cloth, and a pungent smell wafted him into darkness.

Joskyns explained to a porter that his "friend" had been taken ill and would not be fit to travel. He carried Jack to a waiting cab and asked to be driven to Westminster. By the time they arrived, Jack could almost stand and seemed like any other drunk being guided by a caring friend. But Joskyns wasn't kind. Under cover of darkness, he pulled the staggering youth through the cloisters and into the empty abbey by a back door, throwing his body down on the marble floor of the Lady Chapel. He kicked Jack in the side. "Look around you, boy. Look at this place." Jack opened his eyes. In the gloom, he could see almost nothing, but Joskyns struck a match and lit a tiny oil lamp. Its light seemed unbearably bright against the darkness.

"Look at that ceiling," said Joskyns, holding up the lamp to show the intricate pattern of fan-vaulting on the roof. "It's been here for hundreds of years. It watches over what you should be trying to protect. Get up." He kicked Jack again and pulled him to his feet, dragging him among the tombs and monuments listing the kings and queens buried there.

"Henry VII, Mary, Elizabeth I, James I, Charles II, William and Mary. Queen Anne. Are you getting the idea, boy?"

"Yes," mumbled Jack, still stunned but aware that he was in serious trouble.

Joskyns gripped Jack by the throat and bent his head back against the tomb of Henry VII and his wife, Elizabeth of York. "I could show you more, going back almost a thousand years. This is the tradition we are trying to uphold. This is the monarchy we treasure. Is your petty quest for family revenge more important than this?"

Jack said nothing, and Joskyns slapped him across the face. "Is it?"

Jack's nose was bleeding now, but he still could not bring himself to lie. "Yes," he said defiantly. "Yes. My uncle George was worth more than any of them."

Joskyns lashed out again, sending a stinging pain across Jack's cheekbone. "Listen, sonny. I knew your uncle. I shouldn't tell you this, but I know what he did for his country. And I also know what he would think of you running away from the chance to serve the Crown."

"Serve the Crown!" said Jack. "By sorting through ancient paperwork that leads us nowhere?"

"So your efforts have been unproductive? So what? You might or might not stop an atrocity. But at least you will know you have tried. That you chose to put the national interest above your own."

"But killing Malpensa might help the nation. If he were dead, he couldn't mastermind any more attacks."

"Yet the police say he is of more use alive. You know that, but you think your young judgment is better, don't you? You think you know best?"

Jack was silent.

"Well?" said Joskyns. "I'm waiting for an answer. Who knows best?"

Jack said nothing, and Joskyns hit him again, in the stomach this time.

"I said who knows best?" His voice boomed around the empty abbey.

"You do," gasped Jack, struggling for breath.

"Right then. You're coming with me. You'll sleep in the school tonight and be back at your work in the morning."

Joskyns blew out the lamp and guided Jack away.

The next morning, when Montmorency arrived at the school, Jack was already sorting through his card index. Montmorency noticed some bruises, but nothing was said. Inspector Howard arrived a moment later. He'd already heard about the failed raid. "No luck last night, I gather, Jack?"

"No," said Jack. "Benedetti wasn't there. The house had been abandoned long ago."

"Oh well, never mind," said Howard. "We can only carry on."

"Yes," said Jack. "That's what I'm doing. Carrying on."

CHAPTER 19

≫

DORIS

The whole nation waited for news from Osborne. But at Strathgillon Mental Asylum, the patients were protected from the news. The staff chatted about it in their private quarters, but were forbidden to tell the patients, lest some of them became even more deranged with grief. Vi did as she was told and kept the rumors from Robert Farcett. He went about his business, answering only to the name of Francis Fox-Selwyn and spending more and more time tending the pigs.

After the luxury of that first bath, following his dunking in the dirt, his treatment had returned to normal. He was allowed only limited and controlled access to soap and water. So he was careful whenever he visited the sties and managed to stay upright. At first, he would nip in and out as quickly as possible, refilling the troughs and replenishing the beasts' water, but as the days passed, he spent longer with the animals, and with one in particular: the large pink female he now called, in his own mind, Doris. It seemed to him that Doris spent longer than the others nuzzling against his legs as he poured out the food and that she enjoyed it when he playfully scratched the top of her head. After a week, Doris was there waiting for him as he approached the gate. He looked back as he set off after the feed and saw her watching him walk away. He fancied there was a look of sadness in her eyes.

Farcett asked Tom to bring a spade and a broom to the piggery. He spent hours clearing out the muck and spreading clean straw for his new friends. Exhausted, he sat down, and Doris lumbered up to join him. He patted and stroked her and started to talk, telling her thoughts and worries that had tormented him for months. Doris snorted and snuffled, making sounds he interpreted as sympathy. From then on he was there whenever he could get away from the main hospital and Professor Frost's inquiries about his past. He watched the real pigmen tend the beasts, wishing they would be more gentle and hating the way they assumed the pigs wanted to be dirty and eat rubbish. He was there when they let a boar into the enclosure, and he stayed afterward, helping Doris to recover her dignity but hoping for piglets in four months' time.

CHAPTER 20

≫

LONDON MOURNING

t 6:30 p.m. on Tuesday, January 22, Queen Victoria died. Power passed instantly to the Prince of Wales, now King Edward VII, and frantic preparations began for the funeral in early February. A coffin had to be made, soldiers and sailors were drilled, stands were built for spectators, and the special trains were polished, oiled, and tested for their important role in the event. Theaters closed, and shops took down their displays, swathing their windows in black. Visitors arrived from across Britain and all over the world.

Montmorency and Jack continued their mission. They'd silently agreed not to revisit their disagreement and got on with their jobs. Montmorency listened for rumors and scoured faces across London for known troublemakers and for Moretti or any of the anarchists they had encountered in Italy and America. Just a couple of weeks into his new regime, Jack was noticeably fatter. Every night, Cook produced enough food for three, and Montmorency invited Jack up from the servants' quarters to help him eat it. Every day, when Jack went out to study his registers and indexes, Cook gave him some sandwiches and a slab of homemade toffee. She did it to help him add weight, but the sticky sweet served another purpose, too. Jack's uncle, Lord George Fox-Selwyn, had been devoted to toffee. He used to take it with him wherever he could, smashing it into golden shards with his favorite silver hammer and stuffing it into his mouth till his teeth stuck together and the sugary juice ran into his beard. For Jack, the toffee was a secret reminder of Uncle George. Despite Joskyns's brutal persuasion to put public affairs first, Jack treasured this homely symbol of his other task — to get the people who had robbed his boisterous uncle of life. Every morning he smashed up the toffee on the kitchen table, divided the pieces into two piles, and wrapped each pile in a handkerchief. He put the bigger bundle in his pocket and gave the other to Montmorency. It was as if George was with them all day, urging them on to revenge.

They met regularly in Joskyns's room at Westminster School. Now that the queen was dead, Jack had resigned himself to toiling on at his desk. But with a week to go until the funeral, Montmorency was annoyed. He had found nothing, despite walking the London streets for hours.

"What's the point?" he said. "We'd do better to look in Italy. I'd certainly rather be there. Have you heard? Verdi's dead."

"Who? Verdi the composer?" said Jack.

"You know another one?"

"Well, I did, actually. One of the people I used to meet in the cafe in Florence was called Verdi. It's quite a common name. Giuseppe Verdi only means Joe Green, you know."

Inspector Howard laughed. "I don't think all those opera buffs would make such a fuss about him if he called himself that, do you?" he said.

Montmorency sulked.

"*He's* what you call an opera buff," explained Jack. "He loves his Traviatas and his Nabuccos."

"I'm sorry," said Inspector Howard. "I didn't realize you were affected by Verdi's death."

"Well, I never met him. I nearly met Puccini once, but that's another story. . . . It's just that I wouldn't mind being there for the funeral. It's bound to be a big national event. And who knows, I might even spot some of our anarchists."

"Well, if it makes you feel better," said the inspector, "I'm very glad you're here. And at last I can let you know a bit more detail about *our* funeral. We've been told where all the foreign delegations are staying. It looks as if every official residence and posh hotel in London will be bulging with people. And I've got the timetable for the day. Jack, you'll be pleased to hear that I'm expecting you to be out on the streets for the funeral. It will be too late for all this background research then."

He took a sheet of paper from his pocket. It appeared to be a list of all the leading royals and politicians in the world. "This is what we have to protect." He ran his finger down the list. "First we have to get all the royals off the train. That all happens indoors, and we can control who's there to watch them. Then it's going to take two hours for them to parade from Victoria to Paddington. The coffin will be borne on a gun carriage, surrounded by military bandsmen on foot, followed by the kaiser, the new king, and the Duke of Connaught, with all the royal princes, British and foreign, riding behind them."

"Riding?" said Jack. "You mean in carriages?"

"No, on horseback. The royal women are going to follow in six carriages, but the men will be perfect targets. Completely exposed."

Jack was downhearted. "We haven't really got a hope of protecting them, have we?" he said.

"Well, don't forget, we're not the only ones out there trying. Thousands of infantrymen will be marching behind them. The streets will be lined with soldiers and police. Some of the foreign delegations have brought their own protection, I'm sure — though they're not supposed to. And then there are our own secret agents. Even I don't know how many or where, just as they don't know about you. Remember, you don't have to do everything. You are here for a specific job — because you know what a particular set of anarchists look like. Concentrate on looking for them."

"Have you received any threats?"

"Nothing concrete. All the usual crackpots are out there, but we've got men watching them. And there are wild rumors, of course. One bit of good news: The president of the United States won't be coming. He's got influenza apparently. So we don't need to worry about him. The ambassador is going to stand in. I shouldn't think he'd be a target, would you?"

"No. This lot have killed kings and an empress. They'll be aiming high," said Montmorency.

"And I'm afraid they'll have unlimited vantage points. Every balcony, every window, every inch of pavement along the route will be full. Thousands of people, and any one of them could be an attacker."

"So it's all the more important that we intercept them before the big day," said Montmorency. And he returned to the streets, the pubs, the stations, and hotels, hoping for a lucky chance.

Late on the evening before the coffin was due to arrive in London, Jack and Inspector Howard were waiting for Montmorency at the school. They were to have a last briefing on tactics for the next day.

"Would you like a bit of toffee?" asked Jack, holding out his handkerchief to the policeman. "The pieces have got a bit stuck together in my pocket, but you can probably pull one off."

Inspector Howard took a chunk and started chewing. The conversation became indistinct as they both slurped and sucked.

"Is everything ready?" said Jack.

"Just about. There's a certain amount of chaos, of course, and the foreign royals are creating all sorts of fuss about precedence and so on, but I think we've got the crowds under control. Quite a few are out there already. By tomorrow, I doubt anyone will be able to move in the crush."

"Probably just as well. You can't fire a gun or throw a bomb with your arms stuck by your sides!" said Jack.

Howard tried not to laugh, but the tension of trying to look after the largest crowd in London's history somehow made him burst into giggles, and he started to choke on the toffee, spitting it forward so that it stuck out between his teeth. At that moment, Joskyns entered the room and boomed in his most schoolmasterly voice: "What's going on in here? What are you eating? Hand it over at once!"

Jack passed over the parcel of toffee, with the sheepish look of a schoolboy caught out in class, and Joskyns tutted loudly as he examined the sticky mound. He shook his head, then peeled off a bit and popped it in his own mouth. Jack's fear of Joskyns after the violence in the abbey fell away. He began laughing, and the other two joined in. Joskyns thumped Howard on the back as he began choking again.

None of them noticed the solemn figure of Montmorency entering the room. He had to slam the door to silence them, and though the tittering continued for a moment longer, they all fell silent when they saw his face. Joskyns could tell that sensitive matters were likely to be discussed. He quietly left.

Montmorency waited until his footsteps had died away before he spoke. "Gentlemen!" he said gravely. "We have a serious problem. I believe I have seen Malpensa."

Jack reacted first. "He can't be in London," he said. "We would have heard that he'd left Strathgillon."

"I thought so, too," said Montmorency. "But I'm sure it was him. He fit your description exactly — right down to the limp."

"And where was this?" asked the inspector.

"At Paddington. I went to see how they were getting on with the preparations. They were laying down the red carpet and putting up barriers to hold back the crowd. I wanted to make sure there was nowhere for an assassin to hide."

"And is there?"

"Only in the crowd itself. Tomorrow, we are going to be dependent on the people of London to defend us all. Let's hope they react if they see something suspicious."

Jack interrupted. "So you saw him. What was he doing? Where did he go?"

"He was getting off a train."

Now Howard butted in. "Getting off a train at Paddington? But that doesn't make sense. We know he's been in Scotland. Trains to Paddington come from the West Country. Not the north."

"I know. But I'm sure it was him. And he had that look about him. You know. Furtive. Up to no good. You get to sense these things."

Inspector Howard nodded. He knew all about the power of hunches in police work. "How did you lose him? Surely you shadowed him?"

"Of course I did. Out into the street and into the traffic. He followed exactly the route the procession is going to take tomorrow, only the other way around."

"So he went to Victoria Station?"

"I can only assume so. He was pushing his way past all the people settling themselves into position for tomorrow. It was really hard keeping up without being noticed or tripping in the crowd. I lost him somewhere near St. James's Palace. He just vanished."

"Maybe it wasn't him," said Jack, trying to sound hopeful. "After all, you've never seen him before. And we haven't heard anything from Scotland to say that he's left Strathgillon."

Montmorency turned to the inspector. "When did you last hear from your man up there?"

"Well, not for a few days, actually. And I must admit I haven't been in my office today."

"And we left home before the first post this morning," said Montmorency. "So if Vi sent any news, we'll have missed it."

"But Dad's in London now," said Jack. "And Vi would have addressed the letter to him at your house. He'd know."

"But what could he do if he did?" said Montmorency. "He can't risk going to Scotland Yard in case he's being watched, and we haven't been home to see him."

"Let's go now," said Jack.

"You go home," said Montmorency. "But be careful. We've all relaxed a bit thinking Malpensa was out of the way. But for all we know, he is looking for us now, as well as planning a little something for tomorrow. I'll go with Howard to Scotland Yard. If Malpensa's watching the house, we don't want to be seen together. He won't take any notice of you going in the servants' entrance."

Jack went over to a mirror on the wall. He wanted to check that he looked quite unlike Frank, the young firebrand Malpensa had met in Italy and America the year before. He took the hip flask of dye out of his pocket and touched up the roots of his red hair, then pulled on gloves to cover the freckles on the backs of his hands. Montmorency gave him a nod to indicate that he was unrecognizable. "Take care," he said. "Just go in as if it's the most normal thing in the world."

"And then? I can't exactly meet you at Scotland Yard."

"No," said Inspector Howard. "And Montmorency, you shouldn't go there with me either. Suppose Malpensa's been tailing *you*?"

"I see what you mean," said Montmorency. "We'd better leave here separately and meet again."

"But we can't meet here," said Jack. "It'll be late at night. Too quiet. Too obvious."

"Where then?" asked Montmorency. "It's not as if we could go to a pub or something. Everything's closed out of respect for the queen. And anyway, where would it look normal for a policeman, a toff, and a servant to be gathered together for a chat?"

"I think I may have the answer to that," said Howard. "In the cells at Canon Row police station, just behind Scotland Yard. Gentlemen, you are going to act disgracefully tonight. On the eve of the queen's funeral, you are both going to be drunk and disorderly, and I am going to arrange for you to be arrested!"

They made plans for the fake arrests. At ten-thirty, Jack would break a window in Whitehall, and Montmorency would misbehave in the Strand. One by one, they left the school, each checking to see that he was not being followed. Montmorency, who walked the streets to kill the time before the meeting, found himself seeing phantom anarchists everywhere. He tried to stay calm — to persuade himself that the man he'd pursued earlier couldn't possibly be Malpensa. Surely he must still be hundreds of miles away, in Scotland. At a quarter past ten, he swilled alcohol around in his mouth to make himself smell the part, but he arrived at the appointed spot for his arrest perfectly sober, only pretending to be unable to stand. Anyone seeing the policeman tackle him as he urinated against a pillar box would have been disgusted but convinced that the arrest was justified. But in the cell at the police station, Montmorency had all his wits about him. It was just as well. Both the others brought bad news.

CHAPTER 21

≫

BATTLE IN THE DARK

*M*ontmorency was furious. "How can it have happened? We had him so well covered. How can he have gotten away?"

"Keep your voice down," said Inspector Howard, who was pacing up and down the tiny cell. "*I'm* supposed to be interviewing *you*, remember? We don't want to attract attention to ourselves."

"But what went wrong?" asked Jack quietly. "I thought you had a man watching Malpensa up at Strathgillon. Why didn't he raise the alarm?"

"It seems everyone has been a bit too clever for their own good," Inspector Howard explained. "Somehow word seems to have got out that I was tailing a man up in Scotland. I don't know how, but the Scottish police were told, and they got angry. Decided they could do a better job themselves. They traced the suspect to Strathgillon and swooped when he was out of the hotel pretending to do a bit of bird-watching. The trouble is, they picked up the wrong man — my man — when he was taking a couple of hours off to look for some creature called a capercaillie. They locked him up, and he couldn't contact me. By the time he'd convinced them of who he was, the real suspect was gone. The landlady at the inn says someone came with a message for him. He packed, paid his bill nice and calmly, and disappeared."

"Apparently the arrest was the talk of Strathgillon," said Jack, pulling out a sheet of paper in Vi's handwriting. "Vi wrote to tell Dad about it, but of course the story was so difficult for Vi to put into code that Dad could barely understand it."

Montmorency read the note. "And of course, Vi knew nothing of the Scotland Yard man at Strathgillon. When she wrote this, she must have thought the real Malpensa was in custody."

"So," said Jack. "She thought everyone was safer than ever."

"I'll pay for this when the funeral is over," said the inspector. "I'll be in trouble for sending a London man undercover up there. But that's not important tonight. Gentlemen, we have to find Malpensa and stop him from doing whatever he has planned for tomorrow. I will put out his description to all the officers on duty at the procession."

"But what can *we* do?" asked Jack.

Montmorency was gloomy. "All we can do is mingle with the crowds and hope to spot him. Inspector, do you think it's safe for us to go home and get a few hours' sleep?"

"Yes, and if you are going to be sharp tomorrow, you shouldn't lose any time getting to bed. I can let you out of here, one at a time, without being spotted. There's a tunnel that leads down onto the platform at Westminster Underground. I'll send an officer to get you some tickets. If Malpensa is watching the police station, he'll think you're still inside."

They were home by midnight and up by six. Gus was already out of the bath, preparing to play his part in the funeral as

Duke of Monaburn. Chivers, Montmorency's manservant, was brushing down His Grace's ceremonial robes. The duke was grumbling as all the finery was attached to his massive body. "It's going to be a nightmare. Trailing around from London to Windsor. Endless services, and it won't be over till Monday. And for all I know, there are people out there trying to blow the whole thing up."

"Not if we have anything to do with it," said Montmorency — though in his heart he saw little prospect of foiling any plot.

After breakfast they left separately for their chosen vantage points: Montmorency to the spot near St. James's where he had lost track of Malpensa the day before, and Jack to Victoria Station where the royal party would leave the first train and form the procession that would expose them to any assassin in line of sight.

The weather was perfect. Crisp, dry, and clear. Montmorency was thankful that it was cold. The people in the crowd were so tightly packed that they could hardly move, and later in the year, they would have sweltered. Montmorency had intended to dress up for the occasion, in proper mourning clothes. He thought that people might make way for him in the crowd if he looked aristocratic and official. But at the last minute, he had a change of heart and borrowed some clothes from Jack. Better to fit in, he thought. Less chance of being spotted. Easier to creep up on Malpensa if he was there. So he left the house by the servants' entrance. Jack was in his usual disguise. Montmorency watched him walk away from the house and was convinced that no one who had known young Frank a year ago would recognize him now.

They each took up their positions and waited. Around Montmorency, the atmosphere was jollier than he'd expected: good-natured rather than mournful, with excited onlookers perching everywhere, even in the trees on the edge of the park. But then the faint sound of solemn music broke through the chatter, and news spread that the cortege was on its way. A respectful silence fell. Montmorency was relieved — if the procession was still moving, it meant that nothing untoward had happened at Victoria. He scanned the crowd, not really expecting to see anyone suspicious.

But he did. There, just where he had lost him the day before, was Malpensa.

He was about twenty feet away, to Montmorency's right and slightly in front of him. His black cape did not look at all out of place among the shawls and overcoats of the other bystanders. Only his large hat marked him out. As the procession approached, the rest of the crowd were baring their heads as a sign of respect, but Malpensa's hat remained where it was. Montmorency started to squirm his way through the crowd, trying to close the gap with Malpensa without him noticing. But the people around him resisted, angry that he was disturbing the atmosphere at the crucial moment.

Malpensa sensed the movement behind him and turned. His eyes locked onto Montmorency. There was no sign of recognition, just a fleeting look of alarm. He turned away again and started rummaging inside his cloak. Montmorency expected him to pull out a gun, to fire at the king. But the king wasn't in view yet. Only Lord Roberts, the South African War hero, could be seen, leading the procession ahead of the gun carriage, riding at walking pace with the bandsmen behind him. Malpensa's hand emerged again. It wasn't holding a gun, but a walking stick. He used it to part the crowd at his side, and he started working his way out of the throng, with Montmorency shuffling through behind him. People yielded to Malpensa's stick, but they tried to stop Montmorency as his movement blocked their view. He started to explain, tried to shout out something that would get the crowd on his side. But no one took any notice. In the end, he had to struggle to push himself out through the back row and squeezed along a wall just in time to see Malpensa turning a corner, away from the spectacle.

This was Montmorency's territory. He knew all the streets in the area and was thrilled that the foreigner had fled into a cul-de-sac. He would be trapped by the crowds in a small courtyard with a steep downward slope to a high blank wall. Montmorency would have him. And Malpensa could not endanger the procession from there.

But when Montmorency forced his way around the corner, Malpensa was nowhere to be seen.

And all at once Montmorency knew why, and why he had lost Malpensa the day before. He looked down and saw the familiar round disc of a manhole cover. Years before, these had been the doors to Montmorency's private highway through London. They led to the sewer tunnels that linked every part of the capital. Now Malpensa was down there. Was he just fleeing from Montmorency, or did he have another plan, perhaps to set off a bomb underground?

In his rush, Malpensa had not closed the lid behind him, and Montmorency was soon on the ladder leading down into the dark stench. He pulled the cover shut. That would give him an advantage: Malpensa would have no light, but Montmorency knew his way around. He recognized from long ago all the sounds and echoes around him.

"Malpensa!" he shouted, and the name boomed through the dark tunnel. There was no reply, but he could hear his quarry splashing and panting ahead of him, and he knew he was catching up.

Even so, it was hard. The water was up to his knees. In the old days, Montmorency had used tools to help him on his underground adventures. He had worn strong waders. Now he could feel his shoes filling with sludge and effluent soaking into his woolen trousers, so his legs were heavy and slow. Something was wrapping itself around his shins, making it impossible to walk. He forced his hand down into the stinking water to feel what was wrong. It was Malpensa's cloak. Had he thrown it down deliberately to make an obstacle? Or had he slipped in the tunnel and dropped it? Montmorency stopped and waited for the lapping of the sewage to settle so that he could listen. There was no sound, only a trickle from somewhere up ahead, and the strange, distant, almost ghostly rumble of the funeral march resonating through the passages from the band aboveground. He stayed still, hoping that

Malpensa had fallen face first into the slime and was lying there, unconscious or dead. But somehow he could sense another living being near him. There was no light. Neither of them could see a thing. Which of them was more scared? Who would move first?

Just as Montmorency was about to crack, to step forward and untangle himself from the cape, there was a splash, and the liquid formed a wave that unbalanced him for a second. A slithery hand grabbed at his hair, and Malpensa's arm pressed against his throat.

"Who are you?" hissed Malpensa, his lips almost brushing Montmorency's ear. "Police?"

Montmorency said nothing. Even if he'd tried, the pressure against his windpipe would have stopped the words. Malpensa didn't wait for a reply.

"You have to die. And no one will find you here. Your king has been lucky today. But one policeman won't stop me. Never!"

Montmorency thrashed out with his arms, trying to make contact with Malpensa's body. His fist struck against the buckle of a belt. He jerked his knee upward, hoping to make a painful strike. At the same moment, Malpensa's walking stick crashed down across his shoulders, and the two of them fell, bound together, under the surface of the warm, sticking wetness, struggling to get footholds on the curved, slippery floor. Montmorency was up first and tried to stamp on Malpensa, to keep him under the water, but in the darkness, he misjudged his position and was down again, on his hands and knees. Malpensa had wedged himself against the wall, with half his body clear of the water. He gripped Montmorency's jacket and pounded him down, down into the foam, fighting Montmorency's efforts to raise his head, to get at least one gulp of the fetid air. Another slip, and now Malpensa was down, and Montmorency was on his back, dazed, but floating with his face up, gathering strength. He managed to stand, reached into the blackness, and caught Malpensa's belt again, this time from the back, and hung on while both of them gasped for air. He could feel a lump in Malpensa's pocket. A gun. Malpensa's hand came over his own, and they both grappled for it. It spun between them and fell to their feet. Madly, they dived down, groping in the mess of human waste and rubbish, each frantically wanting to be the first to feel that hard lump of metal on the floor. Montmorency was the lucky one, and he pulled his dripping prize from the water with a laugh. Never in his whole time working with George Fox-Selwyn had he killed another human being. But he had no compunction now. This was Malpensa, who might not have murdered George but who inspired those who had. He could hear Malpensa's heavy, gargling breaths to his right. He pointed the gun in the direction of the noise and fired.

And nothing happened. The firearm was useless once the water and slop of the sewer had done their work, but Malpensa was back again, thrashing wildly to find it, to have a go himself. Montmorency hurled it away from both of them just as the grasping hand made contact with his face and a sharp fingernail gouged into his eye. Paralyzed with pain, he was like a rag doll in Malpensa's arms. He felt his head being pounded against the wall again and again, and then his legs being lifted, so that his face was submerged. He kicked, freed himself, and did the only thing he could in his weakened state: He half slithered, half swam away from his attacker.

But Malpensa was there. Even in the dark he could sense it. The man was wounded, but he was mobile, and he was keeping up. Every now and then Montmorency stopped and listened. It was like a terrible, dark, wet, underground game of Red Light, Green Light. For just a moment after he froze, Montmorency would hear the flick of a hand or the drip of a shirt or that breathing again, moist and low. In those still times, Montmorency tried to work out where he was, calling on old memories of the sewers for familiar junctions in the tunnels. He wanted to lure Malpensa away from the parade, up towards Trafalgar Square or Covent Garden, and then kill him and escape up into the streets he knew best. He gathered his strength and stood, ready to wade on.

Malpensa's voice rang out. With the echo, it was impossible to tell where it came from. He was taunting Montmorency. But he sounded tired. He was giving up the chase and letting Montmorency run. "Go, then. Tell your masters you failed. That Malpensa is free and will strike again. But see, I am a generous man. I will let you go back to your little house, your little wife. To your squalid little English life."

"No," Montmorency shouted defiantly into the darkness, panting for breath between his words. "I will not leave, and I will not let you go. I will find you, Malpensa, wherever you are. I am no policeman. I do want to save my king. But more than that, Malpensa, you must pay for the death of my friend!"

The silence that followed was brief but told Montmorency everything. Malpensa had not recognized him, perhaps had not imagined himself a target of Fox-Selwyn's avengers. Malpensa thought aloud and spat out his thoughts. "The Englishman. The Englishman in Florence. His friend. You knew Fox-Selwyn?"

"Yes!" said Montmorency. "You and that monster Moretti killed the finest man I have ever known. And you will die, too. Here. Now."

"Fine words from a coward!" said Malpensa. "A minute ago you were fleeing from me. You say you fight for your friend Fox-Selwyn, but you don't even say who you are!"

"I am no coward. And I want you to know the name of your killer. I am Montmorency. It is the last name you will ever hear. You shall not get away."

"Nor you!" bellowed Malpensa. "Even if we both die in this filth together."

Montmorency turned in the direction of the sound, but as he lunged forward, Malpensa flew at him, knocking him down again. This time Montmorency's mouth opened underwater, and the vile liquid was down his throat and up his nose. But he still had an advantage. He knew the layout of this section of the sewers. He knew that just a few yards away there would be a ladder leading up the wall to daylight and oxygen. He dragged himself along and grasped the bottom rung. He had no strength to haul his body up, and he could hear Malpensa only inches behind him. Then he could feel him pressing against his back, using it as a step for his good leg as he dragged the bad one up the ladder. Malpensa was slow, and Montmorency tried to follow, but Malpensa kicked backward as he went, catching Montmorency's face with his heavy, stinking boot. Three times Montmorency fell down. Each time he swallowed more sewage. Each time it was harder to rise again.

And then the light blinded him more than the darkness had. Malpensa had forced open the manhole cover and was pulling himself out into the street. Montmorency heard him go. He listened on. Silence. They were far from the crowd, who was still watching the procession. Montmorency had done his public duty. Malpensa must be too exhausted to catch up with the procession now, and anyway his gun was lying useless in the sewage. The king and his guests were safe from the anarchist.

Montmorency was tempted to pause, to get his breath back, to let his heartbeat drop and his muscles recover. But he thought again of George's body, hanging from a crane with bullet holes in his back, and he had to follow Malpensa. Had to catch up. The ladder was slippery with the slime from Malpensa's feet, but he reached the top at last. Malpensa had left the hole open. Montmorency had only to pull himself out onto the pavement.

In all his time as Scarper, squirreling his way across London through the sewers, he had never been caught — never been seen entering or leaving his underground domain. He inched his head out of the hole. There was no sign of Malpensa, but he might be hiding in the shadows or staggering along nearby, exhausted and lost. It was still worth chasing him. Using all his remaining strength, Montmorency pushed on his arms until his body was free, then swung himself up into the street. Straight into the arms of a policeman.

CHAPTER 22

≫

PRISONERS

*W*hile Montmorency was wrestling with Malpensa underground, Jack was running across Hyde Park, hoping to get to Paddington before the long, slow procession arrived. He knew he should be glad that the royal party had left Victoria Station without incident, and he had enjoyed the spectacle, but he couldn't help feeling a guilty disappointment that he hadn't spotted an anarchist nor happened on the opportunity to get revenge on George's killers. So he decided to move to where the parade would be and to see if he had better luck on the other side of London.

It was a long way, and he was regretting all the extra weight he'd piled on in the past few weeks. Several times he had to stop, with a stitch in his side, to catch his breath. Later on he realized how he must have looked when he arrived at Paddington Station: hot, sweaty, disheveled, and rather over-eager to force his way through the crowd. He should have remembered what Inspector Howard had told them: There were plenty of plainclothesmen around keeping an eye out for suspicious characters — particularly those of Mediterr-anean or Eastern European coloring, young firebrands with dark hair and staring eyes. So he shouldn't really have been surprised when he found himself grabbed from behind and marched off to a police van. No one believed his story that he was working for Inspector Howard, at least not until after midnight, when the weary inspector arrived to secure his release.

"I'm sorry," said Jack, who could see that Howard was longing to get home to bed. "But I really didn't do anything. They just assumed I was up to no good."

"No. I'm sorry," said Howard. "Sorry I couldn't get to you earlier. I've been rather tied up doing a similar errand for Montmorency. He's in a terrible state. I had to get him moved from the police station to the hospital. It seems he had some sort of fight down in the sewers. He's pretty incoherent, but it sounds as if he encountered one of the anarchists. Maybe even Malpensa himself."

"And did he catch him? Did he kill him?" said Jack, eagerly.

"No. He got away. But I've put out a general alert. We're watching all the roads and the ports."

"And Montmorency?"

"He's been badly beaten up. But worse, he seems to have ingested a large amount of sewer water. He's already got a fever. We're going to have to watch him. He might have picked up some horrible germs."

"Can I see him?"

"He's sleeping now, but I'll make sure you can go tomorrow. We've got some guards there — discreetly, just in case. I'll make sure they know you're coming so you don't get pounced on again. You've already been locked up twice in two days. It couldn't have been fun."

"At least I'm out now. Everyone at the police station seemed pretty relaxed. I take it there weren't any problems with the procession?"

"None at all, at this end. Though we've heard from Windsor that there was a bit of a hiccup there. The coffin was too heavy for its carriage, and the traces attaching the horses broke. Some sailors had to pull it on foot all the way from the railway station up to the castle. I'm told it was quite a moving sight."

"But no anarchists? No arrests?"

"None. Well, one innocent man briefly held in error, but they've let him go now. Just an officer getting a bit jumpy in the crowd."

"I think I understand all about that. I hope they didn't bend his arm up behind his back. My shoulder still hurts!"

"I'm sorry. But suppose you really had been a threat . . ."

"It's all right, Howard. I understand. Imagine what I would have done to Malpensa if I'd found him."

"And what he might have done to you. I think you might get quite a shock when you see Montmorency in the morning."

And in spite of the warning, Jack was taken aback. His friend was incoherent and sweating, so covered in bruises and bandages that he was barely recognizable. The doctors said he would be in the hospital for weeks, and, if he survived, would need intensive nursing at home. Jack wondered what he should do. Should he throw himself into the pursuit of Malpensa?

Where should he start? All he knew was that Malpensa was probably wounded and on the run. While Montmorency stayed locked in his delirium, he could give no clues.

Jack started searching London for the man who had done such damage to his friend. He hung around the areas where Italian immigrants congregated. He visited hospitals, trying to find a patient with symptoms and injuries that matched Montmorency's. After a couple of fruitless weeks, his morale was almost crushed. He began drinking more in the pubs he visited. He stayed a little too long, smoking over games of cards. If Montmorency had been able to see him, he would have recognized that the spirit of the original Scarper was back, tempting a new victim astray.

The lowest point came after a month, when Inspector Howard visited Gus at Montmorency's house. He had a confession to make. In his exhaustion at the end of the funeral day, he had made a mistake. He had, as he'd told Jack, sent all the ports a description and an artist's impression of Malpensa, instructing officers to stop him on sight. It had been quite natural for the officials to assume they were expected to prevent the dark Italian in the drawing from entering the country. It was understandable that they thought he might be coming to England to threaten the guests at the funeral. No one was scanning the faces of travelers going the other way. Indeed, in response to Howard's message, men had actually been taken off that duty to pay extra attention to arrivals.

So Malpensa might well have left the country. Indeed, it

was more than likely that he had. A captain at Harwich remembered a heavily bandaged man on a stretcher sailing for Rotterdam a few days after the queen's funeral, but he could not recall any useful details. Malpensa had slipped through their fingers again, and from Rotterdam he could have gone anywhere in Europe.

CHAPTER 23

➤

THE PAINTER

Up in Scotland, the mood was better. Vi and Tom knew nothing of the dramas in London. Gus had found it impossible to encode the story and decided not to trouble them with it. He told them to continue to look out for infection, but with the flu still doing the rounds, Vi thought he meant the real thing. She believed Malpensa to be under lock and key, an assumption reinforced when the caped stranger failed to return to Strathgillon. Robert — or rather Francis, as he never forgot to call himself — was calm and busy, spending most of his time tending what was becoming the neatest pigsty in the world. Once, when he failed to come back to the main building for lunch, Vi went down to the piggery to take him a sandwich. He didn't know she was watching as he raked the straw and chatted to Doris. Vi hadn't seen him so content since his days on Tarimond with his lost love, Maggie Goudie. Professor Frost might have some funny ideas about curing madness, but they seemed to work.

Doris was blooming, too. Piglets were definitely on the way. It would be her first litter, and Francis was taking particular care of her, fishing out the most nutritious morsels from the swill bin and feeding them to her by hand. When she heard him coming, she would run up and poke her snout through the gate, almost singing a welcome. And when he'd finished cleaning the sty, he would sit and stroke her tummy with her head in his lap. He still liked a good wash when he had the chance and sometimes stole some of the pigs' water for a crafty rinse, but the obsession seemed to be waning. Vi had even seen him enter the dining room with dirt under his nails. Her notes to Gus were full of optimism. She was surprised that she still had to send them to London. She'd expected the duke to return to Glendarvie as soon as possible after his duties at the queen's funeral. He must have found some diversion in town.

In fact, the duke was miserable in London, but while Montmorency was ill, he felt he had to stay. He wanted to keep an eye on his son, too. He could see that Jack was falling into bad habits, and he worried about him, even though he knew he would never persuade him to give up his search for the anarchists. So Gus stayed. And after a patch of boredom, he announced that he had found something to fill the time.

"What's that, Dad?" said Jack, who hadn't been paying attention.

"I said I'm going to get my portrait painted."

"Whatever for?"

"It's a tradition. Every Duke of Monaburn has had his picture done to celebrate a coronation. You just don't know because it's been so long since we've had a new monarch."

"But the coronation probably won't be till next year, Dad. The whole nation is supposed to be in mourning. Is it right to be mucking about with painters at a time like this?"

"Well, it looks as if we're going to have a painter in the house anyway. Beatrice is sending one from Florence. He's the son of an old friend of hers, and she's already told him he can stay with us. He can earn his keep by doing my picture. And as for the propriety of it, I don't see why it should be disrespectful to the old queen to dress up in my formal robes and stand still for hours on end. I bet you the king is having much more fun than that behind closed doors at the palace."

"Who is this painter, anyway?" asked Jack. "Let's hope he's not one of those impressionists who'll make your face look like a tomato in the fog."

The duke pulled his wife's latest letter from his pocket. She'd sent a long account of the Italian national mourning for Verdi. She knew Montmorency would want to know all about the two funerals that had been held in his honor. The details of the painter were on the last page. "Well, he's called Paolo Vannini, and he's very highly thought of in Italy. As far as I know, all those crazy painters are French, aren't they? Beatrice says this Vannini's mother was English and that he went to school here, so he should be a decent sort of chap. She says his work is excellent. I'll trust her judgment. And in any case, he'll just have to do as I wish. This picture's got to fit in with all the others at Glendarvie. I'll see to that."

"And when's he coming?"

"Pretty soon, I'd say. It sounds as if he's already on his way."

"What do we tell him about me?" said Jack. "Do I pretend to be a servant, or do we let him in on the secret?"

The duke thought for a while. "That's a hard one. I've no idea what Beatrice has already said, and I can't ask her. Inspector Howard is still insisting on maximum caution in all communications. If only Montmorency was well enough to ask. Until he is, I think we'd better stay as we are. You'll be Jack Scarper the servant as far as our visitor is concerned."

"Suits me," said Jack. "That will be easier than switching from one thing to the other. And to be honest, I'm getting used to the new me."

A bit too used to it, perhaps, thought Gus, looking at his son's bulging waistline and bloodshot eyes. But he couldn't face an argument, so he made a joke of it. "Well, since you're used to being a servant, perhaps you could pour me another whisky."

"Of course, sir," said Jack, helping himself to a cigar and filling up his own glass as well.

Within a week, Chivers announced Vannini's arrival. Gus went out into the hall to greet him as Jack lugged in several large bags made of fine Italian leather, assorted painting gear, and a paint-spattered traveling easel. The visitor was tall, almost as tall as Gus himself, but unlike Gus he had masses of black glossy hair. He was about half Gus's width, too: exuding the health and vitality of his twenty-five years. The duke held out a hand in welcome, and Vannini gripped it firmly. Gus was surprised to hear him speak in a perfectly modulated English accent.

"Paul Vannini, at your service," he said, with a broad smile.

"Welcome, Mr. Vannini," said the duke.

"Oh, do call me Paul. And it's Paul, not Paolo, when I'm in England. I feel really at home in this country, and that Italian name just doesn't seem to fit the voice!"

"Welcome, Paul," said the duke, relieved that the duchess had sent him a friendly and cultured companion.

He began to relax but tensed up again when the visitor winked and said, "And this must be Jack."

What did he mean? Was Paul trying to say that Beatrice had let him in on the deception and that he knew that Jack was really Frank? How should he react?

Jack saw his father's confusion and decided to step in, keeping up the pretense, as planned. "Yes, sir. Jack Scarper, sir. If you follow me, I will show you to your room."

He carried the baggage upstairs. Paul closed the door behind them. "Well done, Frank," he said. "I was testing to see how well you were playing your part. And you're doing perfectly, by the way. Keep it up."

"Then call me Jack, please. Not Frank. Even Dad realizes we can't risk switching between the two."

"Sorry, Jack," said Vannini. "And you're right to be cautious. I want you and your father to know that the duchess has told me everything. She had to because she's entrusted me with some very important messages. And she's sent me here to help you, if help is what you need."

"Well, help would be useful if we had anything to go on," said Jack. "We're split now between a fruitless hunt for Malpensa and Moretti and trying to lead a quiet life. No real luck on either front, I'm afraid. Poor Montmorency is sick and too weak to tell us how he got that way. Have the women made any progress in Florence?"

"Oh yes," said Vannini. "That's really why I'm here." And he unscrewed a leg of the easel, shaking out a roll of paper from inside. "Take a look at this."

CHAPTER 24

≫

THE DOCUMENT

The page was covered with spidery handwriting, looped in the traditional Italian style. Jack's Italian was good, after his long stay in Florence a couple of years before, but he couldn't understand the document at all. It seemed to be a discussion of ecclesiastical building works, interspersed with reflections on Catholic saints. He was disappointed. "I'm sorry," he said. "I don't understand."

"That's all right," said Vannini. "You're not meant to. It's a code."

"Oh, not another one!" said Jack. "We're having enough trouble with the one we're using already."

"Not our code," said Vannini. "Theirs."

"The anarchists?"

"Exactly. We don't know who wrote it, but it's obviously someone with authority — if anyone can have authority in an organization dedicated to destroying power."

Jack examined the paper more closely. "How did you get ahold of this?" he asked.

"I believe Angelina's father, the police chief, passed it on to Alexander. It's a copy, of course, but a faithful one. Alex, Beatrice, and Angelina worked on it for a long time, and they're pretty sure they know what it means."

He took Jack through the text, unscrambling a story about

medieval monks and church repairs and showing how it must have been written after Queen Victoria's funeral. Switching around the words and substituting letters for some of the numbers, the meaning became clear. After the anarchists' failure to make an impact in London, Malpensa and Moretti would meet in America, to pick off new targets.

Jack was still holding the manuscript. "So they're not here. Definitely not in London?"

"So it would seem."

Jack was downcast. "That means I've been wasting my time again. Searching in the wrong place. I should have gone to America straight after the funeral. I had a feeling that Moretti wasn't in England, and now Malpensa has gone abroad, too. I should have gotten him when he was in Scotland. Yet again, I've failed!"

"No you haven't, Jack. And you've done well to stick with Montmorency while he has been ill. Don't get upset. This is good news."

"How can you think that?"

"Look at the message again. It may be just as important for what it *doesn't* say. There is no reference to you or to Montmorency. It seems you may be able to relax a little. The anarchists may not know you are after them, and it doesn't sound as if they are after you. So you may well be in less danger than you thought — though my advice would be to continue with most of your precautions, just in case."

Jack checked the document to make sure. "I see what you

mean," he said. "Perhaps that is good news, in a way. I think we'd better tell my father."

"Yes," said Vannini, unscrewing a second leg of the easel. "And I have another letter here. The duchess has written explaining properly why she's sent me and what I know. I think we'd better give him this one first."

They went downstairs, looking for the duke. In the end they found him in the basement kitchen, talking to Cook. Gus greeted them warmly. "Good news!" he said, and they both wondered how he could know already. But it turned out he was talking about something else entirely. "Montmorency's awake. He's talking lucidly and asking for food."

Jack went upstairs to see Montmorency while Cook set about preparing some thin soup and Paul Vannini took Gus aside to show him Beatrice's letter. Montmorency was weak but in good spirits, and Jack couldn't resist passing on the intelligence that Malpensa and his sympathizers seemed unconcerned about Montmorency or his whereabouts. He was shocked by the reaction. Montmorency fell back against his pillow and groaned. "Oh no," he said. "If only I had known. If only I hadn't been so vain."

"What do you mean?" asked Jack.

"You're right. I understand now. Malpensa didn't know who I was."

"Didn't and doesn't now, as far as we know," said Jack. "He has no reason to think that we want revenge on him for George's death. If we find him, we can surprise him."

"But he does know about us, Jack. He does. And though I'm not mentioned in that manuscript, I'm sure he'd recognize me if I went after him again. At the very least, I've made him more circumspect, more difficult to catch."

"What do you mean?" asked Jack.

"Malpensa showed no sign of recognition when I spotted him in the crowd at the funeral. He made it clear that he thought I was a policeman. But when I was fighting with him, I couldn't resist telling him who I was. I didn't want him to think I was only protecting the king. I felt certain that one or the other of us would die in that sewer, and I wanted him to know that that death would come about because of George."

Jack could see how distressed Montmorency was becoming and stopped himself from saying what he was thinking: that their hunt for Malpensa and Moretti had been a complete mess. First they'd hampered themselves with unnecessary caution, and now, thanks to Montmorency, they had lost their advantage. But Jack tried to sound comforting. "Don't worry. You couldn't have known that Malpensa didn't recognize you. It's not your fault. The important thing is that you didn't die. And as soon as you are well enough, we will go to America to find him and Moretti."

Montmorency could not be pacified. "But now Malpensa will be expecting us," he said. "All I had to do was stay quiet. And instead I told him who I was and why I was chasing him. I understand it all now. You were right, long ago at the start of all this, when you said that Malpensa didn't do his own dirty work. I should have realized why he'd come to London.

Don't you see? The reason we couldn't find any anarchists here was because there weren't any. The network had collapsed. That's why Malpensa was in the crowd, for once preparing to do the deed himself because there was no one else to do it for him. And even then he wasn't up to it. He ran away as soon as he thought someone was on his tail. All the assassins he's inspired have been braver. They've sacrificed everything to carry out their dreadful acts. But Malpensa fled. He values his own life too highly to let me live now. He'll be watching out for me wherever he goes."

Jack wanted to disagree, but he could see that Montmorency was right. Montmorency's breathing grew faster and shallower. He clung to Jack, shouting random words of abuse and despair. He clawed at the boy's face, calling him Frank, Jack, and Scarper by turns. Jack tried to calm him, answering to each of the names and pretending that he thought all would be well. But as Gus and Vannini entered the room with a hot bowl of soup, Montmorency slumped back into unconsciousness again.

CHAPTER 25

≫

THE PORTRAIT

*T*here's no need to get hysterical!" said Gus, trying to calm Jack as he struggled to revive his friend. "I'll go and call the doctor. Stand back and give him plenty of air."

"Your father is right," said Vannini. "We won't help Montmorency by panicking."

Jack took no notice. "Look at him," he said, pointing to Montmorency's ashen face. "I thought I was giving him good news, and now he's sick again."

"I'm sure he'll recover," said Vannini, feeling Montmorency's forehead. "He hasn't got a fever. He was probably just shocked."

The duke's telephone voice boomed up from the hall. "Very well, we will see you in fifteen minutes. Good-bye, Doctor. Good-bye. Good-bye."

"There you are," said Vannini. "The doctor is on his way. Now relax. We can help Montmorency most by having a proper plan of action ready when he wakes up."

"Action?" said Jack. "But what can we do? Malpensa knows about Montmorency. He knows we're after him. Everything's ruined."

"No it's not," said Gus as he rejoined them. "Think Jack. Before Vannini arrived, both you and Montmorency thought Malpensa was stalking you. You had a short time — less than an hour — when it seemed he was not. Now you know he's likely to avoid Montmorency."

"Avoid! He'll want to kill him after what happened in the sewer."

"Very well, he may be hostile to Montmorency. But we have good reason to suppose he is not in this country. And we can guess that he's in pretty bad shape. I'm sure Montmorency would have given as good as he got in that fight."

"But the fact is," said Jack, "that there's no point in Paul having come here. We're right back where we started."

Vannini interrupted. "No you're not. Alexander is making headway tracing anarchists in Italy. . . ."

Jack snorted with contempt. "Alex! Tracing sculptures and frescoes, more likely."

"And it looks as if the men you are after are in the United States," said Vannini.

Jack was working himself into a desperate panic. "But America's a big place. We don't know where to look. And in any case, Montmorency won't be able to travel for ages. Do you think I should go on my own?"

"No!" shouted the duke. "I absolutely forbid it. You're staying here. We're all staying here until Montmorency is better. And while we're waiting, Paul can paint my picture."

Jack knew there was no point in arguing with his father. And he had no idea how he would search for Malpensa and Moretti alone. He fell into a sullen silence.

Vannini tried to break the tension. "Yes. The portrait," he said. "Exactly what do you have in mind?"

Gus described the other portraits at Glendarvie and was pleased to hear that Vannini was quite happy to paint in a conventional style. The duke would be shown standing in his formal robes, with an appropriate background. The last point presented a bit of a difficulty. Gus's natural habitat was the countryside, and the painting would have to be done in London, but Paul said he'd do the figure first and then put the rest in later, possibly traveling to Glendarvie to get a few local details just right.

"Isn't that cheating?" said Jack.

"Yes. But lots of artists do it. Even really famous ones. In fact, some of the really great painters were the biggest cheats of all. They'd just do the face and get their students to fill in all the rest. At least this is going to be all my own work."

"So how will you want me to stand?" asked Gus, striking a grand pose.

"No need for that sort of thing yet," said Vannini. "I'd like to study you for a bit first — to get a feel for your expressions and how you move. We'll start the more formal stuff in a few days' time. If you don't mind, for now I'll just follow you around with my sketchbook. Take no notice of me. Just go about your business entirely as normal."

The doorbell rang, and they heard Chivers showing the doctor up the stairs. He examined Montmorency and reassured them that this sort of setback was only to be expected after such an illness. He was confident that the patient would be conscious again soon and left behind a couple of bottles of tonic for when that moment came.

And Montmorency did wake up, halfway through the next day. A period of oblivion had done him good. Gus persuaded him that the quest for Malpensa was far from doomed and that if he worked hard at getting strong again, he and Jack would soon be able to go to America. He introduced Paul Vannini, and the two of them struck up an instant friendship. Montmorency was pleased to hear firsthand news from Italy and Vannini's positive interpretation of the coded document. Cook made more soup, and Montmorency's recovery progressed well. After two days he came downstairs and settled on a chaise longue, watching the artist at work.

Paul was still at the sketching stage, following the duke around and insisting that Gus should forget he was there. Gus tried to do that, but every now and then, he caught Paul looking at him when he was slouching or picking his nose. He hitched himself back up into a more dignified position and put on a more serious face.

"Please," said Vannini. "No need for that. Just relax."

But of course, once Gus had been told to relax he absolutely couldn't. He became even more self-conscious, and many of Vannini's sketches were spoiled.

"Can I take a look?" asked Montmorency, maneuvering himself on his crutches behind Vannini's chair.

"You can. But I'm not happy with this one. I haven't caught him exactly yet."

Montmorency leaned over to see. Paul was right. He hadn't captured Gus. He had done something else. He had drawn a perfect representation of the duke's twin brother. "My goodness," said Montmorency. "Look at this, Gus. It's George."

The duke put down the book he had been pretending to read. "Good heavens. How extraordinary. We were very alike, you know, Paul. But you seem to have managed to re-create exactly the way in which we were different."

"I never met him," said Vannini. "It's a complete accident."

Montmorency took the sketchpad and carried it over to the light. "May I keep this?" he asked. "I've got a couple of photographs of George, but nothing that shows his humanity quite so well."

"Of course you can have it," said Paul. "I don't want to keep it. It's one of my failures."

"Not a failure, Paul. A triumph. I shall treasure it. In fact, could I commission you to paint a portrait of George when you've finished doing Gus? Or even a picture of George and me together? Could you do that?"

"Well, it would be most unusual. Painting someone I've never seen. But if you really want me to, I don't see why I shouldn't. I know you were very close."

"I owe everything to George," said Montmorency. "Even my life, I suppose. Between them, George and Robert saved me from death more than once."

"Robert?" said Vannini. Then he realized who that was. "Oh, Doctor Farcett. The man who's in the hospital in Scotland?"

"Indeed. A truly noble man. Even in his sickness, he has given up his very identity to help us. I was worried that we were asking too much, but he seemed determined to act out his part as Lord Francis Fox-Selwyn. Perhaps a little too determined. He seemed to be losing sight of who he really was." Montmorency turned to Gus. "Is there any news from Strathgillon? How dreadful of me. I've been so preoccupied with my own troubles, I've hardly given Robert a thought since I fell ill."

"Apparently he's doing better. Vi's letters are very short. She's being extremely careful about what she writes, just as instructed."

"And has she said anything about Tom?" asked Montmorency, trying to sound casual but longing to know how his son was getting on.

"Not a word," said Gus. "But I expect the boy is fitting in perfectly as a servant. Despite his real origins." Montmorency coughed, to remind Gus that the painter was still in the room, but the duke continued. "Oh, don't worry about Paul. He knows about Tom and how he's all we have left of George. You'd be amazed how being drawn by an artist loosens one's tongue. I told him during one of our sittings." Gus's tone changed. "Think of it. That rough boy is George's son. Unfortunate business. I wonder if I shouldn't get him more of an education. Fit him for the world he'll be able to live in when his money comes through."

Montmorency knew he must tell Gus the truth about Tom — that he wasn't George's son at all. Vi's letter weeks ago had been quite explicit. He should be honest now that Tom himself knew everything. But it was hard for Montmorency to find the words. He was about to start when Jack arrived. He was taking less care of his disguise these days, and the ginger hairs on the back of his hand were quite obvious as he reached for a slice of cake on a silver tray.

Montmorency was suddenly worried. "Jack. Your hair. You must continue to dye it. We can't take chances. What if we're being watched?"

Jack started to argue, telling Montmorency how safe he now felt on the London streets and how he'd certainly pay more attention to his disguise as soon as they set off for America. But he saw the intensity of the anxiety in Montmorency's eyes. It was a reminder of the panic-stricken delirium of a few days before. Jack calmed himself down and promised to take more care. Then he caught sight of Vannini's sketch. "I say! How extraordinary. It's Uncle George. Paul, I'd love a picture of him. Could you draw one for me?"

"I'm sure we'd all like one," said the duke. "Maybe young Tom should have one, too. We were just talking about him. After all, it seems he is your cousin."

Montmorency could bear it no longer and with everyone in the room, he knew the time had come to speak. "Except . . . he isn't, Gus."

"What's that?"

"Tom isn't related to you."

"What do you mean? He must be. Why else would George have left him so much money?"

"I don't know why. And we will never be able to ask him. But I do know who Tom's father is, and the time has come for me to admit it. Tom is my child. Vi has absolutely no doubt."

No one knew quite how to respond. Gus could not tell whether the emotion sweeping through him was relief or disappointment. Jack, who had always thought of Tom as a playmate rather than a cousin, could well believe what he heard. He had never been able to see George in Tom's slim, dark form and had been very surprised by his uncle's bequest to the boy.

Montmorency, still embarrassed, tried to change the subject a little. "You were right, Gus, when you said Tom could do with a bit more education. I should organize something. Perhaps you could advise me?"

"Or maybe," said Vannini, alarmed to be part of such an intimate conversation, "maybe I could help. Perhaps I could travel to Strathgillon and stay there as a tutor for Tom. I can remember enough of my own schoolwork to pass some of it on. I could even teach him to paint, if he showed an interest."

"What a good idea," said Gus, grateful for the lurch back into practicalities. "And while you're in the area, you could see Glendarvie and get the background right for my picture."

"Perhaps you could find out a bit more about what Malpensa was doing there for so long," said Montmorency. "I still can't really make sense of that. And you could give us an opinion on Robert's progress. I meant what I said before. I don't want to put too much pressure on him with this identity swap. Tell us how he is bearing up. Tell us if he needs anything. Of course, we'll have to teach you our code. We mustn't let our guard down. I know you want us to believe that news from Italy, but we can't be sure that Moretti and Malpensa really have gone away."

"Of course," said Vannini. "But perhaps I won't need the code. I thought of another way to communicate when I saw Gus struggling with a letter from Vi the other day. If I went to Strathgillon, I could put it into practice. I could hide messages in pictures."

"What? Draw mysterious visitors?" said Jack.

"I wasn't thinking so much of that as this sort of thing." He took a bright oil painting down from the wall. "This little landscape isn't anything special, is it?"

"To be honest, I never noticed it before you took it off the wall," said Montmorency. "It was there when I moved in. Why do you ask?"

"Because I'd like to do an experiment. Do you mind? I'm afraid if it goes wrong, it may destroy the painting."

"Oh, go ahead. I want to see what happens."

Vannini rummaged around in his bag for jars of ink and varnish. "Now, imagine I want to say something. Something that's not covered in any of the codes you are already using. Let's think of a short phrase, just for this exercise."

"How about 'Frank is on Tarimond'?" Jack suggested.

"Perfect," said Paul. "Now I'll write that here, on these sheaves of corn in the corner, see?" They all watched as he worked. "Now if we just let that dry for a minute, I'm going to darken this varnish and paint it over the whole picture." The bright landscape suddenly looked very dingy and old.

Montmorency laughed. "Rather an improvement, I think."

"So," said Vannini. "Can you see the writing?"

They all examined the painting carefully. Jack thought he could see the T-a-r of Tarimond, but the others were stumped. "I think you'll agree that the script has merged with the body of the picture," said Vannini. "Now let's go away and let that varnish dry."

It was nearly suppertime, so they wandered into the dining room to get away from the smell of varnish.

"I can guess what you're going to do," said Jack. "You'll clean off the varnish to reveal the message."

"I hope that's what will happen," said Paul. "I'm just a bit worried that the ink will come off, too."

"Can't we look now?" asked Gus excitedly.

"No. It's too soon. Strictly speaking we should wait about a week. It might take a long time for a picture to be delivered from one place to another, and in that time, the varnish would harden. It could be more difficult to remove. But I can't wait that long. Let's try after dinner."

They ate quickly and rushed back to the drawing room. Montmorency lifted the picture. "I love the way the varnish makes it look so old," he said. "No one would suspect there's a message in there."

"Well, let's hope there still is!" said Paul. He took a piece of cotton wool and soaked it in mineral spirits from a jar.

"What a stink!" said Gus.

"Yes," said Paul. "It's pretty strong. But it has to be. What I'm hoping is that it will dissolve the varnish." He rubbed at the corner of the painting. "Yes, good, it's starting to soften." They crowded around as he lifted the sticky brown mess off the canvas. Underneath, the paint shone with its old brightness, and there was the message as clear as could be: "Frank is on Tarimond."

"Well done, Paul," said Gus. "If you leave us some of that mineral spirit stuff, you can send messages we'll understand. I can't tell you what a relief that will be!"

"But where will you get all the pictures?" asked Jack.

"I'll paint them, of course. Or Tom and Robert will. I will be teaching them. That's my whole excuse for being at Strathgillon, after all. Now. Let's try to clean off the ink."

Vannini tried, but he couldn't find a mixture of chemicals that would take away the message.

"I'm terribly sorry, Montmorency. I'd hoped I could put the picture back the way I found it. Do you want me to take off the rest of the varnish? At least then you'll have something you can hang on the wall, and I shouldn't think anyone will notice a few words at the bottom."

"No. Don't bother," said Montmorency. "Just make sure the pictures you paint in Scotland aren't great masterpieces! Then we can throw them away when we've read them."

Vannini started packing up his things. The landscape was left leaning against the wall, a strange dark thing, with one bright corner shining in the glow of the fire. "I can't wait to get to Strathgillon now," he said. "I'll go as soon as I've got the portrait finished."

"Oh, never mind about that," said Gus, relieved at the prospect of being able to go about his day without being observed. "It can wait till nearer the coronation, I think."

Montmorency was relieved, too. All four of them had let the business over the painting submerge their embarrassment about Tom. It was done. The news was out, and he would be able to acknowledge his son in public at last. He decided that as soon as he was well enough to travel, he would pay a visit to Strathgillon himself.

CHAPTER 26

≫

DOCTOR DISCOVERED

*P*aul Vannini loved Strathgillon. He painted every day, producing works he was proud of, as well as some rubbish for use if he needed to send messages down south. Professor Frost took to him at once and was happy to let him tutor Tom and to encourage some of the patients to try painting as a way of filling their time. Alone with Tom, Vannini was able to pass on a letter Montmorency had written, acknowledging him as his son and promising to be a better father in the future. Vi told Vannini how glad she was that the years of deception were over, and she, like Professor Frost, enthused about the progress Doctor Farcett, or rather Lord Francis Fox-Selwyn, was making.

But Vannini was worried about Farcett. The man was civil and calm and chatted easily to him about art and the countryside. He seemed genuinely happy when he showed off his pigs, and in particular Doris, the hugely pregnant sow. But every time Paul tried, in the privacy of the hospital grounds, to tell him what was going on in London and how the search for the anarchists was progressing, Farcett seemed to close down. He would not answer to the name of Doctor or Farcett, insisting always that he was Francis — Lord Francis Fox-Selwyn. When Vannini tried to talk to him about his career in medicine, he denied it. At first, Vannini thought Farcett was simply being cautious. After all, how could he be sure that the painter was not an enemy in disguise? But with time Vannini realized that in place of his old obsessive behavior, Farcett had acquired a new illness. He really did believe he was Francis Fox-Selwyn. His genuine identity had slipped away.

Vannini toyed with the idea of sending a message to Montmorency and Gus, asking permission to tell Professor Frost the truth, in the interest of Farcett's sanity. But he couldn't think of a way of hiding such a complex argument in a picture, and, in any case, how would they reply? He remembered how worried Montmorency had been about the false identity and felt that gave him the authority to act on his own initiative. So, one evening, he decided to go to Frost and break the news about who his patient really was.

He knocked on the door of the professor's study.

"Come in."

Vannini entered and was surprised to find the professor more relaxed than he had ever seen him, with his shoes off and his feet on the table, reading a newspaper and smoking a pipe.

"Ah, Paul," said Frost, shuffling into a less undignified position. "Delighted to see you. I was just going to have a cup of tea. Care to join me?"

"Yes. Thank you, Professor. But there is a serious matter I would like to discuss." He stuttered. "It's rather difficult . . . somewhat awkward."

"Oh dear. I hope you're not going to ask for professional advice. I'm sure you'll understand that, even in my work, one does like to be off duty from time to time."

"Of course. And no. Don't worry. It's not about me. It's one of the patients." Vannini outlined the true story of Doctor Farcett and, without going into too much detail, how he came to be in the professor's care.

"Extraordinary," said Frost. "I can barely believe it. I was bemused by him at the beginning. He seemed so much older than his real age. But he's never given the slightest indication that he was anyone other than Lord Francis Fox-Selwyn. He's punctilious about his name."

"Exactly. And it's not good acting. Don't you see? He really believes it. Just as that poor man who makes speeches all day in the garden wholeheartedly believes he is Prince Albert. Robert Farcett is sick. And I don't think it's right to let his illness progress any further."

"Well, I'd like to ask him some questions. Let's go and see him now. I'll just go and get myself tidied up."

The professor went through to a back room and emerged, pulling on his white coat. "Strange," he said, closing a cupboard door as he passed. "That's usually locked. I keep my medical equipment in there. Emergency stuff, you know. Scalpels and things. Just in case they're needed. If there's an accident or something. Not the sort of thing one has a use for in day-to-day psychiatry. I'll just check that nothing is missing." His jolly manner dropped away. "Oh dear. The bag's gone." He became more flustered. "We must check all the patients at once. How could anyone have gotten in here? I don't understand. Nurse! Nurse!"

Someone came running, and soon the whole hospital was in controlled uproar as the staff toured the rooms checking for the missing equipment, secretly panicking but trying not to alarm the patients. Aware all the time that one of them might be on the loose with a knife. Vannini and Frost met Vi, running towards them along a corridor. "It's Francis," she panted. "He's not in his room. I can't find him."

"The whole hospital is being searched," said Frost. "I'm sure he'll turn up."

"One of the nurses said some scalpels are missing. Is it true?"

"Yes, but keep calm, Vi," said Frost. "We've no reason to suppose they're in the hands of anyone dangerous."

"But what about the sad patients?" said Vi. "Some of them don't want to live. What if they've got them? They might hurt themselves."

"I know, Vi," said the professor, trying not to sound too exasperated. "That's why we're trying to account for everyone. When did you last see Robert?"

"At supper. He seemed very agitated. Worried. Oh, Professor, you don't think he's done anything stupid, do you?"

Vannini interrupted. "No, Vi. I'm sure he wouldn't. But I've got a good idea where he might be." He turned to the professor. "Have you got a lantern? I think we should go to the piggery."

When they turned the corner, they could see a faint light

coming from the direction of the sty. Vi ran ahead. "He's here!" she cried. Then the men heard her gasp in horror. When they caught up, they could see why. Robert Farcett was on his knees in the straw, up to his elbows in blood. Before him lay Doris, his favorite pig, unconscious, with a rag stuffed into her mouth and her belly split open. Farcett looked up at them with staring eyes. Then he spoke in a voice of authority that the professor had never heard him use before.

"Come here. Help me," he said. "We haven't got much time."

Vannini entered the sty and looked down at the pig. The incision was deep. *Why?* he wondered. *Why was Francis killing the animal he loved?*

Farcett spoke again. "Hold her head. Make sure she inhales the fumes. I don't want her to feel too much pain."

Frost realized what was going on. The rag was soaked in a rudimentary anesthetic. The cut was not an assault, but an act of kindness.

"She was having trouble," said Farcett, as his hands slithered inside the pig's belly. "The piglets are stuck. This is the only way to get them out."

One by one he lifted seven tiny bodies out into the cold air. Frost, Vi, and Vannini cradled and rubbed each one, trying to get them breathing, while Farcett tended the mother. He was rummaging in the stolen medical bag.

"I must sew her up. Is there anything in here?"

Frost helped him find a suture needle and some twine.

"There's not enough," said Farcett.

"Hold on," said Vi, pulling off one of her stockings. "I'll unravel this." And she pulled out a long strand of cotton.

"We can't use that," said Frost. "It's madness to think we can save this animal. It's been butchered. We should let it die."

"It may be madness, Professor, but in here, we're allowed to be mad," said Farcett, fighting to close the pig's gaping wound. "Humor me. Give me a chance."

Frost turned to Vannini. "Run back and tell everyone that the knives have been found," he said. "At least we can restore calm in the hospital, even if we have mayhem out here. I'll stay and help." And for the next hour, he, Vi, and Farcett formed a strange outdoor operating team, like medics on a battlefield, struggling to save Doris's life.

Vi took the piglets to another new mother, and they latched on, suckling milk right away. Then Paul returned with hot water, towels, and soap. In the dim light of the lanterns, they tried to make Doris comfortable. Farcett refused to leave her. The others stood and watched as he gently stroked her head long after they all knew that she was dead.

Professor Frost finally broke the silence. "You're a doctor, aren't you?" he said.

"Yes," said Farcett. "I'm a doctor. I kill people."

CHAPTER 27

≫

A MESSAGE FROM ITALY

*I*n London, Jack raced to the door whenever he heard the mailman, longing for the delivery of a picture. But it was ten days before they received the first: a still life, set against a particularly dark background. Montmorency and the duke squabbled about who would have the fun of dabbing off the varnish. Gus won and started work on the bottom left-hand corner. Letters soon came into view. *All safe. Tom a fine boy. Learns fast.*

"Is that all?" said Jack.

"It can't be," said Montmorency. "Give me the mineral spirits, Gus. I want to have a go."

They took turns cleaning the picture. In the end it was bright and fresh all over, but they had uncovered only two more words: *Just testing.*

"Well, at least we know we can do it," said Jack, looking on the bright side.

"Yes, but those fumes are making me feel ill," said Gus, lifting the canvas and putting it on the fire. It burned with a raging, chemical flame. They all jumped back from the grate.

"That's a genuine Vannini you're burning," said Montmorency. "It might have sold for a fortune one day."

"I doubt it," said Gus. "Especially with that writing on it.

I think it's worth more as fuel. Maybe the next one will be more exciting."

But there were no more pictures and hardly any letters until the arrival of a note from the duchess in Italy. It was full of gossip about the locals and details of work that needed to be done on her house on the hill outside Florence. The real meat was buried deep within: Gus was not to worry. Beatrice and Angelina were to leave Florence. Alexander would stay there for a while. He had been in touch with the British Foreign Office and had officially started work for them. He had some business to attend to in Italy and would then be moving on himself.

"Typical Alex!" said Jack. "Completely selfish. More interested in his job than in looking after his own wife and stepmother. Where's he going anyway?"

"I don't think it says," said Gus, picking through the letter for signs of a code. "You know, some of this is pure gibberish."

"May I have a look?" said Montmorency. As Gus passed him the letter, a strip of lace fell out of the envelope. "What's this?" he said.

"Oh, she says something about that in the letter. Apparently it's to clean my spectacles with. I don't know what she means. I don't wear spectacles."

"Exactly," said Jack. "That must be the point. She's trying to tell you something."

Montmorency butted in. "Perhaps this lace will help you

see something clearly." He held it up to the light. It was little more than a series of holes held together with delicate threads. Then he noticed marks of ink at the edges of some of the holes. "Look at this," he said. "It's as if someone has used this to blot their writing."

Jack came close. "Or written on the paper through the holes," he said.

"That's it!" said Montmorency. "She's put the lace on the paper and spelled out a message through the holes. All we have to do is match them up."

It wasn't an easy job. Montmorency spread the sheets of paper across the table and laid the strip of lace on top. Letters showed up through the holes, but, however the lace was positioned, they seemed to be purely random characters. There was no sign of a recognizable word or even a coherent code. Then, on the page that talked of the women leaving Florence, the lace lined up perfectly down the page, and on each line a clear letter jumped out. P-a-r-i-s. "Beatrice and Angelina are going to Paris," said Montmorency. "I'm sure that's what this means."

"Let me see," said Jack, and he checked that word, then continued working his way through the letter. When he got to the page about Alexander, even more letters lined up, diagonally across the page. "Washington," he said. "Alex is staying in Florence but then moving on to Washington."

Gus checked the lace. "You're right, you know. It couldn't just be a coincidence. Beatrice must have written out the place names and then built the rest of the letter around them. No wonder it doesn't make perfect sense."

"But why the hurry? And why the secrecy?" said Montmorency.

"Well, they obviously think we should still be careful," said Gus. "And a good thing, too, if it keeps them safe."

"I wish I was going to Washington," said Jack. "I wouldn't spend my time with stuffy diplomats the way Alexander will. I'd get out there and look for Malpensa and Moretti."

"You shouldn't criticize your brother," said Gus. "He's serving his country."

"Well, he should start thinking about serving his family. I don't think he even cares about Uncle George."

"Frank!" said Gus, forgetting for the first time in ages to call him Jack. "I will not hear you saying such a thing."

"You always take his side," said Jack, reverting to the complaint he'd made about his brother throughout his childhood.

"No I don't."

"Yes you do. And I've had enough of it. I hate you all!" He stormed off, down the back stairs and out into the street. Gus and Montmorency both knew that he would be back in the small hours, drunk and dirty.

"I wish I hadn't let him choose the name Jack Scarper," said Montmorency. "I recognize an ugliness I used to share."

CHAPTER 28

≫

GUILT

*P*rofessor Frost gave Doctor Farcett strong sleeping potions to get him through the days after Doris's death. He stopped the pigman from sending her body off to the butcher, knowing that Farcett would want her to have a decent burial and for there to be somewhere he could visit to pay his respects. Tom and Paul dug the grave, and when Robert was strong enough (and none too soon, for the pig was beginning to smell quite badly), he helped them fill in the hole. Spring flowers were just beginning to bloom in profusion, and they transplanted a few onto the mound of earth that marked Doris's resting place.

From then on, Frost spent much of his time with Farcett, whom he found to be a most interesting patient. The shock of the operation had pulled him out of his delusion. He now fully accepted that he was Doctor Farcett and was happy to tell the professor all about his past. But he had a new preoccupation, and Frost came to believe that it was the same one that had led to the obsessive washing. Doctor Farcett was wracked with guilt and self-criticism. He was convinced that he had been a bad, even an evil, doctor. He was ashamed.

"But all doctors make mistakes, Robert," said Professor Frost. "I have myself. Only last week I left my keys in a jacket on the back of a chair. If they'd fallen into the hands of a dangerous patient, there might have been a bloodbath. I was lucky, not good. You took the keys, didn't you? That's how you got the scalpels, isn't it?"

"Yes, and I killed Doris."

"Doris died, Robert, but she would have died anyway. You saved her seven piglets. But for you, they would have died, too."

"But I killed her. Just as I killed Maggie."

"Tell me about Maggie."

And Farcett talked of how his friend and assistant had died because he had made her help him experiment with X-rays.

"But you didn't do it on purpose, Robert. You didn't know the rays were dangerous. No one did then."

"And if I hadn't been obsessed with X-rays and with making a name for myself, I could have been fighting the flu epidemic. I'm sure I could have saved lives there."

"But the flu has beaten many doctors, Robert. The deaths were not your fault."

"There was another man I killed. Sixteen years ago. I will never forget him."

"You say killed. But you are a doctor. You may sometimes fail to save people, but I'm sure you do not kill."

"I killed him. Believe me. I killed him with my ambition." Farcett told the story of the public operation, when he had tried to remove the gall bladder of a healthy man. He'd failed, and the man had died, not knowing that the operation was unnecessary.

Professor Frost said nothing.

"That was wrong, wasn't it?" said Farcett.

The professor nodded and said quietly, "Yes, Robert. That was wrong. But Robert, those people you have told me of are dead. They cannot gain from you destroying yourself. If you shut yourself away in a dark, deranged world, no one benefits. The best way to make amends to the people you think of as your victims would be to get back into the world and do your job well. Go out, and be a good doctor."

"But I have done other bad things. Things that were nothing to do with being a doctor. Things that show I am a bad man."

"Tell me about them. See if I, too, think they are unforgivable."

"There was a priest. On the island of Tarimond. I made a terrible accusation against him. I said he had killed some children — every baby born on the island for seven years."

"And had he?"

"I thought so. I truly believed it when I said what I did. But no. He had not. And if I had waited for the evidence, I would have known he was innocent. Oh, but how he suffered. He was driven from his home, his flock, his livelihood. How can I ever forgive myself for that?"

"Have you asked him to forgive you?"

"We spoke, briefly, once. Not long after the events. He had moved to Glasgow. I meant to visit him regularly and to keep in touch by letter, but I couldn't. I couldn't bear to see the man I had wronged."

"Where is he now?"

"I don't know. Dead perhaps. He was not a young man then, in 1886. He would be in his seventies now, I should think."

"Why don't we find him, so you can apologize properly?"

"I couldn't possibly go out searching. . . ."

"I don't expect you to. You must stay sheltered here until you are better. And don't worry, we will keep up the pretense about who you are. So long as *you* remember you are Robert Farcett, I will let you hide under the name of Lord Francis Fox-Selwyn, and, when you are ready, you can return to the medical world without anyone knowing of this little episode in your life."

"But Father Michael . . ."

"The priest? Perhaps he can come to you. I will ask our friend Paul Vannini to find him and bring him to you here."

Farcett tried to protest, but the professor would hear none of his pleas. He insisted that Farcett should tell Vannini all he could about Father Michael, and the painter went off on his errand. Vannini thought very hard about how to explain it all to Gus and Montmorency. He sent a second painting, talking of some recovery and interesting developments, remembering at the last minute to add the reassurance that no strangers had been seen in the vicinity of the hospital. This new project — finding the lost Father Michael and restoring Farcett to health — was beginning to occupy far more of his time than the task the duchess had given him when she sent him to Britain. He was supposed to keep everyone safe from anarchists, but as time went on and there was no sign of trouble, the threat from Malpensa and Moretti was fading from his mind.

"Can I come with you?" said Tom, as Vannini packed for his trip to Glasgow.

"I don't see why not," said Vannini. "If your mother says yes, I will be glad of your company."

So he and Tom left together, taking Paul's painting gear with them, partly to give them a cover story and so that they were equipped to send messages south.

"I know I'm going to enjoy this detective work," said Tom. "It's what my father does, you know."

"Yes, I do know," said Vannini, "and I'm sure he'll be proud of you when he hears what we have done."

In fact, had Montmorency known what his son was up to, he would have been jealous rather than proud. He was growing tired of being cooped up with Gus and Jack, but he was still too weak to return to his old life. In his own way, he was ashamed. Ashamed of his inability to seek out George's killers and of the need to cower in his own home in case they were out there, looking for him. But Gus was insistent, and he knew Gus was right. Montmorency must wait until he had the strength to act, and then he would be after the killers with all the power he could command.

But for now, the scene grew ever more domestic, and Montmorency was sitting in his dressing gown, knocking the top off a soft-boiled egg when the bombshell came. It was late May, and the French windows were open. The soft warmth and birdsong made Montmorency happy and calm for the first time in ages. Jack brought in the newspaper. He didn't bother to read it himself and Gus was never interested in the news, but Montmorency liked to keep up with what was going on in the world. His eye was taken by a small item in a side column. The print was uneven and the prose terse, as if it had been added at the last minute. Montmorency read it out to the others:

ASSASSIN FOUND DEAD

GAETANO BRESCI, THE KILLER OF KING UMBERTO OF ITALY, HAS BEEN FOUND DEAD IN HIS CELL AT SANTO STEPHANO PRISON ON AN OFFSHORE ISLAND, SOUTH OF ROME. THE OFFICIAL CAUSE OF HIS DEATH IS SUICIDE. BRESCI WAS SENTENCED TO HARD LABOR AFTER MURDERING THE KING AT A SPORTING EVENT IN MONZA ON JULY 29 LAST YEAR. UNDER ITALIAN LAW HE COULD NOT BE EXECUTED. OUR CORRESPONDENT WRITES OF RUMORS THAT HE WAS KILLED BY PRISON GUARDS. AFTER FINDING HIS BODY, THEY THREW IT INTO THE SEA.

Jack, Gus, and Montmorency were all silent. Each had his own memory of the assassination the year before. Gus had witnessed it close up, as a guest in the royal box at the Monza games. Jack and Montmorency had heard only later in Britain. None of them had known then what they all believed now: that George Fox-Selwyn had died trying to stop the outrage. To them, Bresci was the main cause of George's death. He, with Malpensa and Moretti, was to blame. They'd all been angry that Bresci had been allowed to live on, in prison. And now he was dead. But at whose hand?

Unusually, it was Gus whose brain worked fastest. He thought at once of his wife in Italy and how she had left the country hurriedly only a few days before Bresci died. Now he understood that move. Alexander must have sent her to Paris in the knowledge that Bresci was going to be attacked. It was wise to get out of the way in case something went wrong and the anarchists suspected that the Fox-Selwyns were behind Bresci's death. It explained why Beatrice had sent news of the Paris trip in a secret message. And Paris was a good choice. Beatrice and Angelina could blend in among the international visitors. There would be no reason for Bresci's associates to look for them there.

And Alexander was getting out of Italy, too. He had stayed on for some unstated reason but would now be on his way to Washington. A coincidence of timing? Gus thought not. But he kept quiet while the others spoke. Alexander was the last person anyone would suspect of an act of murderous revenge. Best to keep that cover. Best to let people believe that Bresci had committed suicide or been killed by prison guards, out-raged at the assassination of King Umberto. Best not to plant the idea that Alexander had killed Bresci in anyone's head — even, perhaps especially, in the hot head of his younger son.

Jack felt only resentment that the guards had gotten to Bresci first. "I wish I had killed him," he said. "He didn't pull the trigger on George, but if George hadn't been chasing him, he wouldn't have died."

"I know," said Montmorency. "I feel the same. But Bresci's dead, Jack. There are only two of them left now. I can't wait much longer. Come on. You and I are going out for some fresh air and exercise. I've got to get fit, and when I am, we're going after Malpensa and Moretti."

CHAPTER 29

≫

GLASGOW

*P*aul and Tom checked into the most comfortable hotel they could find. The clerk at the desk was surprised when they asked him how to get to St. Aloysius's Church, the last address they had for Father Michael. He showed them where it was on a map. "I know it looks as if there's a shortcut through here," he said, pointing out a zigzag of tiny roads, "but don't take it. Stick to the main street. That's rough enough, I promise you."

They set off. The buildings grew higher and closer together as they got nearer to the church. In the grand square at the center of town, sunshine had sparkled in a fountain. Now the light could hardly penetrate, and the smell of humans packed too close together was overpowering. The church was small, its stone walls blackened from years of exposure to smoky air. Paul tried the door. It creaked open, letting out a strong smell of incense. The lobby inside was dark. Tom fumbled for a door handle and slowly entered the body of the church. It couldn't have been more different from the gloomy world outside. Hundreds of little candles lit statues and paintings of saints, and a single ray of sunlight cut its way through a stained-glass window, illuminating a dramatic image of the crucified Christ. An old lady came towards them with a duster in her hand. She could see at once that they weren't locals.

"Can I help you, gentlemen?" she asked. "Have you come to see the paintings?"

"Alas no," said Paul, though even a quick look told him that there were several worth studying. "We are looking for a priest who used to work here. Perhaps he is here still. His name is Father Michael. He used to work on Tarimond."

The woman shook her head sadly. "Father Michael is no longer with us," she said. "A sad business. A very sorry business."

Paul had known from the start that there was a chance that Father Michael would be dead. But the news hit hard. He knew how important it was for Farcett to get the priest's forgiveness if he was to recover. "Oh dear. I'm very sorry to hear that," he said. "When did he pass away?"

The woman looked surprised. "Oh, he's not dead," she said. "Though there are those who might wish he was. Father Michael has left the church."

"Is he still in Glasgow?"

"Aye. If he's not off gallivanting with that show of his."

"I don't understand," said Vannini. "What show?"

"Father Michael has turned himself into some sort of music hall artist. Reading minds. Telling stories. That sort of thing. He had to leave here. We liked him when he first came. He was a kind man. He could be funny, too. But then there was a bit of trouble. The drink, you know, and rumors. Rumors about gambling and about a woman in the choir. And then one Sunday he went into the pulpit and said he no longer believed in God. We'd put up with all the other things, but God, you know — well, believing in God is a bit of a qualification for the job. If you're a priest, that is."

"And you say he's gone into the theater?" Tom asked.

"Yes. He's on at that big music hall in Trongate. They say he pulls in quite a crowd. I've never been, though. It would hurt too much to see him prancing around and posing at his time of life, just to earn a living."

She told them how to find the theater, and Vannini made a large donation to the church maintenance fund. Then he remembered the squalor and suffering outside and put even more money into the poor box.

"Thank you, sir," said the woman. "And if you find Father Michael, tell him Mrs. McCracken sends her best regards. We have to love sinners, sir. Father Michael was always very insistent about that."

"I'll tell him," said Vannini as she showed them out into the dirty street.

The music hall was a high, square building with several stories of grand, arched windows. Posters advertised everything from dancing girls to animal acts, and there, on a lavish advertisement headed KEEP IT CLEAN! HE KNOWS WHAT YOU ARE THINKING! was a picture of an elderly man, with slicked-back white hair and a twinkle in his eye, wearing a long cloak covered in silver moons and stars.

"That must be him," said Tom, reading the rest of the poster. "*Shocking! Shocking! Magic, Memory, and Mind Reading with Micky McGuire!*"

"*Twice Nightly, at six-thirty and nine*," read Paul. "Well, let's see if we can find him inside."

They went to the stage door, where a grumpy man did all he could to keep them out.

"We would like to speak to Mr. McGuire," said Paul. "My name is Vannini."

"Vannini," said the man. "Now what sort of name is that? Italian or something?"

"Yes, Italian," said Paul, dropping a little extra music into his accent. "I need to speak to Mr. McGuire on most important business."

"We've had a Frenchman after him, you know. You've got competition. He'll drive a hard bargain."

Paul had no idea what the man was talking about, but he went along with the assumption that he must be some sort of impresario. "We'll see about that. Now is McGuire in the building?" He heard a rustle behind a partition, then a tall, thin man swept around to greet them. He was wearing the cloak they'd seen in the poster, but the white hair was sticking up wildly, as if he had just woken up. When the cape flapped open, they could see a tatty shirt and suspenders underneath.

The doorman was more respectful now. "Mr. McGuire, sir. This is a Mr. Vannini come to see you, sir."

"Pleased to meet you, Signor Vannini," said McGuire, who had obviously been listening to the earlier exchanges and wanted to ingratiate himself with the foreigner. "And this is?" he added, holding out a hand to Tom.

"Tom Evans, sir. We would like to talk to you."

"And you shall, you shall. Come this way to my dressing room, gentlemen."

They followed him down a hallway to a tiny room stuffed full of newspapers and empty bottles. McGuire gave Vannini the only chair and cleared a space on top of a crate for Tom. "Now, what can I do for you?" he said. "I must tell you from the start that I have had an offer from the *Folies des Anglais* in Paris. 'The English Follies.' They don't seem to mind that I'm Scottish. I seem to have hit on something unusual with my act. People like to see a respectable old man being a bit saucy — making a spectacle of himself. The manager of the *Folies* thinks it will go down well with the British tourists over there. Are you thinking of doing a similar thing in Italy?"

Paul couldn't resist a joke. "I suppose if you really could read minds, you'd know the answer already."

"Ah!" said McGuire. "You are clever. But I am a business-man as well as an entertainer, and people have to pay to see my mind reading. Mr. Vannini, I have yet to see the color of your money."

"Well, as it happens, I have none to offer. And I'm afraid I am not the man of the theater you take me for. We are here on a quite different matter. We are searching for a priest. A man who once had the care of souls on the island of Tarimond. His name is Father Michael."

McGuire hung his head. He let out a long, low sigh and closed his eyes. Tom thought he was never going to speak.

But at last he looked up and nodded. "I was Father Michael," he said. "I no longer have the right to use that name. I have ceased to be a man of the cloth. Though if you look at the label in this cloak, you will see where it started life: in one of the best clerical outfitters in Scotland. I sewed on the decorations myself when I first started out in this game."

"Father Michael," said Paul, deliberately using the man's clerical title in the hope of appealing to his good nature and of awakening memories of the past. "We need your help with a friend of ours. A friend who is in serious trouble. He is someone you knew on Tarimond."

"Of course I will help. If I can. Who is he?"

"He is someone who has done you great harm, Father Michael, and who is destroying himself with guilt about his actions. His name is Doctor Robert Farcett."

Father Michael flinched. "Robert Farcett. I know who you mean. You are right. His allegations changed my life. He brought me great sorrow. But that was long ago. You say he is in trouble? How so?"

Vannini told the story of Farcett's mental collapse and how the professor felt that Father Michael's forgiveness might be the key to recovery.

"Ah, forgiveness!" said Father Michael. "I used to deal in forgiveness all the time, urging it on my flock every Sunday. It's a funny thing, forgiveness. They don't tell you the truth about it. Forgiveness works best on the forgiver, not the forgiven. I have forgiven Doctor Farcett. I forgave him years ago, for I knew how vengeance can eat away a soul. He already has my forgiveness. Tell him that. I forgave him for my own sake. The real question is, can he forgive himself?"

"Not without your help, Father Michael. Will you come with us to Strathgillon to see him? Will you take the time to try to restore him, despite what he has done to you?"

Father Michael was thoughtful. "It's not that easy. I have a contract. You've seen the posters. I am here 'twice nightly.' I can't just walk away. If I break my engagement, I will have to find somewhere else, perhaps take that offer from Paris. But I'm not as young as I was. And I need to keep earning. If I came, you'd have to house me and feed me."

"Oh, I'm sure the Duke of Monaburn would take care of that."

"The duke? How does he come to be involved?"

"He's looking after Doctor Farcett. He has done so ever since Lord George Fox-Selwyn died."

"George is dead?" said Father Michael. "I liked that man. He visited me in prison, you know, when everyone else thought I was a killer. He used to keep in touch, but I stopped replying to his letters when I broke with the church. When did he die?"

Paul told the story of the murder and of events since.

"And Montmorency?" Father Michael asked. "He must have been hit hard by all this. He and George were very close. If you'd asked me whether he or Farcett would end up in a mental hospital, my money would have been on Montmorency. How is he?"

This time Tom spoke. "He has been ill, sir. He was hurt

fighting one of the men who had George killed. But there's something else I should tell you. Montmorency is my father."

The old priest took Tom's face in his hands. "Yes, yes, I can see it," he said, gazing into Tom's eyes. "Well, I never. Montmorency has a son. And a fine boy, by the look of you. You must have a wonderful mother!"

Tom looked offended, and Father Michael added, "Only joking, son."

Paul changed the subject. "So will you come? Say, at the end of the week?"

"I will think about it," said Father Michael. "I will say no more than that now. But will *you* come to my show? I'll get you two tickets for the late performance. Now, I'm afraid I must do some preparation. Mind reading takes a lot of work, you know. Pass me the evening paper. I need to take a look at the births, marriages, and deaths."

"What does he do that for?" asked Tom as they made their way out.

"I don't know," said Paul. "But perhaps we'll find out tonight."

CHAPTER 30

≫

THE MIND READER

The music hall was hot and smelly, with lines of benches for the rowdy crowd. Paul and Tom were jostled and squashed and had a good deal of beer spilled on their clothes. But they enjoyed themselves, joining in the singing and whistling at the dancing girls. Then, after the jugglers, it was time for the last act. The jolly master of ceremonies stepped onto the stage.

"Ladies and gentlemen, have you had a good time?"

The audience shouted, "Yes!"

"I can't hear you. Have you had a good time?"

They shouted louder. "Yes!"

"Do you want to see some more?"

"Yes!"

"Well, you've been a great audience, so I'll see what I can do. Ladies and gentlemen, you've seen a comic from England. You've seen a fire eater from Wales. I'm told that the prettiest girl in the dancing troupe is from Ireland. Don't you think it's time we had someone from home?"

"Yes!" they bellowed, even Vannini, who was far from Scottish.

The master of ceremonies carried on. "He's not just from Scotland. He's not just from Glasgow. He's not just a man. He's a man of magic. A man of magnificence. A man who can read your mind. So keep it clean, everybody. Even you, madam! For he used to be a man of God! Ladies and gentlemen, I can read minds, too. I know what you're thinking. You're thinking, 'Shut up and get on with it.' You're thinking, 'Bring him on. Give us the man. Give us the magic. Give us — Micky — McGuire!'"

The crowd roared, and the orchestra struck up a rousing beat. Paul recognized the tune but couldn't place it at first, then he realized what it was: a souped-up version of "Dear Lord and Father of Mankind," a hymn he remembered from school. Father Michael took the stage, his face thick with makeup and his cloak flapping and sparkling in the lights.

"Shocking, shocking!" he cried, leaning over the orchestra pit with mock horror. "Quite outrageous. What would the cardinal say? He'd have me defrocked all over again."

Someone shouted something from the gallery.

"What's that, madam? I can defrock you any time? Ooh! Shocking. Shocking. You Glasgow people. What am I going to do with you?"

Someone got up to leave. Paul recognized him as the man from the stage door and realized he was a plant. Father Michael shouted out to him. "Leaving us, sir? I don't blame you. It's shocking. Shocking."

The man turned and shouted back, "Disgraceful. Shouldn't be allowed!"

"I know," said Father Michael. "It's . . ." He signaled to the audience to join in. "Shocking. Shocking!" they cried as the man blustered his way up the aisle. "Let him leave!"

shouted Father Michael. "I can read his mind, and I tell you, ladies and gentlemen, you don't want to know what's going on in there, it's . . ."

"Shocking! Shocking!" The audience laughed as the door swung shut.

Paul knew what Father Michael was doing. He was using all his old skills as a churchman to work this crowd. They were on "call and response" now. He was sure there would be singing, fear, and mysticism to come.

But Father Michael was still building up the atmosphere, getting the crowd on his side. He was into the "memory" section of his act, offering to recall the details of any event shouted out from the audience. They all hollered at once, and he picked out items from the noise, repeating the questions as he answered them. "The date of the Massacre at Glencoe? 1692. How many plays did Shakespeare write? Thirty-seven. Maybe more. Maybe some were too shoc — No, no, we haven't got time for that! How many books are there in the Bible? Sixty-six, and I've read every single one. Who was prime minister in 1800? William Pitt the younger, sir. I said Pitt, Madam. I know what you're thinking. . . ." Again, Paul worked it out. The questions were either planted or not being asked at all.

As he bobbed about the stage, Father Michael did rudimentary magic tricks, pulling a bunch of flowers from his sleeve, a string of flags from behind his ear, a cigarette from his nostril. With each pathetic stunt, he urged on the cries from the audience: "Shocking! Shocking!" Then he would be back, answering questions. "Who was I with last night? Madam, that's something you and I don't want to remember!" And he whipped up the crowd again: "Shocking! Shocking!"

Suddenly, amid all the laughter, he went very still. He held up his hand for silence and got it immediately. He'd transformed himself with a few gestures from a figure of fun into a source of authority. "That's enough, my friends. I feel some messages coming through. Strong messages. Someone here is not happy. Someone is in pain. There is grief in the room."

He thrust his arm forward, closed his eyes, and spun around slowly till he settled with his finger pointing to the left-hand side of the crowd. "Here. Over here. Someone is worried about a boy. A boy whose name begins with J. Are you that person?"

Four hands went up, and the rest of the audience turned to face them.

"The second letter is 'o.'" Two hands went down. "It's John. John. Who is worried about John?" He opened his eyes. "I see your hand, madam. I'm getting an age. Twelve years. Is John twelve years old?" The woman nodded. The crowd gasped. "Now, he's not your son, is he? Not a relative? He's someone you know. A neighbor, perhaps?"

"Yes," she shouted. "He lives on my street."

"And he's been hurt, hasn't he? I see horses' hooves. I see a carriage. I see blood."

"Yes, yes. He was run over on his way home from school yesterday."

There were more gasps. Father Michael put his hands to his head as if he were receiving a new message. "Find his mother. Tell her that all will be well. He will get better."

Everybody cheered.

"Now," said Father Michael, shutting his eyes and spinning again. "I feel another strong thought. It's coming from over here." He pointed to a couple in the front row. His voice lightened. "Oh dear, sir. I can hear what you're thinking. And madam! You, too! You're not concentrating. You're thinking about what you're going to do after the show. Ooh, ladies and gentlemen. I'll tell you what it is. It's . . ."

"Shocking! Shocking!" they all cried.

He spun again and started a rapid fire of readings, pointing at random into the crowd. "The lady there. Did you leave the gas on? No! Will you catch the bus, sir? Yes! Did you leave the washing out, miss? Yes, you did, and it's raining outside. Let me know if I'm wrong. Tell your friends if I'm right."

Then he stopped again, closed his eyes, and held his head. "Hush now," he said, and they quieted down. "I feel a big worry in the air. Tom. Is there somebody here called Tom?" Several hands went up. "This Tom is young. He's thinking about someone whose name begins with an R or an F." Two hands stayed up. "It's a man he's thinking about. A man whose initials are R.F." Tom was bouncing on the bench, thrusting his hand into the air, totally taken in by the performance.

Father Michael spoke again. "I see a hospital. I see a patient who needs a visitor. Am I right?"

"Yes!" Tom shouted. Every eye in the house turned on him.

"I have a message for you, Tom. A message about RF. The visitor will come. The visitor will come tomorrow."

Tom jumped to his feet. "Oh, thank you, thank you," he yelled as the audience around him clapped and whistled.

Father Michael called for silence. He stepped right to the front of the stage. "My friends. I can feel more brainwaves. I feel them very strongly. Someone in this hall has just made a big decision. He is hoping he will not regret it, but it cannot now be changed." He dropped his voice, and the crowd stilled with him. "My friends. I am that man. And my decision is that this will be my last performance here. You people have been wonderful to me. But I have to go!"

The crowd were stunned for a moment. Then a joker in the gallery shouted, "Shocking!" and everybody laughed.

Father Michael went into his final patter. "That's all for tonight. That's all for a while. I hope it wasn't too . . ."

"Shocking! Shocking!"

"And remember, I know what you're thinking! You're thinking you've had a great time! Now be good, be kind, and forgive my foolish ways!"

The band struck up again, and Father Michael bounced off the stage, returning to bow a few times.

The master of ceremonies returned. "Micky McGuire, everybody. Give him a big hand. And don't believe what he said about leaving. He was just having you on. He's here twice a night. So tell your friends. But warn them he's really shocking. Now let's close the show with a song. . . ."

As the audience bellowed out an old favorite, Father Michael returned to his dressing room and the wrath of the theater manager. He stood his ground. "I'm an old man," he said. "There's something I must do. I'm sorry, but I have to go."

The manager stormed away, cursing, as Paul and Tom arrived backstage.

"It was wonderful," said Tom. "You knew exactly what I was thinking."

"It was just an act, Tom," said Father Michael. "I'm good at it, but it's not real."

"But that woman worried about the boy in the accident. You read her mind. Did you know she was going to be there?"

"No, but I knew what I said would ring a bell with someone." He pushed the newspaper over to Tom. A small story about an accident was ringed with pencil. "It happened less than a mile from here. The boy is local. I knew somebody in the audience was bound to know of him, and I knew it wouldn't be a close relative. They wouldn't go to the music hall when their child was in the hospital." Tom looked disappointed, and Father Michael tried to cheer him up. "But what I said to you was true. I will come to Strathgillon. I'd be obliged if you would help me clear up in here. I've burned my bridges, and now the manager wants me out straight away."

They collected Father Michael's sad belongings. The room

was full of rubbish, and the things he wanted to keep filled only one cardboard box. Then they walked out into the Glasgow night. The poster for Micky McGuire's shocking act was still there, but a banner saying "canceled" had already been pasted diagonally across it.

CHAPTER 31

≫

FORGIVENESS

*F*ather Michael stayed at Strathgillon for three weeks. Farcett didn't recognize him at first. He was feeding the piglets when he saw the professor walking towards him accompanied by a stranger. He started tidying the sty for their arrival. As they drew closer, the visitor seemed strangely familiar. There was something about his gait and the way his hair fluttered around his head. But Father Michael was reaching out in friendship before Robert realized who he was. "Father Michael. You look different without your clerical robes," he said, wiping his palms on his trousers. "Surely you don't want to shake hands with me."

"I do, Robert," said the old man, cheekily adding, "Even with that muck on you."

They shook hands formally. Then Father Michael pulled Farcett into a warm embrace. "Robert, I'm pleased to see you. It's been too long. If I'd known where to find you, I would have come before. I want to thank you."

"Thank me? Whatever for? I blackened your name and lost you your home. Why should you thank me?"

"Because, though you may not have meant to, you changed my life, Robert. Because of you, I returned to Glasgow and met people who made me think about my calling. I realized I wasn't meant to be a priest."

"But you were a good priest, Michael. I saw you on Tarimond. The people were in awe of you. I can remember sitting spellbound through your sermons."

"Yes, I admit it; I was good at that side of the job. And that was why it was wrong for me. I loved the theatricality of it, Robert. I loved being the star. But I was not a good enough man. I proved that in Glasgow. I let people down. I let myself down. I got a good kicking from the church, and now at last I am doing something that suits me better."

And Father Michael told Farcett about his new life on the stage and how he would be going to Paris. "It's not often a man gets a fresh start at my time of life, Robert. And for that, I want to thank you."

Over the days that followed, Father Michael used all his old pastoral skill to persuade Farcett that he, too, could start again. They had long conversations about the past and the future, and for the first time the doctor started to contemplate life outside the asylum. After a week, the professor experimented with leaving the bathroom door open and put a washstand and soap in Farcett's room. Robert used them, but no more than anyone else would. Professor Frost was always reluctant to say the word "cured," but he was very happy with Farcett's progress. Very happy indeed.

Eventually, Father Michael's thoughts started to turn towards Paris. He, Paul Vannini, and the professor gathered over a drink late one night to discuss his departure.

"Robert has recovered greatly while you have been here," said the professor. "He'll miss you when you've gone. We all will."

"I've been wondering," said Father Michael. "Is there any way that I could take him with me? Does he really have to stay here?"

"To be honest," said the professor, "if it weren't for the special circumstances surrounding his admission, I would let him leave. But remember, he is supposed to be here as Lord Francis Fox-Selwyn. I can't discharge him without putting his lordship in danger. I certainly could not do it without the authority of His Grace, the duke. Perhaps I should telephone him."

"No," said Vannini. "Don't do that. I have a secure way of contacting the duke. I will ask him to come up, and we can discuss the matter here."

So a painting was dispatched south, and in response to its cautious message, Gus arrived with the minimum of fuss. Vannini collected him at the nearest station and drove him to the hospital in a simple carriage. He looked like a visiting doctor arriving for a professional chat.

"Welcome, Your Grace," said the professor, when the door to his study was closed. The duke kissed Vi and shook hands with Tom. Vannini introduced him to Father Michael.

"Oh, what a joy to be in Scotland!" said Gus. "I hadn't realized how much I was missing clean air and soft rain. Now, Professor, Paul has explained the situation. You think it is time for Robert to leave your care."

"I do. But of course I will not do anything to endanger your son."

"I think we can take the chance," said Gus. "Frank has

made a new identity for himself — not an entirely desirable one, it has to be said — but a new one, nonetheless. And presumably Robert now looks quite unlike the Francis Fox-Selwyn your unexpected visitor saw?"

"Oh yes, quite different. Robert now looks like the eminent doctor he really is."

Vi chipped in. "If you give the go-ahead, I'll shave off his beard. No one who knew him when he was sick will recognize him then."

"And Vi," Gus asked, "you've known Robert for years. Do you think he's fit to travel?"

"I do. And more than that, I think he should get away from here. No disrespect, Professor. But it's not a normal place to be, is it? Surely he's never going to get really sane if he's surrounded by madmen all day."

The professor laughed. "As usual, Vi, you have gotten right to the point. I sometimes wonder how far *I'm* drifting from 'normal' in this company!"

Gus made his decision. He slapped his hands down on his knees. "Well, Professor, I think we should let him go to Paris with Father Michael if he wants to. Under his real name, of course. My wife is there, and my daughter-in-law. They could keep an eye on him."

"Perhaps you could go, too?" suggested Paul.

"Do you know," said the duke, "much as I am missing my womenfolk, I don't think I will. Coming here has brought home to me how much I dislike city life. I'd rather stay in the country."

"Why not come with me to Tarimond?" asked Vi. "The house has been empty for too long. I'd like to open it up for the summer and give it a good airing. You could have a rest and get back to town in time for the coronation."

"That sounds wonderful," said Gus. "Yes, I would like that."

Tom cleared his throat. "Mam? Do I have to come to Tarimond?"

Vi looked hurt. "Why? Where do you want to go?"

"I'd like to go to Paris, too," he said.

"But you can't expect Robert and Father Michael to look after you!" said Vi.

Paul intervened. "I could look after him. And on the way, we could stop in London and ask Montmorency and Frank to come, too."

"Jack," insisted the duke, "you must call him Jack, or I won't let him go anywhere."

Vannini corrected himself. "Jack, of course. I'm sure Beatrice and Angelina will be pleased to see them."

"Well, that all sounds rather satisfactory," said Gus. "Just do it all with the minimum of fuss. No great farewells or baggage wagons. Vi, if you don't mind waiting to clear up after the others, we will stay until they are gone."

"Certainly," said Vi. "Would you like me to go and get Robert? I think someone had better break the news to him."

CHAPTER 32

≫

THE LIBRARIAN AND THE STRANGER

*I*n Paterson, New Jersey, Mary Gibson opened her dressing table drawer. The letter was still there, hidden under her silk handkerchiefs. It was becoming quite fragile. She had folded and unfolded it several times a day for months now, and yet she had never replied. It was a year and a half since she had seen Montmorency, and this letter was all she had heard from him. He begged her forgiveness but promised to leave her in peace if she wished. She wanted to forgive him, but she couldn't find the words, and the letter she constantly composed in her head had never found its way onto paper.

But now, surely, she would have to write. She had a duty. Montmorency had sent her a picture of a dangerous criminal. He had asked her to watch out for him, just in case he had fled from Florence to hide among the Italian immigrant community in Paterson. His name was Antonio Moretti. He had full features and thick-rimmed round glasses. He was well educated, quiet, and personable. He matched in every particular the efficient clerk who had helped her in the Paterson Public Library that morning. She had asked his name. It was Agostino Grasso. He sounded and looked Italian. She had inquired where he came from. He said Rome, not Florence. But then, a real criminal *would* lie about his origins and change his name. Surely she should let Montmorency know about him and ask what to do next.

She sat down to write to him at last.

At Strathgillon, the man in the dark cape was back. He waited by the main gate, hoping to spot the servant boy, but he was nowhere to be seen. Eventually, a nurse came out, pushing a wheelchair. "Excuse me, miss," he called.

"You startled me," she said. "Who are you? What do you want?"

"I have come to visit Lord Francis Fox-Selwyn."

"He is no longer a patient here," she said.

"Has he gone to another hospital?"

"Oh no. He's quite recovered. He might have gone anywhere. He's gone home, I expect. But of course people like him have so many homes, don't they?" She laughed.

"Yes. You're right. I suppose they do. It seems I have had a wasted journey."

"What a shame. It was good of you to visit." She pointed at the slobbering man in the chair. "This poor soul never sees anyone. You wouldn't think he had any family or friends at all. I hope you find Francis. I'm sure he'll be pleased to see you. He's such a nice man."

"Yes," said the visitor. "I hope I find him, too."

CHAPTER 33

≫

PRIORITIES

*M*ontmorency's London house was buzzing with preparations for the Paris trip when Mary's letter arrived. Montmorency found Jack drinking down the dregs from the abandoned wineglasses on the lunch table. He showed him the letter. "We'll have to go straight to Paterson," he said. "If it really is Moretti, it's too good an opportunity to miss."

"Are you going to tell the others or shall I?" Jack asked. "I don't think they'll be very happy about us setting off on our own at the last minute."

He was right. Paul and Tom were both very disappointed. But Father Michael's reaction was worse. He was angry and worried.

"Look at yourselves," he said to Montmorency and Jack. "You're like a couple of schoolboys desperate to have a scrap."

"Michael, we've got our first real lead on Moretti," said Montmorency. "Of course we're excited. He's the man who killed George!"

"And?" said Father Michael.

"And we're going after him, of course," said Jack.

"To do what?" Neither Jack nor Montmorency spoke. Father Michael said it for them. "To kill him. That's what you want to do, isn't it?"

"Yes," said Jack. "I'm not afraid or ashamed to say it. To kill him. I want to see him dead."

"And what good will that do?"

"Well, it will make me feel better for a start," said Jack.

"Will it? Will it really? Do you think it would have made me feel better to have lashed out at Robert here?"

"It might have. Maybe you should have tried it."

"Don't think I didn't feel like it. Don't think I wasn't angry with him. But Jack, I was a priest for long enough to see what rage and vengeance do to people. I had to care for people whose lives were wrecked by their own anger."

Montmorency interrupted. "So are you saying we should do nothing? That we should let that monster walk the streets of Paterson in peace for the rest of his natural life?"

"No. Not necessarily. There are authorities, there are forces of justice who can take action."

"Authorities! Police!" said Jack. "How can they possibly give us the revenge we seek, the revenge we need?"

"I'm trying to tell you that you don't need revenge. That you don't need to get blood on your hands. There are other ways, and you have other obligations."

"Oh really? And what are those? How can there be any obligation greater than the service I owe to my dead uncle?"

"You have duties to the living. The duke has asked you to look after the duchess and Angelina. You should be caring for Robert. And Montmorency, you should be showing your son how a civilized man behaves, not rushing around like something out of the Wild West."

"So you would have us forgive Moretti?" said Jack.

"Eventually, yes," said Father Michael. "Forgiveness can be a hard burden to live with. Ask Robert here. He has to live with mine."

"I suppose he's right in a way," said Robert. "I sometimes wish he'd just hit me. Then I could feel I'd paid my debt."

"You're mad, all of you," said Jack, slamming the door and striding out into the street.

Father Michael grew calmer. "I mean it, Montmorency. Don't let yourself get eaten away by revenge. When was the last time you enjoyed a sunset or a great piece of music? You'll be only half the man you were if you don't let go of this rage. And that poor boy," he said, pointing at the door. "That poor boy is in danger. He's got a hate in his heart that frightens me. If you let him kill, he may kill again. You are older, Montmorency. You can show him the lead."

"And Moretti?"

"Moretti is thousands of miles away. You cannot reach him quickly. Alexander can tell the authorities in the Foreign Office about him. Then the American police can deal with him as they see fit. Meanwhile, you and Jack can spend some time thinking about the living, not the dead. George would not want you to neglect Beatrice and Angelina on his account. He would not have wanted you to suffer the injuries you have already sustained. I beg you. Come to Paris. Give peace and forgiveness a try."

Montmorency looked around for someone to speak in his defense. Paul and Tom were both staring at their shoes.

Farcett looked him in the eyes. "He's right, you know," said Robert. "And I need you, Montmorency. I want you to be there in Paris in case anything happens to me. I don't want to worry about you roaming America with guns. And I don't think George would have wanted his nephew to be wallowing in a sea of hate. If you can't pacify your own heart, you owe it to George to pacify Jack's. What sort of man are you letting him grow up to be, Montmorency? A vengeful, drunken libertine. How long before he's in the gutter? You know what it's like there. Stop him. Show him some of the finer things in life."

Montmorency thought for a long time. "All right," he said at last. "I shall pass Mary's information to Alexander in Washington, and I will come to Paris. But I'm warning you all. If we can't stand it there, Jack and I will be off to America."

Montmorency composed a letter to Alexander and carefully addressed it to him using his full title: the Marquess of Rosseley. He marked it *Urgent and Confidential*, to be delivered to the Washington Embassy in the diplomatic bag. Jack returned just as he was placing it on the hall table, ready for Chivers to take it to the Foreign Office. "What's this?" he said, reading the envelope aloud and slurring the many *S*'s in his brother's name.

"I've written to Alex," said Montmorency. "He's better placed than we are to do something about Moretti. Father Michael is right, you know. Our place is in Paris for the time being."

Despite his drunkenness, Jack managed to control his rage. "Oh," he said. "I see. So Paris is back on, then?"

"Yes, we're all leaving in the morning."

"Then we'd better get this letter off safely," said Jack. "I'll run it around there now."

"I'm sure Chivers can do it."

"No, no. I'm on my feet, and Chivers will be more useful helping with the packing. I'll be back in no time."

Jack walked out into the street. He couldn't bear the idea of his boring brother taking on the task of hunting Moretti. Jack would go to Paris all right, but from there he would find a way to America. He walked all the way to the Foreign Office, stopping off briefly at a couple of pubs along the way. He didn't want to make Montmorency suspicious by getting home again too soon. Diplomats were entering and leaving the building: steady, dependable, unexciting people just like his older brother. What use would they and their kind be for giving Moretti what he deserved? Yes. Jack would do it himself. This was not a job for Alexander.

There was a drain in the gutter alongside him. The grille that covered it formed slots, just like the mouth of a mailbox. Slightly unsteady on his feet, Jack bent over and dropped the letter down into the sewer. Scarper's sewer. Where it belonged.

CHAPTER 34

≫

FREGOLI

They'd all expected the duchess and Angelina to be anxious and miserable. Instead they found them having the time of their lives in Paris. When Alexander had confided in her that they must all leave Italy, Beatrice had guessed that he had a plan that might put them in danger there. But she knew better than to ask for details or to alarm Angelina by discussing her fears. Instead, she had suggested that the two of them should go shopping in the French capital while Alexander prepared for their move to Washington. Angelina, who had never been to Paris, was glad to go.

The duchess had rented the lower floors of a large town house on a central boulevard. The upper floors had been taken by an international celebrity: Leopoldo Fregoli, the famous Italian impersonator, who was on a world tour with his one-man show. At first, the women had been annoyed by his wild lifestyle. Hangers-on arrived day and night, and the great man himself seemed to need no sleep, suddenly deciding to sing or play loud musical instruments in the early hours of the morning. Beatrice had gone upstairs to complain, only to be invited in by the dapper little man who always seemed to have a carnation in his buttonhole. He was delighted to discover that she spoke Italian and even happier when he met Angelina, too. Soon they were regular features at his nonstop parties, and when Montmorency and the others arrived, they were adopted into the gang as well.

Fregoli got them all tickets to his show, which was a sell-out at one of the grandest theaters in the city. Father Michael, whose own stint at the smaller, vulgar *Folies des Anglais* was yet to start, hoped to pick up a few tricks of the trade. "I've heard he's very gifted," he said.

"He's certainly very popular," said Montmorency, elbowing his way through the crowds towards their box.

"Yes," said Vannini. "But don't forget, this is the town that spent the nineties lionizing a man whose entire act consisted of farting."

"Ah, *Le Petomane*," said Father Michael. "Now he *was* good. I thought of doing something similar myself, but I just didn't have the control."

The duchess cleared her throat. "Let's just concentrate on Fregoli, shall we? I won't spoil it for you by telling you what's going to happen, but I can assure you you're in for a treat."

The curtain rose, revealing a young woman on the stage. She was bidding farewell to her husband, off on a business trip. Seconds later, her lover arrived, only to be forced to hide when the husband returned unexpectedly. The three of them, and their maid, were caught up in a frenzied farce of suspicion, deceit, and panic. It was fast, it was funny, and it was only halfway through the romp that young Tom realized the point. Although the characters all spoke to one another, even had arguments, there was only ever one of them onstage at a time. Fregoli was playing all the parts, darting off the stage for complete costume changes that took only seconds. All the time he kept talking, throwing the voices of each of the characters out into the auditorium. The whole thing was meticulously timed and choreographed, and the audience was in stitches. The play moved at breakneck speed, scene changes happened imperceptibly. Backdrops flew up and down and back again. At the end, Montmorency and his friends cheered with the rest, desperate for more.

"Just you wait," said Beatrice in the interval. "The next part is different."

And it was. Now Fregoli impersonated all the famous music hall artists of the day: singers, dancers, jugglers, magicians. In what seemed like no time, he went through sixty costume changes, from male to female and back again, altering everything about himself — his look, his voice, his walk — so that the audience recognized all their favorite performers. He even sang an excerpt from the soprano part of the opera *Carmen*, dressed up like a flamenco dancer, complete with a headdress and an enormous fan.

And then there was another intermission, and a huge screen was set up on the stage. The lights dimmed, and Fregoli came on to introduce the third and final part of the program: his own creation, the Fregoligraph. Flickering images began to play before the audience. Here was Fregoli again, but now on film, acting out more sketches. Everyone was entranced. They applauded throughout the spectacle and cheered and threw flowers to the great star when he came back in person at the end to take a bow.

"And now the best bit," said the duchess. "Leopoldo has invited us backstage. We may even see a little of how it's all done."

The wings of the theater were stacked high with shelves of wigs, hats, beards, gloves, and shoes. Costumes hung in orderly row after orderly row, meticulously labeled: ready for action. A team of dressers was busy checking that everything was back in place, ready for the next performance. Fregoli, the jolly, rowdy host they knew at home, was sternly presiding over it all, making sure that the tools of his trade were all in perfect condition. Montmorency and his friends were fascinated and begged Fregoli to let them come again.

They waited until the fans had dispersed from the stage door. "What did you think of it, Michael?" asked Fregoli, as they walked around the corner to the house. "I always treasure the opinion of a fellow professional."

"I'm humbled, Leopoldo. Truly humbled. By contrast, my own work is — as my audience would tell you — shocking. Shocking."

"And you, young Tom? Did you enjoy yourself?"

"I loved it. But do you know which part I liked best?"

"Was it the little play? Or perhaps the Fregoligraph?"

"No. It was behind the scenes afterwards. Oh, Mr. Fregoli, do you ever need people to work for you? I would do anything for the chance to be part of all that."

"It's a hard job, Tom," said Fregoli. "And I am a severe master. It takes years to build a team I can really trust."

"I understand," said Tom, trying not to sound too disappointed.

"But I do happen to need an extra pair of hands at the moment," said Fregoli, letting his face broaden into a smile. "Could I trust you to take the job seriously?"

"Oh yes!" said Tom, glancing at Vannini to get his approval for the venture.

Fregoli followed his eyes. "Will you let him do it, Paul? I know you're supposed to be tutoring him. You could sit in to make sure he is not exploited. And I will pay him, if he works well."

"If I'm sitting in," said Paul, "might I sketch and paint? I would love to capture your energy. Would you let me try?"

"Delighted and flattered, sir," said Fregoli, as they arrived home. "Now. Let's have a party!"

Everyone was exhausted. But Fregoli, who had spent the whole evening in an athletic frenzy, still seemed to have enthusiasm to spare. Actors and musicians from shows all over town dropped in to join them, and they drank and joked into the night. Watching it all, Doctor Farcett had an idea. It was the first truly professional thought that had passed through his head since he had been ill. He wondered how Fregoli's body could stand the pace. How his heart and lungs sustained him through his stagecraft and what his vocal cords looked like before and after the show. He asked Fregoli if he could study him, building up a dossier, possibly for publication. Fregoli agreed with glee.

The next day, Tom, Paul, and Doctor Farcett started work backstage. Montmorency joined them, just to watch, while Father Michael went off to meet his new masters at the *Folies des Anglais*, and Jack loped off to find a bar. He was angry — more obsessed than ever with the need to get to America and search for Malpensa and Moretti. And he was worried that Montmorency would never leave Paris. To his mind, Montmorency was too convinced of his obligation to take care of Farcett and the ladies and too keen to stay with Tom, who was mesmerized by theatrical excitement and wouldn't want to leave his new job. But Jack was wrong. In the end, it was everyone's attachment to Fregoli that enabled Jack and Montmorency to go to America at last. Fregoli's engagement in Paris had only two more weeks to run. The next stop on his tour was New York. Late that night, at yet another flamboyant party, he asked everyone to join him on the trip.

CHAPTER 35

≫

CORNERED

Angelina loved the idea. She would be able to join her husband, now that he was settled in Washington. But Beatrice didn't want to go. It was time, she thought, to get back to Gus. It was hard for him to keep in touch from Tarimond, and she knew he must be worried about her, not knowing that she was having fun. Paul said he would take her to Tarimond and paint his portrait of the duke there, so long as Montmorency promised to keep an eye on Tom.

"Of course I will," he said. "He's my son."

"Yes, but this will be the first time you've really had to look after him. You can't just go running off after anarchists at the drop of a hat, you know. You have to think of Tom, too."

"I will," Montmorency promised.

"And I will make sure he does," said Doctor Farcett. "I want to go back to America. I'd like to visit Edison again."

Father Michael had to stay. He could not walk out on another job, and Fregoli kindly boosted his audience by adding a hilarious parody of his act into his nightly show. Thanks to Fregoli, "Shocking! Shocking!" was becoming a local catchphrase, even if most Parisians had no idea where it came from.

The last days of the Paris run were fun for everybody, even with all the preparations needed for the trip to New York. Jack was happier and more involved with the others now that

he knew he would be leaving. He made himself useful, packing props and costumes into huge wicker crates.

On the last night, he and Montmorency strolled out at the
first intermission for a cigarette by the banks of the river.
It was just getting dark, at the end of a hot day, and the water
was giving off the legendary Paris pong.

"I can't understand why their sewers smell so different
from ours," said Montmorency. "I meant to go down and
have a look. I don't know where the time went. I'll have to
come back again someday."

"I'm surprised you want to go down a sewer ever again,"
said Jack, "after what happened last time."

"I should think the chances of being beaten up down there
are almost nil, wouldn't you?" said Montmorency.

"Yes," agreed Jack.

They both heard noise behind them. A nasty, involuntary
exhalation quickly stifled.

They turned and simultaneously saw the twitch of a cloak
in an archway. Instinctively they moved towards it; then
Montmorency recognized, and Jack guessed, who it was.

"Malpensa," said Montmorency, and the man turned slightly.
It must be him.

Montmorency and Jack didn't need to say anything to each
other; they both realized they had an advantage. There were
two of them. Jack was fat and out of condition, but he was
young. Montmorency was fit again. And Malpensa had a bad
leg. They would get him. They both leaped forward, ready to
make a grab.

But Malpensa was up and away, moving faster than either of them. How could they have missed him? How could he move so fast?

Jack saw it first. He was on a bicycle. They would have to run as fast as they could to catch him, even though he was bumping along on the cobblestones with one leg sticking out. He led them through a maze of streets. They were almost on him when he turned the bike, steadied himself, flicked out a gun, and fired.

They dived away. "Split up," cried Montmorency, turning and running the way he had come. He could hear the bike behind him and now and then Malpensa's heavy breath, just as deep and wheezy as it had been in the sewer. Montmorency kept to the side of the road, in the shadows. He was almost back at the theater again, and there, beside him was a low wall. He knew it backed onto a courtyard by the box office. If he could find the strength to jump it, he could turn Malpensa's advantage into a liability. Malpensa would be cut off, stuck on his bike. He leaped, and Malpensa fired again, but he missed, and Montmorency heard the sound of the bicycle falling to the ground behind him. He had bought some time. He should use it wisely. He could hide in the theater. But Jack was still out there and might need his help. Montmorency had to get back onto the street, but he couldn't risk being spotted again.

He knew what to do. He could hear Fregoli inside, screeching his way through his opera sketch. He forced his way through a window and along the understage passages, up to the wings. Tom was there, waiting to rip off Fregoli's costume, while another dresser swapped it for a clown's suit.

"Help me," mouthed Montmorency, trying to indicate with his hands that he wanted a change of clothes. Tom could see from the grime and sweat on his face that his father was in trouble. Fregoli saw it, too, as he stepped behind the curtain, using his ventriloquist's voice to shout out jokes and keep the audience on the boil for the few seconds he would be offstage. As Tom tore off the dress, he held it out for Montmorency. He plunged his arms in and turned around. Fregoli himself fastened it at the back, still talking, ad-libbing extra lines to fill the time. While Fregoli's new wig was being pulled over his ears, Montmorency was tugging on the old one. He grabbed the fan and ran, just as Fregoli thrust his feet into gigantic shoes and lolloped back onstage, to roars of laughter from the crowd.

Back in the street, Montmorency pressed himself against the wall, with the fan covering most of his face. His eyes darted from side to side, looking for Malpensa and his bike. There was no sign of him or of Jack. In the distance he heard two bangs. Gunshots? Fireworks? Sounds from the stage?

Three men approached from the end of the road. They looked drunk. He moved farther into the shadows. But they'd seen him and, lured by the flutter of his skirt in the dark, they walked towards him.

"Hello, my pretty," said the first. "My friend here thinks you're a stunner."

"I like a strapping lass," said the friend.

The first man reached out towards Montmorency's wig.

Montmorency raised the fan. He would have hit the man with it, but he didn't want to show his face, with its evening stubble. "Go away," he said, in the highest voice he could muster. "Leave me alone."

Someone came running around the corner. The three men stepped back a pace, not wanting to be seen accosting a woman. The running man was followed by a bicycle, which was gaining on him all the time. Montmorency wanted to break away from the drunks and give chase, but he couldn't risk drawing Malpensa's attention. For the moment, the three oafs were the best possible cover.

But he had to get rid of them. He had to follow Jack. From the corner of his eye, he could see him turning into the next street, with Malpensa only a second behind. Then, just after they disappeared from view, there was the unmistakable sound of a gunshot.

The three men rushed towards the noise. Montmorency followed, as unobtrusively as he could, his legs getting tangled in his skirt as ran. When he got to the corner, he saw what he dreaded: Jack was on the ground, clutching his arm. He had been shot. Malpensa was standing over him, with the gun still in his hand. He turned Jack faceup and stamped his foot on his chest. The drunks had been shocked into silence, and Malpensa's words rang through the street.

"You are the wrong one!" he said, as if it was Jack's fault that Malpensa had made a mistake. "I would finish you off, but I have only one bullet left, and I am going to keep that for your friend." He turned to the three men, and Montmorency pulled himself back out of sight. Malpensa spoke with venom and authority, bringing out all the cowardice in the drunkards' souls. "Leave him here. Do not help him. Go away. You saw nothing. Do you hear me? Go." He couldn't resist firing his weapon to frighten them off. Then he cursed as he realized he'd wasted his last bullet. He picked up his bicycle and rode away. The three men ran in the opposite direction. Montmorency was alone again and rushed to Jack, dragging him along the pavement and into the safety of the theater, despite his agonized cries at being touched at all.

Doctor Farcett was there, preparing to take Fregoli's temperature as he came offstage. He scooped Jack into his arms and carried him to a dressing room, tearing away his shirtsleeve to expose the wound.

"I know it hurts, but it's actually not that bad. There's a lot of blood, but the bullet passed straight through. It's missed the bone."

"How did he find us?" Jack asked frantically. "I thought he was supposed to be in America."

"I don't know," said Montmorency. "Maybe he's been and come back. Or maybe someone in Italy told him Beatrice was here."

"Perhaps he was watching us in London," said Jack. "Perhaps we weren't careful enough."

"No, Jack. You were good. You kept your disguise perfectly. Malpensa didn't even recognize you tonight. I'm the one to blame. I told him my name, and I've kept that name, trailing it in the open from London to Paris. You and Robert have given up your very selves to fight these people. I've clung to my identity, even though it isn't really my own. I'm the one who has let us down. I have no one to blame but myself."

Doctor Farcett disagreed. "No, Montmorency. Blame Malpensa. Decent human beings shouldn't have to skulk around in disguise. Malpensa is the person who shot Jack. Turn your anger on him, not yourself."

"Can I still go to America tomorrow?" asked Jack.

"Maybe we should stay here now," said Montmorency. "We should track Malpensa down."

"But Montmorency," said Jack, "Malpensa could be anywhere by now, and we know where to look for Moretti. Even if the Italian manuscript was wrong, we know Mary Gibson thinks he's in Paterson. Please. I've waited so long. We've got the tickets, and we're ready. We must go to Paterson to find him, while we have the chance."

"But what about Malpensa? He could have killed you. I have to get back at him."

"I think we know now that Malpensa will come to you!" said Jack. "Please. Don't make me wait any longer. Please let me get at Moretti."

"All right," said Montmorency. "I'll tell Paul to warn your father that Malpensa's on the loose in Europe." He turned to Doctor Farcett, who was washing Jack's wound. "Robert, do you think Jack is fit to travel?"

"Yes. We can take the risk," said Farcett. "At least on board ship you'll both be safe from Malpensa, and a few days' bed rest will probably do Jack good, even if he's seasick again. I'll be with you. I'll dress the wound. And I think Jack's right. Malpensa is after you. Get away from him. Deal with Moretti if you must. He's the man who murdered George, after all. But don't put yourselves in danger deliberately. Jack's too weak to fight him off now."

"All right," said Montmorency. "We'll go." He watched Farcett bandaging Jack's arm. He was horrified by what had happened that night. But he was thrilled to hear Robert talking like a doctor again.

CHAPTER 36

≫

AMERICA AGAIN

They traveled on the SS *Campania*, the same ship that had taken them to New York two years before. It was all very familiar, although there was one change: The photographs decorating the passageways had been replaced since their last trip. The *Campania* had been the only ocean liner allowed to take part in the great flotilla that had escorted Queen Victoria's coffin from the Isle of Wight to Portsmouth, and the shipping company had put up black-framed pictures of the event and of the foreign royals and British dignitaries who had been on-board that somber day. But the passengers for this transatlantic voyage were definitely not in funereal mood. They had the best entertainment imaginable. Fregoli had insisted to the captain that he would not do any performances, but he couldn't help himself, and even without costumes he made people laugh at informal gatherings all over the ship.

Under Robert's care, Jack's wound started to heal, but his arm was still useless after a week at sea. He wanted to go straight to Paterson when they landed, but Montmorency was adamant. Jack must recover first. They would stay in New York, where Tom would be helping Fregoli with his show. Moretti could wait till they were both fit. And anyway, perhaps Alexander had dealt with him already.

Montmorency let Tom go straight to the theater with Fregoli and his team. Special trucks had been sent to carry all the props and costumes into the city. They would need every available minute to get unpacked and organized in time for the first show. Montmorency, Jack, and Doctor Farcett made for the hotel. They were surprised to find a visitor waiting for them. He was obviously American: tall and healthy with a handsome tanned face and a broad smile glistening with straight white teeth. He wore a smart suit whose cut and light color intrigued Montmorency. The jacket was shorter than was the fashion in Europe, the waistcoat tighter and the trouser legs narrower. His high shirt collar was bound loosely with a short necktie. He was holding his hat. It was soft, with a narrow brim and a low crown. He took out his wallet and discreetly flashed some identification that was meaningless to Montmorency. "My name is Jerrold Armitage. I work on behalf of the federal government, sir," he said. "I wonder if I might have a word with you all in private."

"Certainly," said Montmorency. "Perhaps it would be best for you to come up to our suite? The bellboy is taking us there now." He began to introduce his friends. "This is Doctor Robert Farcett, and this is my assistant, Jack Scar —"

"I know who you are," said Armitage, silencing him as they walked to the elevator.

In the privacy of the suite, he passed Montmorency a telegram. It was from Inspector Howard in London.

Montmorency Farcett Scarper arriving Friday on
Campania STOP know nothing STOP feel free to
use my name STOP Howard Scotland Yard STOP

"What does he mean 'know nothing'?" said Jack.

"You were on the ship, and we couldn't tell you," said
Armitage. "Inspector Howard has suggested you may be able
to assist us with a security matter. We have had a series of
threats to the life of the president. Of course we get them
all the time, but you will appreciate that with all the recent
anarchist activity we have to take them seriously. Howard
says you were very helpful at the time of Queen Victoria's
funeral."

"Well, we tried to be," said Montmorency. "But I can't say
we did much. I may have foiled one attacker, but he got away."

"I know. Inspector Howard has told us everything. And,
Lord Francis, I've spoken with your brother . . ."

"Please don't call me that," said Jack. "It's very important.
No one must know who I really am."

"I'm sorry, Mr. Scarper. The Marquess of Rosseley has
assured me you will help. He's confirmed that you can recognize some dangerous people who are not known to us and
that you believe those men to be in the United States."

"We did," said Montmorency. "But we know that at least
one of them, Malpensa, was in Paris a few days ago. Of course
that doesn't mean he won't come here. Indeed, if he's found
out where we've gone, he may be on his way now. I think at

first it was just a question of us pursuing him, but now he's on our trail, too."

Armitage continued. "The president has a very busy public schedule in the next week or so. He likes to get out and meet the people. We need all the help we can get, watching the crowds for threats. Will you help us?"

"Well, we were on our way to Paterson, New Jersey," said Jack. "We have some important business there. I think going to Washington might be a bit awkward."

"Actually, we wouldn't be sending you to Washington. And if you were thinking of going to Paterson to find anarchists, I can tell you now that there's no point. We've cleaned out the entire cell there. No, I want to take you to Buffalo. That's in New York State: We can get there easily by train. President McKinley is on his way to visit the Pan-American Exhibition there. He's going to see Niagara Falls and tour the exhibition itself. He has all his usual aides and security men with him, but they could do with a couple of extra pairs of eyes at a time when he's so exposed to the public. Will you help us?"

Jack looked reluctant, but Montmorency said yes.

Armitage thanked them. "I noticed that the hotel has tourist information about Niagara Falls and the exhibition. Perhaps you'd like to take a look. And Doctor Farcett, there should be plenty to interest you at the Buffalo fair. It's a huge show, about everything that's wonderful in all the Americas. So of course there are displays about science and inventions and so on. I gather you are rather an admirer of Thomas Edison. Maybe you would like to come, too."

"Yes," said Farcett, slightly uncomfortable that this stranger seemed to know so much about them all.

"Well, perhaps I could meet you in the lobby tomorrow morning, and we'll get the train to Buffalo."

"Oh," said Montmorency. "I hadn't realized you wanted us so soon."

"I'm afraid so. Is there a problem?"

"No, none at all," said Montmorency.

Doctor Farcett interrupted him. "But what about your son?" Montmorency looked blank. Farcett had to remind him about Tom. "You can't just leave Tom here, can you?"

"Oh no," said Montmorency, ashamed that he had already fallen into the trap Vannini had predicted and forgotten his new parental responsibilities. "But I'm sure we will be able to make some sort of arrangement with Fregoli . . ."

Armitage was anxious to get away. He didn't want to give them a chance to change their minds. "I'll let you get yourselves settled," he said, picking up his hat. "As you say, you'll probably get something sorted out. I'll meet you in the lobby tomorrow morning at ten."

The Englishmen were too polite to do anything other than agree. But when the door closed behind Armitage, Jack exploded. "Are we never going to get to Paterson? How many more things are you going to allow to come between us and Moretti? We've only been here an hour or so, and now all our plans are upset again. I can see Alexander's at the back of this, volunteering our services without asking. Who does he think he is?"

"He's a British diplomat offering help to a friendly power," said Montmorency. "He's only doing his job. And don't forget, he knows our suspicions about Moretti being in Paterson. He may well have dealt with him already. You heard what Armitage said."

Jack got quiet. This was no time to admit that he'd destroyed Montmorency's message about Moretti and that Alexander knew nothing about Mary Gibson's suspicions.

"And anyway," Montmorency continued, "who knows? If Malpensa comes to America, this great exhibition might be exactly where he would go to get at the president. Remember, it's not just me he's after. His real aim is the destruction of authority. I'm just an irritation on the way to his goal."

"So we're back to putting public duty before our own ends?" said Jack. "I'm getting sick of this."

"We have no choice," said Montmorency. "It's the correct thing to do. Father Michael was right. Our desire to avenge the dead must come second to the protection of the living. President McKinley is alive, and it seems he needs us."

"I'm alive, too," said Jack, "and I've got my arm in a sling. I want revenge on the man responsible for that!"

Farcett wanted to get away from the argument. "I'm going down to the lobby to find those leaflets about the exhibition. Do you want me to visit the theater, too, to see if Fregoli is willing to look after Tom while you're away?"

"Would you mind?" said Montmorency. "From what

Armitage said, I imagine we'll only be gone for a week or so." He knew that Tom would have a good time, working backstage for Fregoli. But he was new to fatherhood and had never had a father himself. He had no idea how hurt Tom would be that Montmorency was going away without him and that he had not even broken the news himself.

CHAPTER 37

≫

CZOLGOSZ AND NEIMAN

While Jerrold Armitage was talking to Montmorency and his friends in New York, a young, unprepossessing American was buying a gun at the Walbridge Hardware Store in Buffalo. The salesman congratulated him on his choice. The tiny Iver Johnson .32 revolver was a neat little thing, small enough not to make a bulge in a pocket. It could fit into the palm of one hand. The customer was attracted to it for another reason. It was the make of gun Gaetano Bresci had used in Monza a year ago, when he had assassinated King Umberto of Italy.

The customer was Leon Czolgosz, the American-born son of a Polish immigrant. He'd grown tired of explaining to people how to say his name, which, to American eyes looked like a random jumble of the least compatible letters in the alphabet. "Shole-gauze," he would say, and folk would try to get their tongues around it, but the next time they saw the strange word they were stumped again. He'd taken to using a different name: Fred Neiman. Neiman translated as "Nobody." It summed up his place in this world. How until now he had made little impact. And it was a useful disguise, too. As Fred Neiman, he had mingled with anarchist supporters across the nation. He had drunk in their message about the injustice of one man wielding power over another and the glory of the assassination in Italy. It was as Fred Neiman that he took a room at Novak's Hotel in Buffalo and waited for the arrival of the president.

Montmorency, Jack, and Farcett reached Buffalo the next day. The train took them right into the exhibition, and Jerrold Armitage showed them around. The place was swarming with people. News that the president would be visiting had boosted attendance after disappointing figures since the opening in May. The Englishmen had read the hotel pamphlets. They'd heard that this was one of the greatest expositions ever erected, but they were quite unprepared for what they saw. The Pan-American Exhibition was a city in its own right, with wide avenues, railway lines, and giant buildings housing celebrations of every imaginable form of human achievement and all aspects of American life, from an Eskimo settlement to a Wild West show. There were zoological displays, horticultural demonstrations, art galleries, fairground rides, a sports stadium, fountains, boating lakes, restaurants, and shops. Farcett wanted to see the medical exhibits. The brochure said they had all the latest equipment, including special heated glass incubators that could keep premature babies alive. "Apparently they have real babies in them. You can pay to go in and look," he said.

"The city of Buffalo spent ten million dollars building the exhibition," said Armitage, "and most of it will just be knocked down at the end of the year when it's all over."

"But how could they demolish such wonderful buildings?"

said Farcett, admiring what appeared to be a palace adorned with cherubs, angels, fantastic animals, and a gilded dome.

"It's not real stone," said Armitage. "They use a mixture of paper and wood. They had terrible trouble with rainstorms before they got everything finished and sealed. But it's quite something now, isn't it?" The Englishmen had to admit that it was. "Just wait till it gets dark," said Armitage. He pointed to strings of white globes covering the fronts of the buildings so that they looked as if they were dressed up as pearly kings. "See all those lightbulbs? They're real. The whole place sparkles at night. When they turn on the electricity after dark, that huge tower is aglow from top to bottom. You'd think it was daytime. And all the power comes from the great Niagara Falls. We'll be going there when the president comes. It's a sight to see. But we'll have to keep our eyes on the protestors. There are plenty of people who think it's wrong to take power from the waterfalls. They'll be out in force when McKinley's here, trying to make their point."

Two days later, Czolgosz was at the falls, too, hoping to get near enough to the president to make good use of his new gun, but the Secret Service were indeed being careful, watching so closely that he knew he had no hope. He had already followed the president around the exhibition, hearing him enthuse about it as a monument to America's prosperity and increasingly dynamic place in the world. He had seen McKinley reviewing parades of troops, watching a ballet, trying ice cream and popcorn, smiling, waving, and thrilling bystanders with a nod or the lightest touch of his hand. The president was still at it now, here at the falls, full of energy, though the first lady had told him that it was all getting a bit much for her and she wanted a rest.

McKinley was determined to keep going, despite the sun and the discomfort of his heavy city clothes. He toured the power station and confirmed that after lunch he would return to the exhibition for a reception at the Temple of Music, to shake some more hands. Czolgosz left the falls to catch a train back to the exhibition, determined to get a place in the line for a handshake.

Returning from Niagara, Montmorency and Jack took a break for a glass of cool sarsaparilla while President McKinley was off changing his shirt for the reception at four o'clock. Jack yawned. "I can't stand this heat much longer," he said. "The sweat's running into my eyes." He lifted his wounded arm and wiped his face on his sling.

Montmorency passed him his handkerchief. "Here. Have this." Jack mopped himself gratefully and tried to hand it back. "No," said Montmorency. "Keep it. There's a stall over there selling hankies with the exhibition crest embroidered in the corner. I'll go and buy a couple. It looks as if they're doing a roaring trade in this heat."

A line was forming outside the Temple of Music. Armitage led Montmorency and Jack in through a back entrance, to meet the Secret Service agents and bodyguards who would be policing the event. A nervous man was organizing the placement of potted palms and drapes around the spot where the president would stand.

"Mr. Quackenbush," said Armitage, "these two gentlemen will be helping us in here this afternoon. They'll be monitoring the line for undesirables. Where would you like them to stand?"

"Pleased to meet you," said Quackenbush. "Let me show you how it will work. You see how we've moved the chairs to make a sort of L shape? The president will stand here." Quackenbush took up position at the center point of the L, as if he were McKinley, miming handshakes with invisible members of the public. Then he walked over to the east door. "This is where people will come in. I'm going to have some military guards here and at all the corners, to give a sense of occasion and to impress upon the public that they are expected to behave. Visitors will walk along this path to the president, shake hands, keep going, and exit along the other leg of the L, over there. I suggest you stand opposite the president and to one side, towards the door where they come in. That way you'll get a good look at their faces." Quackenbush looked Montmorency and Jack up and down. Montmorency was wearing the smart clothes of an English gentleman. Jack was in the "Sunday" version of his servant uniform. Quackenbush obviously thought they were policemen in disguise. "Good, good," he said, straightening Jack's jacket. "I've got plenty of uniformed men. I could do with a few more like you. You'll fit in with the newspaper reporters we're going to put in this section. I like the sling; it's a good touch," he said, slapping Jack's injured arm so hard that Jack had to bite his tongue to stop himself from howling with pain. Quackenbush didn't notice. He'd moved on to Montmorency and brushed some dust off the shoulder of his coat. "And if you stand up nice and straight, you might even be taken for some sort of Washington official. Good, good. You'll blend in nicely. Now I really must get on." He looked at his watch. "The president will be arriving in five minutes. Stand by, everyone. Stand by." The military guards took up their places, and Montmorency and Jack nodded unobtrusive greetings to plainclothesmen they had met earlier on the president's tour.

They heard the murmur of the crowd outside grow louder until it reached a crescendo of shouts and applause. The news-papermen were ushered in through a side door as McKinley took up his position at the spot Quackenbush had prepared for him, surrounded by ferns and bay trees, with the Stars and Stripes draped behind him. McKinley nodded to an aide, who nodded to Quackenbush. Quackenbush nodded to the organist, who started to play. The doors were opened, and the line filed in.

McKinley reached out to the first in line, shook his hand, and said a few words as he firmly steered his admirer for-ward and along towards the exit. Then he turned to take the next hand. Everybody in the crowd got the same treatment, the same mixture of sincerity and efficiency. There were a few breaks in the tedium. A woman who arrived laden with souvenirs dropped one, and the president helped her pick it up. A little girl charmed everyone with her lisping cuteness. An old man wanted to stay and chat and had to be led away. But it was a wearying process for all concerned. Everyone was sweltering in the heat, dabbing their faces with handkerchiefs and sleeves, trying not to appear too damp in the presence of the Great Man.

Just as at Queen Victoria's funeral, Montmorency and Jack found it hard to stay alert, to scan every face, when most of the time there was nothing remarkable to see. Then all at once there was a flurry of activity. One of the president's own bodyguards noticed someone suspicious in the line. He nudged a colleague and gestured towards the man. His dark complexion and excited expression spelled "anarchist" to them, and they quietly pulled him to one side. Montmorency watched them go through his pockets. Nothing. They apologized and let him back in the line. Soon he was shaking hands with McKinley, who steered him on past, towards the exit.

An aide standing near Jack was holding a stopwatch. "The president likes to do fifty handshakes a minute," he whispered. "We need to speed up." He walked over to the entrance and urged people to walk faster, so everybody could get through before McKinley had to leave. Outside, Czolgosz was worrying that he wouldn't make it to the front of the line before the doors were closed. But he didn't want to draw attention to himself by pushing. Everything was in place. The gun was in his pocket, and he had a handkerchief ready to wrap around his fist so that the weapon didn't show when he reached out towards McKinley. He mentally rehearsed the move. Step forward, aim, fire. He was only a few feet from the entrance.

Inside, Jack was stifling another yawn when an electric charge ran through him. In his lapse of concentration, he had started looking at the line of people who had already shaken hands and were making for the exit. There was something about the way a short, round man was walking: a certain roll to his gait, with his small feet turning in towards each other so that the round toecaps on his shoes almost touched. There was a familiar circular bald patch on the back of his head. Jack couldn't see his face, but he was certain — it was Moretti.

But what was he doing? He had passed right in front of the president and had merely shaken his hand. Had he intended to attack but been put off when the man just in front of him was tugged from the line? Had he lost his nerve at the last minute? It didn't matter. He was there, now, and Jack had the chance to catch him and to make him pay for what he had done to Lord George Fox-Selwyn. There were plenty of policemen and soldiers in the room. Quite enough to spot any troublemakers in that line of sweaty people.

Jack knew for certain where he should be and what he should do. He would pursue Moretti. Montmorency was looking the other way, paying special attention to a new arrival in the hall, a young man who seemed to have a bandaged hand. Jack tapped Montmorency on the arm, mouthed, "Moretti," and inched his way through the newspapermen and guards towards the exit. He didn't want to make a commotion. He didn't want Moretti to sense someone was after him nor to disrupt the presidential occasion. He had to go in slow motion, and Montmorency, who was following him now, crept along, too. By the time they got outside, the man was a good twenty yards away, on the other side of a crowd that was forming to watch the president leave. Montmorency and Jack began elbowing their way through to catch up with Moretti.

Inside the Temple of Music, Leon Czolgosz was only a few feet from McKinley. No one took any notice of the cloth wrapped around his hand. He reached forward and fired two shots. The handkerchief over the gun caught fire. A bodyguard jumped on top of Czolgosz, only to be grabbed by a soldier, who mistook the guard for the attacker. The next man in the line punched Czolgosz in the face. The president put his hand against his chest and felt a wetness that could only be blood.

As Jack and Montmorency caught up with their man, they heard the shots. He heard them, too, and turned back towards the Temple of Music. A collective scream of horror swept the crowd. For Montmorency and Jack, the shock was twofold. The president had been shot. And the man they had been chasing wasn't Moretti.

CHAPTER 38

≫

EMERGENCY

$\mathcal{D}$octor Farcett was viewing the incubator babies when the shots were fired. He'd paid twenty-five cents to get in and felt a little uneasy about tiny patients being displayed for financial gain. But he was fascinated. He had never seen anything like this exhibit, a two-story building tucked in among the fairground attractions. Twelve glass boxes lined the walls, each with a pipe for letting in filtered fresh air and a thermostatic mechanism for keeping the babies at the optimum temperature. Every incubator had a notice on the front, telling the public all about the little person inside, the circumstances of its birth, and its prospects for survival. Upstairs, there was a nursery, showing off babies who had grown strong enough to leave the incubators.

Someone ran in, jabbering that the president had been shot. He was calling for medical help. "I'm a doctor," said Farcett, and in no time, he was running across the grass with one of the nurses, in the direction of the Exhibition's medical center.

The president had not yet arrived, but there was word that he was being driven over, still alive, but in need of urgent attention. Farcett looked at the facilities: They were perfectly adequate, exemplary even, for dealing with the sort of mishap that might be expected at a big public event. But they would be quite unsuitable for operating on gunshot wounds. There were insufficient instruments, and the lighting was poor. The eminent surgeon who headed the unit was out of town, in the middle of an operation. Until he could get there, the most senior person involved in the president's case would be a gynecologist who had been halfway through a haircut when the news of the shooting reached him. Things didn't look good. Farcett felt sure they would transfer the patient to the big hospital in town.

But when the carriage carrying McKinley arrived, the decision was made to treat him on site. One bullet fell out when they removed the president's shirt, leaving only bruising on his chest. But the other wound was more serious. Farcett explained who he was and offered to help. He did menial tasks while the American doctors struggled by the light of a single window to repair the damage caused by the second bullet. It had gone right through the president's stomach and lodged deep in his abdomen. They couldn't find the bullet and decided to leave it inside. Farcett was surprised that they didn't put in a drain to help prevent infection, and he worried what effect the lost bullet might yet have on the president. But he kept quiet, did as he was told, and hoped for the best.

Jack and Montmorency were in the hushed crowd outside. Montmorency was full of guilt. For the second time, he had abandoned his public duty to pursue a private vendetta. The first time, at Queen Victoria's funeral, he had caused no harm. The procession had passed without incident, even though he hadn't been looking. It might even be true that by chasing Malpensa he had stopped him from shooting the king. But this time Montmorency had followed his rage, left his post, and now the president was injured. McKinley might even die. Montmorency had seen the culprit being taken away to the police headquarters. He had surrendered without a struggle and admitted his crime. It was the man Montmorency had been watching before he left the hall. He remembered feeling uneasy about that bandaged hand. If only he had followed his first instinct and intercepted Czolgosz. He was ashamed.

Jack was sorry, too, but he was angry. The whole Buffalo enterprise had been a failure, and it had distracted him from what he really wanted to do. And now Armitage had told him that he wouldn't be allowed to leave town. There would be legal proceedings and probably an inquiry. Everyone in the Temple of Music that afternoon would be interviewed, probably more than once. Jack and Montmorency would be stuck in Buffalo, and somewhere out there Moretti was going about his business unhindered, unpunished for killing George.

CHAPTER 39

≫

AFTERMATH

*F*or the first few days after the shooting, the news was good. The doctors issued optimistic statements about the president's condition, and the atmosphere in the town was excited rather than fearful. The president was a good patient, cheerful and cooperative. No one knew that the tissue around the lost bullet was decaying, that gangrene had set in, and that McKinley's body was gradually poisoning itself. Eight days after the attack he was dead, and the whole country threw itself into an orgy of mourning and recrimination. In the public mind, the Buffalo doctors were transformed from heroes to buffoons. The papers ran long articles about Czolgosz's background and lifestyle. They criticized the people in charge of the president's safety, who responded by insisting that little could be done to guard against a determined assassin acting alone.

The vice president, Theodore Roosevelt, rushed into town from his vacation in the Adirondack Mountains and was hurriedly inaugurated at a simple ceremony in a private house, wearing a borrowed jacket. There was to be a grand funeral, larger even than Queen Victoria's, involving long train journeys, a parade in Washington, and finally the burial, in McKinley's hometown in Ohio. Montmorency asked Jerrold Armitage if he and Jack could be of any assistance. Armitage tried to sound polite when he turned them down. He would not forgive the two Englishmen for leaving their posts just before the president was shot. "No thank you," he said. "I think we have everything covered. When the trial is over, you will be free to go."

"But what about Moretti?" said Jack. "He wasn't at the exhibition, but he's still out there somewhere. He might be plotting something. Shouldn't you at least check in Paterson?"

"I told you before," said Armitage. "The anarchists in Paterson were cleaned out after the Italian assassination. We did another sweep there this week, of course."

"And did you check out the man I told you about, the man in the library?"

Armitage was getting cross. "We did, and all his papers were in order. He's from Rome, not Florence. A charming man, apparently, and an asset to the town. It seems that your informant was mistaken. Has it not occurred to you that your Moretti might not be in the United States at all?"

"Yes," said Montmorency. "For one thing, Alexander might have tracked him by now if he were here. We've heard nothing from Alexander since we arrived in the country."

"I should think he's very busy," said Armitage. "Washington is in an uproar with all the arrangements for the funeral and coming to grips with a new president. Maybe you should visit him there when things calm down. Now I really must go." He shook their hands but couldn't make himself thank them.

"We'll look you up if we come to Washington," said Montmorency.

Armitage smiled sadly. "If I'm there. They're keeping me on for the funeral, but after what's happened here, I can't be sure I'll have a job after that."

Montmorency realized that his failure to stop the Czolgosz tragedy would have repercussions for many people he hadn't thought of before.

Doctor Farcett had followed all the medical bulletins on the president very closely. He had realized early on that all was not well. McKinley's heart rate was too high. There might be an internal infection. He wished he had spoken up during the operation and insisted on the need to drain the wound. But he had been reluctant to say anything. He had nothing with him to prove he was a doctor. Why should the surgeons have believed him? Only a few months before, he wouldn't have believed it himself.

Now he was fascinated by Czolgosz, or Neiman, as he had called himself when he was arrested. Why had he killed McKinley? If it was in pursuit of a crazy theory, could he really be described as sane? And if he was insane, should he be held responsible for his action? Shouldn't he be in a mental hospital rather than a prison? He condemned Czolgosz's crime, but he felt he understood a little about the man. It was those two names: Czolgosz and Neiman. Perhaps the man didn't know who he really was. Perhaps Czolgosz was doing Neiman's bidding. Farcett could sympathize with that. At Strathgillon Hospital, he had not been the only patient unsure of where his real identity lay. He knew now that the self was a fragile thing.

He wanted to talk to someone about it. Buffalo had a splendid mental asylum. A grand building, like so many in that prosperous city, it was the home of some of the most respected psychiatrists in America. Farcett approached them, and they were happy to discuss the mental state of the assassin with a fellow professional. But no one felt they could stand in the way of Czolgosz going to trial. The public was angry, and the killer was perfectly prepared to pay for his deed.

And so, within weeks, Leon Czolgosz went to the electric chair. Farcett's friend at the hospital offered to get him a pass to watch the execution, but the doctor couldn't face it, even though his professional self was curious to see the effects of 1,800 volts on a human body. In the spirit of innovation that dominated Buffalo, the electric city, this was to be the first time that alternating current would be used to kill a criminal. Farcett read afterward how Czolgosz offered no resistance as his body was strapped into the chair and the electrodes were attached. He'd shouted, "I killed the president because he was the enemy of the good people — the good working people. I am not sorry for my crime." Then his body snapped into a spasm as the power was turned on, slumping lifeless when the current stopped.

Farcett did accept an invitation to the autopsy. He particularly wanted to see the assassin's brain. The doctor in charge,

Dr. E. A. Spitza, made a note of the state of the body, describing twenty-eight-year-old Czolgosz as "youthful, good-looking, with a pleasant expression." The top of his skull was sawed away. His brain was removed, weighed, and closely examined. It was judged to be "above normal," with no abnormalities that might excuse Czolgosz's actions. Dr. Spitza declared that Czolgosz was "socially diseased and perverted, not mentally diseased," adding, "the wild beast slumbers in us all. It is not always necessary to invoke insanity to explain its awakening."

CHAPTER 40

≫

A CLUE

*I*n London, Montmorency's house was dark and shuttered. The staff were away and the furniture had been covered with dust sheets. A tiny lantern threw the shadow of a caped intruder up on the walls. He searched everywhere for something that would give him a clue to where Lord Francis Fox-Selwyn had gone. He had asked at inns on the road from Strathgillon to Glendarvie, but no one had seen him. The duke had been spotted, in the company of a Doctor Farcett, but no one had seen his son. He had almost given up. But he'd visited Scotland one last time. A maid from Glendarvie Castle had mentioned the name Montmorency, and, for a little money, had found his London address. But the house had obviously been empty for some time.

In the library, he started sorting through a pile of papers on the desk. They were bills, mainly. This Montmorency clearly had expensive tastes, especially in clothes and wine. He was behind with his subscription to Bargles Club but, wherever he was now, he was obviously intending to return. He had ordered wallpaper for the dining room and some champagne for the cellar.

The prowler suddenly jumped in alarm and pulled a gun from under his cloak. A strange noise was coming out of the dark, on the other side of the room. He stood still. It was a frantic flapping, rustling sound, a metallic clatter, and a thump. Then it stopped. He picked up his lantern and moved slowly towards the fireplace. There in the grate stood a filthy pigeon. It had fallen down the chimney, causing a shower of soot. It cocked its head to one side and flew off, perching on a tall bookcase.

The light from the lantern fell across a picture leaning against the wall. There was something odd about it. One corner was brighter than the rest, as if the grime of years had been wiped away. The man lifted it up to the light. It was a landscape, with sheaves of corn in the arc where the dark surface had been cleaned off. And across the corn there was writing. A signature, perhaps? No there were four words, in black ink. "Frank is on Tarimond," it said. Strange. A message in a picture. But what a clever way to communicate! He thought back. On his second visit to Strathgillon, the landlady at the inn had told him about a painter who had stayed at the hospital for a while. He had gone to the post office frequently, with large oblong parcels, addressed to London. "Frank is on Tarimond." It couldn't be clearer. He went to the shelves and found an atlas. There it was, an island far out to sea off the west coast of Scotland. He had tried everything else. He would have to go there. He climbed out of the house through a back window, leaving the pigeon flying around inside.

CHAPTER 41

≫

TRAVELING THEATER

Jerrold Armitage had been sure there was no point in look-ing for Moretti in Paterson, but Montmorency had another reason for going there. He couldn't let himself leave America without trying to see Mary Gibson. She was the only woman who had ever won his love and admiration. He had lost her in a crazy collision of misunderstandings and bad timing, and now he wanted to know if there was any hope of winning her back.

Jack was pleased at the idea of going to Paterson. He knew that Alexander could not have investigated Agostino Grasso, the librarian. Thanks to Jack he had never heard of him, and Jack didn't trust the American Secret Service anyway. Jack knew Moretti. He would be able to tell if Moretti and Grasso were one and the same. He looked in the mirror. Surely Moretti would not recognize this plump dark-haired young man as the "Frank" he had known in Florence? Jack realized how much he had changed in nearly a year of chasing around the world trying to get revenge. He checked the roots of his hair. The American dye he was using these days was good. It was stronger than the British stuff. He took out his hip flask and poured a little of the black liquid onto a cloth. He touched up his eyebrows, beard, and the hairs on his arms. He checked the scar on his bullet wound. It had healed well, but it would always be with him now, a reminder of Malpensa and his kind.

Jack and Montmorency started making plans for their trip. Farcett interrupted them.

"Haven't you forgotten something or, rather, somebody?"

"I'm sorry?" said Montmorency.

"Tom, Montmorency. Tom, your son? He's still in New York. Surely you should go there, if only to see him. Perhaps you should take him with you to Paterson. But you can't just abandon him to the care of others. He's only just found out he's got a father. He deserves to spend some time with you."

Montmorency was ashamed. He had hardly given Tom a thought in recent weeks. And he knew why Farcett was so angry with him. For years the doctor had thought Tom might be his own child. Robert must be thinking how much better he would be for the boy. He might be right.

"We should go to New York, shouldn't we?" said Montmorency, not expecting a reply.

Jack was irritated at yet another delay in getting to Paterson, but he understood. "All right," he said. "But briefly?"

"Yes, briefly. We'll just check on Tom and see how Fregoli is getting on."

Tom was pleased to see them, and Fregoli was the hit of the season, playing to full houses every night. But his contract was nearly up, and he was thinking of returning to Italy to take a break from performing for a while. "But I might travel a bit here first. I've had offers from theaters all over America," he told Montmorency, showing him a stack of letters from cities thousands of miles apart. Montmorency shuffled through them. "There are some wonderful places here. San Francisco. New Orleans. How are you going to choose? I've always wanted to see Chicago myself," he said. Then he stopped. "Paterson," he said. "They want you in Paterson."

"Never heard of it," said Fregoli, who was plucking his eyebrows to make his female impersonations more convincing.

"I know Paterson well," said Montmorency. "It's in New Jersey. The next state to this one. It's full of life. Lots of factories, people with money. And this theater," he said, showing Fregoli the heading on the letter, "they call it the Opera House. It's a great place; you'd love it."

"And Tom tells me you are on your way there anyhow." Fregoli laughed. "I see your game. You want me to perform in Paterson so you can have your son at your side."

"Well, yes," said Montmorency sheepishly. "And if Jack and I were part of your entourage, it would help explain why we've suddenly arrived in town."

"Well, those are as good reasons as any. I couldn't make up my mind, and now you have done it for me. It will cut the costs, too, to go somewhere so close. You are doing me a favor."

Fregoli telephoned the manager of the Paterson Opera House. He was so keen to get the show everyone was talking about that he offered to throw out the Shakespearean troupe he had booked. Montmorency broke the good news to Jack, who could hardly believe that they would finally be revisiting the town where his life had been changed so profoundly and where Montmorency's life might yet take a new turn. Montmorency and Jack joined the Fregoli crew, packing up the props and arranging hotel rooms for everybody involved. The theater manager had organized a special welcome for the great star, with a band at the station and posters along all the streets. Tickets were already selling well, and a bottle of champagne was waiting in the biggest dressing room, to celebrate in advance Fregoli's great success.

Montmorency and Jack got to bed late. The next day they would have to help sort out all the costumes for the first performance. But they each planned to do something else first. Montmorency wanted to visit Mary Gibson. And Jack would be going to the library.

CHAPTER 42

TROUBLE ON TARIMOND

*G*us, Beatrice, and Vi were enjoying the quiet of Tarimond after all the excitement of the past few months. Paul Vannini was pleased with his portrait of the duke. He had found it easier to capture Gus's true personality in the island setting, even if it had been a little strange to see the big man dressed in his formal regalia in such a spartan place.

They all worried, of course. Far away from the news, with no telephone, their imaginations had plenty of scope. "Anything could be happening," said Vi. "I find myself waking up in the night thinking that Tom might be in trouble."

"I know," said Beatrice. "Gus's boys are very brave, but we can't be entirely sure that they're safe."

"And Doctor Farcett. Suppose his nerves have given way again? Perhaps we should have brought him here with us?"

"We'll just have to hope for the best," said Gus. "You know what they say. 'No news is good news.'"

"But it isn't, is it?" said Vi. "Not on Tarimond. On Tarimond no news is no news."

"Well, at least the others can relax about us. Nothing is going to happen here. They can be sure we're safe."

Down on the beach, a stranger was struggling to land his boat. It was dark, and no one had seen him arriving. He called out for help, but the noise of the waves drowned out his voice. He was wet. His wool cloak was soaked with icy water. It was heavy. He felt like dumping it into the sea, but it was the only warm clothing he had. His bag had been washed over the side hours before. It was a miracle that the boat hadn't overturned. At last he was safe. He took his first steps, and the sand sucked at his boots. Even crossing the beach would be exhausting, and then there was a cliff to climb. But at least he could see a light up there. The warm glow of the big house had been all he'd had to guide him on his way. Perhaps they would welcome him there, give him dry clothes and a hot drink. Maybe even a bed for the night. He staggered forward and reached the cliff. He pulled himself up onto the steep but well-worn path. A clump of gorse nodded at his side. He grasped it, stupidly expecting it to take his weight. His foot slipped; he fell back and landed on the rocks at the bottom, unconscious.

The next morning a child hammered on the door of the house, calling for Vi. They slithered down the cliff and examined the stranger. Vi thought at first he was dead, but she found a faint pulse. She was relieved but then shocked when she realized who the man must be. She had only seen Malpensa once, ages ago in America. Even then she'd only had glimpses of part of his face under a big hat. But she knew, looking at the body, that this was Malpensa. He matched the description Tom had given of the stalker at Glendarvie and Strathgillon. She sent the little girl back up the cliff to get Gus and Paul.

Gus arrived in his bathrobe. He used the belt to tie Malpensa's hands behind his back, though the dazed man could barely move. When they had carried him into the house, Paul threw him onto a sofa. He looked terrible, on the point of death. They discussed what to do.

"We'll have to give him something to eat or at least something to drink," said Vi. "He's in a dreadful state."

"Feed him, and then kill him?" said Gus. "Perhaps I should just shoot him now."

"You can't kill him, Gus," said Paul. "Not in cold blood."

Beatrice appeared, awakened by the commotion. She understood at once who the stranger was.

"We must take him to the mainland and hand him over to the police. It's the only way, Gus. They're bound to lock him up. They've already got Montmorency's evidence about what he was prepared to do at the queen's funeral. He'll be put away forever."

Gus was deflated. "It doesn't seem right that he should continue to live when George is dead."

"But he'll live with punishment. He'll pay for what he's done every day of that life. Killing him might be too merciful. And if you kill, you will have to live with guilt for the rest of your days."

"All right," said Gus. "But let's do it straight away. I'll go and get dressed. Paul, you get the boat ready."

"Are you just going to leave him lying there?" said Vi. "Suppose he comes around, with just me and Beatrice in the room?"

"Don't worry," said Gus, "I'll make sure he can't hurt you." He found a scarf and made a tight gag around Malpensa's mouth. He took back his bathrobe belt and used some strong rope to tie Malpensa's hands and feet. Then he quickly got ready, and within half an hour, he and Paul were on their way. They were lucky. They reached a bigger island in time to catch a cargo boat that was on its way to Oban. By nightfall, their unwelcome visitor was languishing in a police cell. He was too sick to talk and grew sicker the next day as he bumped about in a prison van on his way to Glasgow.

Paul and the duke followed behind in a carriage. When they got to Glasgow, Gus sent a telegram to Alexander at the British Embassy in Washington. It asked him to find Montmorency and Jack and to break the news that Malpensa had been captured.

CHAPTER 43

≫

WASHINGTON

*J*errold Armitage sat in a leather armchair, waiting for his contact to arrive. He liked the Wilkie Club. It had all the privacy and convenience of gentlemen's clubs in Britain but none of the stuffiness. Its position, near many of the main embassies, meant that diplomats from all over the world used it as a place to relax. Serious business could be conducted under a cloak of informality, without raising a single eyebrow. No one would think it at all strange for him to be chatting with the new young member of the British diplomatic team, Alexander, Marquess of Rosseley.

"I'm sorry I'm late," said Alexander, settling into the chair Armitage had prepared for him in a corner away from the bustle of the bar.

"It's not a problem. Gave me a few minutes to gather my thoughts." He gestured towards a waiter. "Drink?"

"Just water, for me, please," said Alex. "I like to keep a clear head."

"Let's have a jug of water," Armitage said to the waiter. "And I'll have another one of these." He passed over his glass, which was empty except for a slice of lemon lurking in the bottom.

Once they were alone, Alexander apologized again. "I'm so sorry my brother let you down. When I recommended him, I thought his obsession with catching Moretti would be an advantage. I didn't think for a moment it would turn into a distraction."

"I don't blame you. And I'm not as angry as I was. After all, who's to say that Czolgosz wouldn't have managed to get to the president even if Jack and Montmorency had been in the room. There were plenty of other agents there. Nobody stopped him."

"It's funny to hear you calling Frank 'Jack.'"

"It's all I've ever called him. He carries off his new identity perfectly. Never lets the mask slip. He'd make a great agent. If he could control his passions a bit better."

"His obsession with the anarchists, you mean?"

"That and the drink. He doesn't always think clearly late in the day."

The waiter returned with their order: the jug of water and the glass of gin. Armitage laughed. "Not very good timing, eh? Perhaps I should stick to water, like you." He nodded to the man. "Thank you. That will be all."

"So your job is safe?"

"Yes, Roosevelt's keeping us all on. He doesn't see the assassination as a major security failure. It seems this Czolgosz was just an oddball. A bit of an outcast even among the anarchists. We're convinced he was working alone. We're never going to catch people like that. Not without a great deal of luck. And luck wasn't on our side that day."

"Well, there's been some good luck in Britain. That's what held me up on the way here. I've had a telegram from my father. They've caught Malpensa. He's under lock and key, and if they get the right judge at the trial, he should never be released."

"So he was in Europe all the time? That Italian document placing him and Moretti in America was wrong."

Alexander bit his lip. "I've got a bit of a confession to make about that," he said. "The document was a fake. I wrote it myself."

"Whatever for?"

"I wanted to lure Montmorency and Frank over here so that I could offer you their services. Being new here, I thought it would give me a bit of a leg up — putting you on to people who could actually recognize some of the anarchists. I truly believed Malpensa and Moretti probably were in the United States, though."

"Of course, Moretti still could be here," said Armitage. "Jack seems to think so. He's insisted on going to check out that lead in Paterson, even though I told him we'd ruled out the librarian."

"I'm sorry," said Alexander, confused. "What librarian? What lead?"

"Montmorency told me he'd written to you. They had a tip-off that someone answering Moretti's description was working as a clerk in Paterson Public Library. We checked him out. He's legitimate. A middle-aged guy from Rome."

"First I've heard of it," said Alex. "So Frank and Montmorency are in Paterson then?"

"That's where they were off to when I last saw them. I

don't keep tabs on them though. To be perfectly honest, I wouldn't mind if I never saw either of them again."

"But I'd better find them. I need to pass on the good news about Malpensa." Alex looked at his watch. "Oh dear. Time to get back to the office. Shall we meet again when I'm back from Paterson?"

"Yes. Give me a call. I'd appreciate it if you'd pass on anything the British police get out of Malpensa. Unofficially, you understand."

"Oh yes. Unofficially. And it would be a great help to me to hear about your government's stand on the trade talks. Just informally, you know."

"Of course."

Alexander went off to find a train timetable. He wanted to get to Paterson as soon as he could.

CHAPTER 44

≫

MARY

*M*ontmorency walked to the Gibson house, nervous about meeting Mary, fearful that she might be out, and terrified in case her mother was there. The maid took his hat. She seemed lighthearted. The whole house lacked its old air of sickness and gloom. Mary soon explained why. Mrs. Gibson had passed away more than a year ago, gone to complain to God about the shortcomings of heaven. As the only unmarried daughter, Mary had inherited the house and all that was in it. She had redecorated. She wanted to make the place as comfortable as possible for herself. After all, having lost Montmorency, she expected to be living alone there for the rest of her life.

They talked and cried together. Mary passed on all sorts of Paterson news. The biggest shock was the death of Curtis Bayfield, the man whose money and factories had dominated the town. He had died of influenza the previous winter. His widow, Cissie, had been forced by grief into the arms of another businessman, a weapons trader from Virginia. The big house on the hill had been taken over by Harrison Bayfield, Curtis's younger brother. After a lifetime dealing in insurance, he was struggling to manage the family's silk factories and was thinking of selling them.

They walked in the garden. It was chilly, just as it had been two years before, when Montmorency had asked Mary to marry him. He reminded her of that day and asked, "Is there any hope? Could I possibly persuade you to consider my offer again?"

Mary looked away. "It's strange; I have dreamed of this moment a thousand times, and yet I find I'm not ready to say yes. We need to get to know each other better. We have to decide important things. We haven't even discussed where we would live."

"Anywhere. Anywhere you want. If you wish to stay in America, I will start a new life here."

"No, Montmorency. I don't want you to start a new life. I want to get to know and understand your old one. I need to hear everything about you, everything that has made you who you are today. I know you had secrets from me before. Are you willing to reveal your whole history before I commit myself to care for you forever?"

"Yes," said Montmorency.

But she could see in his eyes that it would take time for him to let her into every corner of his world. She raised the issue that had split them before. "That boy. Tom. Is he your son?"

"Yes, Mary, he is, though I did not know it when I was here before, I swear."

"Would you wish me to accept him as my own?"

Montmorency could not answer.

"If it were him or me, which of us would you choose?"

Montmorency was shocked. He could not believe that Mary

could be so cruel. He knew he should choose Mary, but however bad a father he had been, he couldn't make himself renounce Tom. He felt his hopes for Mary draining away.

But she smiled. "Thank heavens for your silence. If you had turned your back on the child, I would have rejected you. Of course I would not force you to make such a choice. And Tom is almost an adult. He has a mother already. If we were to marry, I would not expect to supplant her in his heart. But I would want him to be part of our lives, open and acknowledged, like everything else in your past."

"So you will say yes?"

"Not yet. Let me think, and come again and tell me all those things you haven't found words for before. When I am truly certain of who you are, and if I love that man, I will consider your proposal once again."

She showed him to the door. She had been strong. Her heart was longing to say yes, but her head was cautious after having had such a long time to think. Montmorency left in a turmoil of hope and fear, praying he could at last admit to the parts of his character that Mary would not like, so that he could discard them and the real Montmorency could take Mary to the altar.

CHAPTER 45

≫

WRONG

*G*us and Vannini stayed in Glasgow, waiting for Malpensa to come around. They told the whole story to the local police, and since the allegations against the prisoner involved crimes in England and a threat to the life of the sovereign, they contacted Scotland Yard. Inspector Howard caught a train north, relieved and excited that Malpensa was in custody at last. He visited Malpensa in the prison hospital. He still couldn't speak, but Howard recognized him from their encounter at the inn near Strathgillon.

The next day, the prisoner could sit up. His attention span was short, and he rambled, repeating incoherent sentences about Lord Francis Fox-Selwyn, Italy, and America. Howard decided to give him another night's sleep and try again. In the morning he was looking better. The nurse had washed and shaved him. He was sipping a drink of water. Howard introduced himself. The prisoner seemed impressed that Howard was from Scotland Yard. "Oh, thank goodness," he said. "Perhaps you can get me out of this mess."

"That's not why I'm here," said Inspector Howard. "I'm here to make sure you stay in prison. Probably for the rest of your life."

"But why? I have done nothing wrong."

"Nothing! You call threatening the lives of the royal family nothing? Practically killing a man down in the sewers nothing? And who knows what else you have done in your own country and abroad. I know about the shooting in Paris. We can't punish you here for that, but it tells us what kind of man you are. The kind of man who should be locked away, for everybody's safety."

"But I don't know what you're talking about. What shooting? What sewers? What threats?"

"Oh, for goodness' sake. How can you expect me to believe that? I saw you at Strathgillon, remember? I thought then that you knew too much about the queen's health and the arrangements for her funeral."

"But . . ."

"And you were seen there again and at Glendarvie, trying to get your hands on Lord Francis Fox-Selwyn. I have witnesses. They will testify. You cannot escape this time, Malpensa."

"Malpensa?"

"Yes, Malpensa. We know who you are."

"But that's not my name."

"Did you seriously expect me to believe the name you used in Strathgillon? Do you really think I was fooled? Can you look me in the eye and say you are Max Bartok?"

"No. I'm not Max Bartok. That was an alias, of course."

"Well, thank you for admitting that at least," said Inspector Howard sarcastically. "Now cooperate, Malpensa. We can bring the Italian Embassy in to help you, if you wish, though I have to warn you that they are likely to be less than friendly. But if you want support from your own country, it is your right."

"I do want support from my own country," shouted the prisoner. "And I want it now. But my home country is not Italy. Inspector Howard, my home country is the United States of America. I am Miles Beck of the U.S. Secret Service. I have been in your country to gather intelligence about anarchist threats to our president. I have operated undercover. It is true that I told lies to you at Strathgillon, but, except for one case of breaking and entering, I do not think I have broken any of your laws."

Inspector Howard was stunned. "You are not Malpensa? But you were recognized . . ." He thought back. The first identification had been from Tom's description at Glendarvie, and Tom had never seen Malpensa before. Then Howard himself had inadvertently endorsed the assumption after the meeting at the inn. He remembered their conversation there and how "Bartok" had shown too much knowledge. It was true that, if he were an American agent, he might have had access to the daily briefings supplied by the government. Was it possible? Could there have been a terrible mistake?

Surely not. This must be why Malpensa had avoided capture so successfully in the past. He could be plausible, charming even, as he was at the Strathgillon inn. The evidence was still against him. Hadn't he run away from there just before the queen's funeral, when he heard the Scottish police were on his tail?

"Run away?" said the prisoner. "What do you mean?"

"We have a statement from the landlady. Someone came with a note, and you suddenly left."

"Yes. I received a message when I was there. It told me that President McKinley had the flu and wouldn't be going to the queen's funeral. The surveillance job in Britain was scaled down. I was sent back to America. I only returned months later when we wanted to get more background on the European anarchists. That was why I had to look for Lord Francis Fox-Selwyn again."

"But why are you so preoccupied with him? Why have you gone to such lengths to find him?"

"Because I was told that he had direct experience of the anarchists. That he'd actually lived among them and could recognize them firsthand."

"Told by whom? Nobody knows that."

"I can't say precisely who told me. But I can say this. It was somebody who works with you at Scotland Yard. Someone who was involved in that phony shoot-out at the Hippodrome."

"One of my men?" said Howard, shocked.

"One has to have contacts in this job," said the prisoner.

"So that's why you went to Glendarvie?"

"Yes. I wanted to interview Lord Francis Fox-Selwyn. But I was too late. He was already ill. And then I waited at Strathgillon for him to get well enough to talk, but he was discharged when I was out of the country."

Beck's story was horribly plausible. Inspector Howard tried

to clarify in his mind where the real Malpensa had been while he had been obsessed with the wrong man. Frank (or Jack, as he now wanted to be known) could place him firmly in America at the end of 1899. It was from there that he had organized the attempted atrocities in Rome and London in 1900, which Montmorency and the Fox-Selwyns had foiled. In America, Malpensa had links with Gaetano Bresci, who had assassinated King Umberto of Italy in July 1900, but that was the end of the chain. No one had heard of — or seen — the real Malpensa again until he'd turned up in London on the eve of Queen Victoria's funeral in February. He had definitely been in Paris in August. That's when he had shot Jack. So, since Howard had been working with the Fox-Selwyns — since he had stirred them into believing they were under threat — the real Malpensa had, in fact, been seen only three times: in London on two consecutive days in February and in Paris in the summer. All the other sightings had been of the man who sat before him now — this Miles Beck.

Inspector Howard stared at the wall. What a shambles. The British authorities had wrongfully imprisoned an American citizen. There would be trouble at the highest level, and Britain's own agents in the United States might pay the price. Howard had devoted time and money to chasing the wrong man. He had plunged Montmorency and the Fox-Selwyns into a quagmire of secrecy, codes, and double identities at a time when they could have been emerging from their grief into peaceful family life. He had inadvertently stoked their lust for revenge. And worse than that, he had turned them into targets. Somewhere out there, maybe in Europe, maybe in America, the real Malpensa was on the loose, and, because the hunt had been called off, nobody was looking for him.

CHAPTER 46

≫

BROTHERS

*J*ack overslept. He'd been up half the night with Fregoli, drinking, playing the trumpet, and singing, to the fury of the other guests in the hotel. It was nearly lunchtime before he was dressed and ready to go off on his trip to the library. He climbed the stairs to Montmorency's room and knocked. There was no reply. He must have gone to see Mary. Jack would go in search of Moretti by himself.

In the lobby, he heard a familiar English voice.

"But surely you must have a room. Is there nobody you could move to fit me in?"

"I'm sorry, sir. We are completely full. We have an entire theater company staying at the moment."

The visitor coughed and put on a pompous voice. Almost before he heard the first syllable, Jack realized who it was. "I am the Marquess of Rosseley," said the man. It was Alexander, trying to pull rank.

Jack rushed to the desk, hoping to keep his brother from embarrassing himself any further. "Alex," he said, pulling him over to one side. "That name won't cut any ice here. They really are full."

"I know. It seems they've got some sort of circus troupe taking up all the rooms."

"Don't worry. I'll see if you can stay with me."

Jack persuaded the desk clerk to arrange for a cot to be set up in his room. The clerk was puzzled that the two men seemed to know each other so well. They couldn't have been less alike: one smartly dressed to the point of caricature, the other almost too scruffy to be accepted as a guest. Jack took Alex's bag and asked the bellboy to take it upstairs, then he led his brother out into the street.

"What are you doing here, Alex? I thought you were in Washington."

"I was. But I've come to see you. I was expecting to spend the whole day looking for you. What a stroke of luck to find you so soon."

"But why have you come? There's nothing wrong is there?"

"No. Far from it in fact. I've brought good news. Malpensa has been arrested. He's in prison in Britain, and they've got a rock-solid case against him. He won't be coming out for a very long time."

Jack hugged his brother. It was years since they had even touched each other, and Alexander flinched at the unexpected show of affection.

"Thank heavens!" said Jack. "Do you know, it's only now that you've told me he's locked up that I realize how scared I was that he'd find me again. You heard about Paris, I suppose?"

"A bit. But no details. How is your arm?"

Jack rolled up his sleeve and showed off the scars where Malpensa's bullet had gone in and out. "So that's Bresci dead and Malpensa in prison. Who knows, maybe the British prison guards will give him the same treatment Bresci got in Italy."

Alexander shrugged.

"Only one to go," Jack continued. "Moretti. No one's heard anything of him since George died. We had a report that he was here, working in the library under the name of Agostino Grasso. The Secret Service say it isn't Moretti. But I have to see for myself. Do you want to come?"

"I can't," said Alexander. "You may have changed your appearance, but Moretti knew me in Florence. I'm sure he would recognize me straight away."

"Wait here then. Go up to my room." He gave Alexander the key. "I'll go and have a look at this Grasso character."

"But don't do anything. If it is him, I mean. Promise me, Frank. Hold back."

"Please call me Jack."

"I'm sorry."

"And no. I won't make a scene. But believe me, Alex. If Grasso is Moretti, he won't get out of this town alive."

Jack walked along to the library. He'd never gone inside it when he'd lived in Paterson before, and he was amazed by the number of books on display. Somehow he'd never imagined much reading went on in the town. The rich people he'd met there had been complete philistines. Their grand house contained almost no books. Living among the poor, he had been unaware that the library was free. He'd always thought of it just as a landmark, blind to the possibilities it held for all.

He wandered around the silent reading rooms, pretending to look at the shelves but watching out all the time for the round, friendly little man he had known in Florence. The staff seemed to be entirely female. He wondered if he should go and inquire about Grasso. But would he take flight if he heard that someone was looking for him? He decided to wait a bit longer. He took a book at random and settled down at a table to wait and see if Grasso appeared.

The woman at the main desk kept looking at her watch. She was getting agitated. She opened a drawer and took out an apple and a package wrapped in greaseproof paper. Jack guessed that she was desperate for her lunch. She drummed her fingers on the desktop and looked up at the clock, sighing. Twenty past one. Someone was late.

And then Jack saw him. Puffing from the effort of rushing back to work. He knew at once it was Moretti.

"Mr. Grasso," said the lady in a whisper so shrill that everyone could hear it. "That's the second time this week!"

"I'm sorry, Miss Petrie. Lost track of time. I had to stand in line. I was buying a ticket for that Fregoli show."

"Well, I'm glad you have time to do such things in the evenings, Mr. Grasso," she said. "I have to look after Mother. My lunch breaks are the only times I get to myself."

"I'm sorry," said Grasso again, this time so loud that she shushed him.

She flounced out, and Jack followed, off to tell Alexander and Montmorency that Moretti was at their mercy.

CHAPTER 47

≫

THE LAST PURSUIT

*T*om was thrilled that his father wanted him to help catch Moretti. Montmorency, Jack, and Alexander had made a plan. They had worked out a way to deal with Grasso without being disturbed, and it all depended on Tom. They would wait till the evening, when the show had started. Tom was to approach Moretti with a message.

As the audience took their seats, Jack looked through a hole in the curtains, trying to spot Moretti. He was on the end of a row, halfway up the main stalls. Perfect. Backstage, Montmorency took over for Tom, helping Fregoli in and out of his costumes while the boy was away. Moretti was howling with laughter as Tom approached.

Tom tapped him on the shoulder. "Mr. Grasso?" The librarian was startled, but looked around and nodded. "There's a message for you from a Miss Petrie. She says you are needed urgently." Moretti hesitated, and Tom added an extra line. "She says it's a matter of life or death."

Moretti rose from his seat and followed Tom outside. He looked around for Miss Petrie. She wasn't there. Tom ran back into the theater as Jack approached. "Mr. Grasso," said Jack, relieved that Moretti didn't recognize him. "Miss Petrie sent me to get you. There's a problem at the library. Someone has reported an intruder, and she can't leave her mother to open up for the police. You must come at once."

Moretti followed Jack, trying to keep up with his urgent footsteps. He took out his keys and opened the library door. He reached for the light switch, but Jack grabbed his hand. "No," he said. "Don't do that. If there's someone inside, we don't want them to know we are here."

They crept into the main reading room. It was silent, with only a little light from the street. They heard the front door creak, and Moretti turned to see if the intruder was escaping. Instead, two figures were coming in, and they closed the door behind them. Moretti recognized them as soon as they were close enough for him to see their faces.

"Montmorency? Alexander?" he said, bemused. Then he lashed out behind him, knocking Jack in the belly, and ran between the bookcases to the back of the room. Before Montmorency could catch him, he threw open another door and ran down a flight of stairs. The others were close behind, but he knew where he was going and they did not. He led them into a labyrinth of shelves and cupboards. They were down in the basement, where the library kept the books it had no space to display. Chasing him was hopeless. They were simply running in a line. There was no room between the shelves to overtake him. Whenever they caught up with him, he found a gap in the shelving, another place to turn. They could hear a low rumble growing louder as he led them to the back of the building. He lurched towards the noise, down another flight of steps, so narrow, flimsy, and dry that it couldn't take the weight of all four of them at once. It splintered and twisted its way from the wall, and they all fell together into the boiler room.

Montmorency understood at once why Moretti had run there. There was a coal chute at the back. It sloped up to the pavement outside, and he could see streetlights at the top. Moretti was hoping to escape that way. But Moretti was still on the ground, so Montmorency stood in the mouth of the opening, blocking his way. They had done it. They had him trapped.

"You killed George!" shouted Alexander.

"And you will pay!" said Jack.

"No," said Moretti. "George was a clever man, but I beat him, and I will beat you, too." He picked up a rail from the broken stairs and thrust one end into the embers of the boiler. It caught immediately, flaring up into a burning torch. He swung it around, forcing the three men to pull back as he edged towards the coal hole. All four faces shone in the light of the flames. The glass in Moretti's spectacles blazed with hate.

The plan had gone wrong. Back at the hotel, Alexander had persuaded the others not to kill Moretti outright. With three against one, he had been sure they could capture him and maybe rough him up a bit but keep him alive, so that Armitage and his men could interrogate him. Moretti would be worth more alive than dead. He was an academic. A weak man. With a little forceful persuasion, he might reveal all sorts of secrets about the anarchists' campaigns. And then he could be tried. Tried, convicted, and locked up, like Malpensa, or even sent to the electric chair.

But now, here they were, trapped halfway underground, and Moretti had the upper hand, threatening them with fire.

Alexander dived forward, trying to grab the burning stick. Moretti pushed it towards him, and Alexander yelped in pain as his hand caught in the flame. He jerked his arm upward and knocked off Moretti's spectacles. Montmorency stamped on them as they slid across the floor.

Jack grasped his hip flask, hoping that in the semidarkness it would look like a gun. "Drop it, Moretti," he shouted, pointing the silver box towards him.

But Moretti would not let go of his torch. Montmorency took a stick of his own and set it alight. He pointed it at Moretti. The burning poles struck against each other like swords. Sparks flew and started little blazes around the floor. The room began to fill with smoke. They all coughed. Moretti made for the coal chute, trying to force his way past Montmorency. But Montmorency stood firm and pushed him back into the smoke.

"You two. Get out now," he said to Jack and Alex. "It will do no one any good if we all suffocate in here. Get some air, and be ready to come back for me." Moretti tried to stop Alexander and Jack, but Alex got past and forced himself upward with his jacket on fire. At the top, he rolled on the ground to put out the flames and waited for his brother to escape, too. Moretti was waving his stick in front of Jack. Jack tried the gun trick again, but it was no good. Had it been a real gun, he would have fired it. But it was only a hip flask. A metal bottle full of chemical dye. And now Moretti knocked it from his hand. But his move had put him within range of Montmorency, and Montmorency ducked beneath the flaming stick, pulling Moretti to the floor.

"Run, Jack!" Montmorency coughed through the smoke. "I'll deal with him." He wrenched the torch from Moretti's hand and hurled it across the room to where the stairs had been. Flames raged upward, into the storerooms, and along the wooden floorboards towards the shelves and the books.

On the floor, Moretti, half blind, could just make out the metal lump that had dropped from Jack's hand. Spluttering and wheezing, he stretched out to pick it up, ready to fire at Montmorency as soon as the gun was in his hands. He was furious to find that he had been held at bay by a hip flask. He swore, but the smoke left him without enough air to make a sound.

"Come on, Montmorency," Jack shouted from the street. "It's not safe. Get out of there."

"I won't come without Moretti," he said. "Alex was right. We need him alive." Then he, too, was overcome by coughing, with no strength to pull Moretti out of the room.

Moretti's throat was burning. He needed water, but anything wet would do. He unscrewed the lid of the hip flask and swigged the liquid back, expecting the taste of whisky or brandy.

Outside, Alexander and Jack heard his strange, gargled, howl of agony as the harsh chemicals in Jack's hair dye scoured away his final breath. Montmorency felt Moretti's body slacken into death. It was over. A second later, Montmorency lost his own fight for air and collapsed, unconscious alongside him.

Alexander and Jack rushed down the slope to pull Montmorency out, praying that he would still be alive when they got him onto the pavement. Jack blew into his mouth, trying to replace the foul smoke in his lungs with oxygen. At last he was breathing on his own. Just in time for them to pull him away from the library as the upstairs windows started exploding in the heat of the roaring blaze.

CHAPTER 48

≫

THE FIRE

The whole building's gone up," said Alex, as glass crashed down around them. "We'd better move. It's blowing this way." The wind was strong, and flames were already licking the roof of the next building. It was a wooden structure, which caught on fire at once.

Jack looked along the road. "The theater!" he said. "It's full of people; we have to get them out."

Montmorency was still spluttering, but he ran behind them as they raced along the street. Jack crashed through the double doors at the front and pushed his way into the auditorium. The audience was laughing so loud he could hardly make himself heard.

"Fire!" he cried. "Get out! Fire!"

At first the crowd thought he was part of the show. Then people stood up and tried to push their way out. On the stage, Fregoli could see that only he could prevent a panic. He shouted as loud as he could. "STOP!" The audience obeyed him long enough for him to appeal for calm, and though there were shouts and crying, Montmorency, Alexander, and Jack were able to keep some degree of order, holding open the doors and ushering people into the street. They could hear fire engines. Help was coming. But the wind was high, and the blaze was only a few buildings away, jumping from roof to roof. At the back of the theater, Fregoli and his team were desperately trying to rescue costumes and props before the flames reached the theater, but in minutes they had to run, driven away by the smoke and heat from next door.

The audience fanned out through the streets of Paterson, knocking on doors and warning everyone to get out and away. They ran up to the waterfall, instinctively feeling that the rushing torrent would save them from the fire. High above Paterson, Harrison Bayfield stood at the window of his mansion, watching the city burn. He knew he should be worrying about the human tragedy that might be unfolding below him. But he couldn't take his mind off the other costs of the blaze. His insurance company would face a hefty bill in the morning.

The firemen stopped the blaze from spreading, but at daybreak buildings were still burning. Twenty-four hours later, smoldering wreckage gave off an acrid smell. Churches, shops, and five hundred homes were lost, though Bayfield's great silk factories were spared. The *Paterson Guardian* praised the men who had raised the alarm, evacuated the theater, and turned the audience into an army of good Samaritans, urging everyone to get out of the way of the blaze. In the excitement of the event and believing that their mission was over, Montmorency and Frank spoke freely to reporters, Frank using his real name for the first time in months. But it was Alexander who really captured the editor's imagination, and, thanks to a long interview about himself, with pictures, the young Marquess of Rosseley became a celebrity in Paterson.

The New York papers picked up the story the next day. Any hope of a quiet life was gone.

Fregoli was photographed in tears outside the gutted theater, lamenting the loss of almost all his precious costumes. Later on at the hotel, which had escaped the blaze, he admitted to Montmorency that there was a silver lining to his cloud. There would be insurance money, and he was spared the expense of shipping everything back to Europe.

Miraculously, only one person had died in the fire. His body was found in the burned-out library, under the ashes of thirty-seven thousand books. People who had been sitting near Agostino Grasso at the theater remembered him being called away. They assumed he had gone to fight the fire and to try to rescue his precious volumes. Miss Petrie told the newspapers that he had been an exemplary colleague: knowledgeable, courteous, and punctual. She seemed to have forgotten how he had ruined her lunch break twice that very week.

CHAPTER 49

≫

THE FUTURE

Mary Gibson's house was well away from the fire zone, and she came to Montmorency's hotel early on the morning after the blaze to check that he had survived. They spent the day together, helping distraught citizens salvage what they could of their burned belongings. At the end of the day, she had made up her mind. They were sitting on a wall behind the theater, their clothes smudged with soot, when she told him her decision. "I will marry you, Montmorency. I learned my true feelings for you when I thought you might be lost again."

Montmorency's reaction took her by surprise. "No, Mary. You were right before. Don't commit yourself until I have explained everything about my life. I will write it down for you, and when you have read it, we will see if you still want me."

Tom emerged through what was left of the stage door. "Tom," said Montmorency. "What were you doing in there? It's dangerous, you know."

"I just wanted to see if there was anything I could keep as a souvenir," he said, holding out the charred remains of the fan Montmorency had used for his disguise in Paris. "I suppose that's the end of it all, isn't it? We'll be going home, and I'll have to stop working with Fregoli?"

"Well, I was thinking of sending you to school, Tom," said

Montmorency. "There's a man I know at Westminster who might take you on."

"But I don't want to go to school, Dad. I want to stay in the theater and to work with you sometimes, like Frank does. I suppose we can call him Frank again now?"

"Yes, Tom, we can. And you're a good boy. Of course you can help me, though I'm not sure what work I will do in the future or even where I will live. But you know, there is someone else you can help. Help Frank. He needs someone to keep him steady, the way his uncle George once looked after me. You be his George, and he can be your Scarper. Stick together, Tom. He's going to need you."

"Are you two going to get married?" asked Tom, making Mary blush.

"Perhaps," said Montmorency. "We'll see. Would you like that?"

"Yes," said Tom, "I think I would."

For the next few days everyone worked hard, helping the city clean up. Mary and Montmorency set up a shelter for people who had lost everything in the fire. Frank ran a soup kitchen inside, and Fregoli gave free shows there every afternoon. In the evenings, he traveled to neighboring towns to raise money for the victims, with special performances introduced by the Marquess of Rosseley, who spoke eloquently about the fire in his sonorous English voice. Alex knew nothing of the telegram waiting on his desk in Washington. In it his father warned that someone called Enid might be on her way after all. Alexander's assistant had read it but assumed it was about some tiresome aunt and could wait until he returned from the important business that had taken him away from the office in such a hurry.

Every night, at the Paterson hotel, Fregoli gave one of his noisy parties in the room underneath Montmorency's. Frank was always there, but Montmorency would sit upstairs, as the music blared from the floor below, writing down the story of his life for Mary. After about a week of this, Frank and Alexander went up to try and persuade him to relax.

"Come downstairs, Montmorency," said Frank. "We've got wine and food. You need to rest, even to celebrate."

"Celebrate?" said Montmorency. "How can I celebrate when I set half the town on fire?"

"That wasn't your fault," said Frank. "Moretti lit the first blaze."

"I was part of it. And I think I set fire to the stairs."

"Do you know who you sound like?" said Alexander. "You sound like Robert when he was blaming himself for everything. Don't get like that. Think of what you've achieved. Because of what you did in that library, the world may be a safer place. Now come down and have some fun. Toast the future. Our nightmare is over. Bresci, Malpensa, and Moretti are gone. We've gotten our revenge for George."

"But Father Michael was right, wasn't he?" said Montmorency. "Revenge doesn't make you feel better. I still miss George every bit as much as I did before."

"Well, if you can't toast revenge," said Frank, "at least drink a toast to safety. At last we can walk the world without look-ing over our shoulders all the time."

"All right, I'll drink to that," said Montmorency. "But I don't want to go down to Fregoli's party. Could you just bring some wine up here?"

Frank went downstairs and came back with a bottle and three glasses. They talked of the future. Alex hoped that he would be an ambassador one day, and Montmorency hoped that he and Mary might settle down together. Frank had no ambition at all. "I've spent so long just trying to stay alive," he said, "I've forgotten what the future is for."

"Well, in the immediate future, I'm going to have some-thing to eat," said Alexander, trying to break the maudlin atmosphere. "Can I bring you up a plate of something, Montmorency?"

"Yes, thank you, Alex. That would be nice."

Alexander and Frank went back down. Montmorency heard the upsurge of laughter as the two of them entered the room below. He got on with his work, despite the racket.

The manuscript in front of him already contained the bald facts about his parallel lives. He had written of his upbring-ing at the Foundling Hospital and how he would never be allowed to know who his real parents had been. At that insti-tution, he had been given the name Stanley Kemp — a name he had never used or revealed since the night that had changed his life, when he had been injured and fallen into the hands of Robert Farcett more than twenty-five years ago.

He had described his years of stealing, first through the

need to survive, but later as part of a careful plan to turn himself into the man he struggled to be proud of today. He confessed to his past addiction to drugs, told of his time in the sewers and how he had thrown off the police by letting another man take the blame for his crimes. He tried to convey his shame without making it sound like an excuse.

Reading it through, he wondered how he could ever expect Mary Gibson to overlook his many faults and take him on as a husband. Why should she accept that the identity he inhabited now was the real Montmorency? Could even he be certain that Scarper's selfishness had been erased from his soul? Maybe this catalog of misdeeds — showing how he had repeatedly let down himself, his son, and his dearest friends — simply proved he was unworthy of her. Perhaps he should burn it and return to London alone or send it to Mary to explain why he had gone.

And yet, it could all have another meaning. Perhaps, at last, he had truly found himself. Maybe this urge to run was Scarper's last attempt to lure him away from responsibility and a settled life. The time had come to turn his back on Scarper forever, to rejoice that he had survived so much and acknowledge that this autobiography was a plea to himself, as well as to Mary, to embrace the future and live in hope.

He took up his pen again, to invite Mary to forgive him and to share with him the name of Montmorency, the only name he would use from now on.

Downstairs, the party romped on. Someone was playing a trombone, and a woman was singing. There was a slow thumping noise, strangely out of time with the music: one beat loud, one beat soft. It stopped. Then Montmorency heard the doorknob turn behind him. It must have been Alex carrying his food upstairs.

"Just put it on the table, Alex," he said without turning around. "Thanks very much."

There was no reply, and yet he was sure there was someone in the room with him. From the corner of his eye he saw the edge of a black cloak. Then he felt the pressure of cold metal against the back of his head.

Montmorency grasped the arms of his chair, closed his eyes, and tried to feel brave.